The
RECOVERY
AGENT

BY JANET EVANOVICH

THE STEPHANIE PLUM NOVELS
One for the Money
Two for the Dough
Three to Get Deadly
Four to Score
High Five
Hot Six
Seven Up
Hard Eight
To the Nines
Ten Big Ones
Eleven on Top
Twelve Sharp
Lean Mean Thirteen
Fearless Fourteen
Finger Lickin' Fifteen
Sizzling Sixteen
Smokin' Seventeen
Explosive Eighteen
Notorious Nineteen
Takedown Twenty
Top Secret Twenty-One
Tricky Twenty-Two
Turbo Twenty-Three
Hardcore Twenty-Four
Look Alive Twenty-Five
Twisted Twenty-Six
Fortune and Glory
(Tantalizing Twenty-
Seven)
Game On
(Tempting Twenty-Eight)
Going Rogue (Rise and
Shine Twenty-Nine)

**THE FOX AND O'HARE
NOVELS**
(with Lee Goldberg)
The Heist
The Chase

The Job
The Scam
The Pursuit

(with Peter Evanovich)
The Big Kahuna

(with Steve Hamilton)
The Bounty

KNIGHT AND MOON
Curious Minds
(with Phoef Sutton)

Dangerous Minds

**THE LIZZY AND DIESEL
NOVELS**
Wicked Appetite
Wicked Business
Wicked Charms
(with Phoef Sutton)

**THE BETWEEN THE NUMBERS
STORIES**
Visions of Sugar Plums
Plum Lovin'
Plum Lucky
Plum Spooky

**THE ALEXANDRA BARNABY
NOVELS**
Metro Girl
Motor Mouth

(with Alex Evanovich)
Troublemaker
(graphic novel)

JANET EVANOVICH

A GABRIELA ROSE NOVEL

THE
RECOVERY AGENT

Pocket Books

New York   London   Toronto   Sydney   New Delhi

Pocket Books
An Imprint of Simon & Schuster, Inc.
1230 Avenue of the Americas
New York, NY 10020

This book is a work of fiction. Any references to historical events, real people, or real places are used fictitiously. Other names, characters, places, and events are products of the author's imagination, and any resemblance to actual events or places or persons, living or dead, is entirely coincidental.

This Pocket Books paperback edition August 2023

POCKET and colophon are registered trademarks of Simon & Schuster, Inc.

For information about special discounts for bulk purchases, please contact Simon & Schuster Special Sales at 1-866-506-1949 or business@simonandschuster.com.

The Simon & Schuster Speakers Bureau can bring authors to your live event. For more information or to book an event, contact the Simon & Schuster Speakers Bureau at 1-866-248-3049 or visit our website at www.simonspeakers.com.

Interior design by Jill Putorti

Manufactured in the United States of America

1 3 5 7 9 10 8 6 4 2

ISBN 978-1-9821-5493-6
ISBN 978-1-9821-5494-3 (ebook)

The
RECOVERY
AGENT

CHAPTER ONE

Gabriela Rose was standing in a small clearing that led to a rope-and-board footbridge. The narrow bridge spanned a gorge that was a hundred feet deep and almost as wide. Rapids roared over enormous boulders at the bottom of the gorge, but Gabriela couldn't see the river because it was raining buckets and visibility was limited.

She was deep in the Ecuadorian rain forest. Her long dark brown hair was hidden under an Australian safari hat, its brim protecting her brown eyes from the rain. She was a martial arts expert. She ran five miles every morning. She was a crack shot and a gourmet cook. None of these skills were keeping her dry. She was wet clear through to her La Perla panties. Her camo cargo pants and

Inov-8 Bare-Grip hiking shoes were caked with mud. She was carrying a Glock .38 in a Ziploc bag tucked into a hip pocket. Other pockets held her passport, a folding Buck knife, and moisturizing lip gloss. Her daypack held a useless waterproof poncho, protein bars, her Ziploc-bagged cell phone, and assorted other necessities for jungle trekking.

She was with two local guides, Jorge and Cuckoo. She guessed they were somewhere between forty and sixty years old, and she was pretty sure that they thought she was an idiot.

"Is this bridge safe?" Gabriela asked.

"Yes, sometimes safe," Jorge said.

"And it's the only way?"

Jorge shrugged.

She looked at Cuckoo.

Cuckoo shrugged.

"You first," she said to Jorge.

Jorge did another shrug and murmured something in Spanish that Gabriela was pretty sure translated to "chickenshit woman."

Let it slide, Gabriela thought. Sometimes it gave you an advantage to be underestimated. If things turned ugly, she was almost certain she could kick his ass. And if that didn't work out, she could shoot him. Nothing fatal. Maybe take off a toe.

It had been raining when she landed in Quito two days earlier. It was still raining when she took the twenty-five-minute flight to Caco and boarded a Napo River ferry to Nuevo Rocafuerte. And it was raining when she met her guides at daybreak and settled into their motorized canoe for the six-hour trip down a narrow, winding river with no name. Just before noon, they'd pulled up at a crude campground hacked out of the jungle. They'd immediately left the river behind and followed a barely there trail through dense vegetation. And it was still raining.

"Insurance Fraud Investigator" was printed on Gabriela's business card, and she had an international reputation for excellence in the field. As an independent contractor she had the luxury of accepting jobs not related to insurance fraud, whether because they paid well or because they were fun. Her current job had checks in both boxes.

She'd been hired to find Henry Dodge and retrieve an amulet he was carrying. She didn't have a lot of information on the amulet or Dodge. Just that he couldn't leave his jobsite, and he'd requested that someone come to get the amulet. Seemed reasonable since Dodge was an archeologist doing research on a lost civilization in a previously unexplored part of the Amazon Rain

Forest. The payoff for Gabriela was a big bag of money, but that wasn't what had convinced her to take the job.

She was possibly a descendant of the infamous pirate Blackbeard, and she was fascinated by seventeenth- and eighteenth-century pirates and the civilizations they touched. The opportunity to visit the site of a lost city was irresistible. It was also her thirtieth birthday. What better way to celebrate it than to have an adventure?

"How much further?" she asked Jorge.

"Not far," he said. "Just on the other side of the bridge."

Twenty minutes later, Gabriela set foot on the dig site. She'd been on other digs, and this wasn't what she'd expected. There was some partially exposed rubble that might have been a wall at one time. A couple of tables with benches under a tarp. A kitchen area that was also under a tarp. A stack of wooden crates. A trampled area that suggested it might have recently been used as a site for several tents. Only one small tent was currently left standing.

There were no people to see except for one waterlogged and slightly bloated man lying on the ground by the rubble, and a weary-looking man sitting on a camp chair. The first was clearly dead. The second stared at them as they approached.

"This is not good," Jorge said. "One of these men is very dead and something has eaten his leg."

"Panther," the man in the chair said. "You can hear them prowling past your tent at night. This site is a hellhole. Were you folks just out for a stroll in the rain?"

"I was sent to get an amulet from Henry Dodge," Gabriela said. "I believe I was expected."

The man nodded to the corpse. "That's Henry. Had some bad luck."

"What happened?"

"He was checking on an excavation in the rain first thing this morning, fell off the wall, and smashed his head on the rocks. Then a panther came and ate his leg before we could scare it away. Everyone packed up and left after that. Too many bad things happening here."

"But you stayed," Gabriela said.

"They couldn't carry everything out in one trip. I stayed with some of the remaining crates and the body. Cameron said he would be back with help before it got dark."

"Do you know where Henry kept the amulet?" Gabriela asked.

"Usually on a chain around his neck," the man said. "He felt it was the safest place. Right now, it looks to me like he's got it in his hand. You can see the chain hanging out and part of the gold trim."

Gabriela looked at the dead man's hand. It was grotesquely swollen and clenched in a fist. The amulet was barely visible.

"Someone needs to get his hand open," Gabriela said.

No one volunteered.

Gabriela flicked a centipede off her sleeve. She knew the rain, the mud, the bugs, the sweltering heat were all part of the Ecuadorian experience. The dead man with the swollen hand was not. The question now was, how bad did she want the amulet? The lost-cities site had turned out to be a bust, but there was still a payday attached to the amulet. So, the answer to the question was that she wanted the amulet pretty damn bad. Without the amulet, there would be no big bag of money. She was well respected in her profession, but big paydays didn't come along every day.

"I've come this far," she said. "I'm not going back without the amulet." She looked at the man in the chair. "I need to pry Dodge's hand open. I need gloves and a baggie. Archeological sites usually have them."

The man shrugged as an apology. "They were all packed out. Truth is, we were shutting down before Henry happened. Henry was the holdout. He found the amulet, and he thought there was more here. The rest of us didn't care."

"We need to leave now," Jorge said. "It will be bad to be in this jungle after sunset. Hard to find the way, and panthers will be hunting at night. We have maybe five hours of daylight left."

"I'm not leaving without the amulet," Gabriela said.

Cuckoo took his machete out of its sheath and *whack!* He chopped Henry Dodge's hand off at the wrist.

"I suppose that's one way to go," Gabriela said. "I would have preferred to try my way first."

"He's dead," Cuckoo said. "He doesn't need the hand."

He picked the hand up by the horribly swollen thumb, grabbed Gabriela's daypack, and dropped the hand in.

"Problem is solved," Jorge said.

"He's right about the jungle at night," the man in the chair said. "If you're going back on the same path you came on, you don't want to go alone. And you don't want to stray from the path."

"If everyone packed out this morning, why didn't we see them?" Gabriela asked.

"They took the road behind the wall," the man said. "Forty-five minutes to walk, and it cuts the river trip in half."

Gabriela looked at Jorge and Cuckoo.

"Road has bad juju," Jorge said. "Anaconda highway."

. . . .

The walk back to the motorized canoe took a little under four hours. Easier going without the rain.

Gabriela stopped at the river's edge and dropped her daypack. "I can't take the smell coming out of my pack. One way or another I'm going to get the amulet out of Dodge's hand," she said to Jorge and Cuckoo. "Hopefully the swelling has gone down and the rigor has relaxed."

"Not good to stay here," Jorge said. "The hand will draw predators."

"No problem," Gabriela said. "The predators can have the hand as soon as I get the amulet."

Gabriela removed a folding Buck knife from her cargo pants pocket and opened the blade. "This shouldn't take long." She unzipped the daypack, held her breath against the smell of decomposing flesh, and looked in at the hand.

Jorge and Cuckoo inched away from Gabriela, moving closer to the canoe. Gabriela couldn't blame them. This was going to get worse before it got better. She was about to do surgery on some necrotic fingers, and it wasn't going to be pretty. She dumped the hand onto the ground and tossed the pack toward Jorge and Cuckoo.

She didn't want to grab the hand without gloves, so she stepped on it to secure it and tried to pry the hand open with the knife. No luck. She took a moment to assess the situation.

"I hear something in the brush," Jorge said. "We should right away go now."

"We've been hearing things in the brush for four hours," Gabriela said.

"Even worse," Jorge said. "Could be the panther stalking the hand you are standing on."

"That's ridiculous," Gabriela said. "He would have attacked by now. The brush is filled with small animals doing whatever it is they do."

As she bent down to try the knife one more time, a panther crept out of the jungle. He was thirty feet away and he was in a crouch. His bright yellow eyes focused like lasers on Gabriela.

Jorge jumped into the canoe and started the engine. Cuckoo was at the bow, pushing off from the bank. Gabriela had her gun trained on the panther.

"Very bad to shoot panther," Jorge said from the canoe. "They are on critically endangered list."

"He ate Henry Dodge," Gabriela said.

"Humans aren't endangered," Jorge said. "Okay for panthers to eat them."

Gabriela took two steps back. The panther

rushed forward, snatched the hand, and disappeared into the jungle with it.

"I would have shot him," Cuckoo said.

"We can track him," Gabriela said. "He won't eat the amulet. He'll leave it behind."

Jorge and Cuckoo exchanged glances.

"You track him. We'll wait here for you," Jorge said.

They aren't going to wait, Gabriela thought. They're going to take off the instant I'm out of sight. I'll be stuck here with no cell service and no canoe. And by the time I walk back to the dig site tomorrow it'll be completely abandoned. And the truth is, the cat was terrifying. Magnificent, beautiful, and terrifying. It would be terrible to have to shoot him, and even worse to be his main course after he enjoyed the hand as an appetizer.

· · · ·

It was a little after 9:00 p.m. when Gabriela climbed out of the motorized canoe and onto the dock at Nuevo Rocafuerte. She paid the guides and tossed her empty daypack into a trash barrel. Not one of her better outings but not the worst, either, she thought. She got to see a wild panther on her birthday. How often was that going to happen?

She powered up her cell phone and was about to check messages when her mom called.

"Hi, honey," Maeberry Rose said. "Happy birthday. We've been trying to call you all day, but you haven't been answering."

"I'm in Ecuador," Gabriela said. "I didn't have cell service until just now."

Gabriela could hear her grandmother Fanny in the background shouting *happy birthday*.

"It sounds like Grandma is still living with you," Gabriela said to her mother.

"At least for a while," Mae said. "We're thinking of selling. We can't afford to fix the damage. No one can."

Six months ago, a cat 4 storm blew over Scoon, the little South Carolina coastal town where Gabriela grew up. Double-wides were moved off their foundations, boats were beached, cottages that had stood for generations had their roofs stripped off and windows blown out. It was said that the fishing wharf was swept all the way up to Ocracoke Island.

"What about insurance?" Gabriela asked.

"We weren't insured. Just about no one in the town had insurance. It's too expensive."

"Where will you go?"

"We haven't figured that out yet. Wherever

your father can find work. Even if he could get the boat put back together, there's no place to dock it. The boat docks are gone. Only the pilings are left."

Gabriela's father owned a charter fishing boat. When Gabriela was ten years old, she started working as mate on the boat. She put herself through college with the wages she earned every summer. When she left to live in New York, her cousin Andy took over the mate job.

"When I was home at Christmas you didn't seem to be worried," Gabriela said.

"We all thought the town would qualify for emergency funding, but the funding never came through," Mae said. "And now there's a real estate developer making offers on all the houses. They're really low offers, but most of us have no other choice."

"I'm not giving up my house," her grandmother Fanny said into the phone. "It was my mother's house and her mother's house."

"It doesn't have a roof," Gabriela's mother said. "It's got a blue vinyl tarp over it. There's a tree in your living room."

"It can be fixed," Fanny said. "All the houses and boats and the dock can be fixed. We just need some money, and I have a way to get it if Gabriela will help us. I have a plan."

"Your plan is crazy talk," Gabriela's mother said. "It's not a plan."

Gabriela checked the time. She needed to get into clean clothes, and she needed to make some phone calls.

"I'm leaving Ecuador tomorrow," she said to her mother. "I'll change out my ticket to New York for a ticket to Charleston and we can discuss this when I get home."

• • • •

The ticket change had required taking a red-eye out of Quito. It dropped Gabriela in Charleston at 1:30 in the afternoon. She'd rented a car and taken her time driving through her hometown of Scoon. Not that there was a lot to see. It was a hardworking little town located an hour out of Charleston. The storefronts were mostly brick. Some of the windows were still boarded up. The houses were clapboard. Nothing fancy. It wasn't a picturesque tourist town, but the fishing was phenomenal. Backwater fishing to the west and perfect ocean currents to the east. A natural harbor.

Gabriela was thinking that this was sweatshirt weather if you were born in Scoon. Gray sky with cold drizzle. If you were in from Atlanta or Tampa, you might have wanted a winter jacket. There was a scattering of cars in the Publix parking lot.

Lights were on in Eddie's Coffee House. That was about it for activity. A year ago, things were different. A lot more cars at Publix and more foot traffic on Main Street. The parking lot for the wharf would have been packed.

Her parents lived on the town's outer edge. Close enough to the shoreline to smell the briny mist on a day like today, far enough inland and on a slight rise to be protected from the surge tides. It was a small clapboard house on a quarter acre of land. A Ford F-150 pickup and an empty boat trailer sat in the driveway.

Gabriela knew exactly how the inside of the house would smell. It would smell like her childhood. Febreze air freshener, store-bought powdered-sugar donuts, and cat food.

She'd been away for enough years that the smell of her childhood was no longer the smell of home for her. Home was a condo in Soho. It had no smell.

She parked behind her dad's truck and twenty minutes later she was at the small kitchen table with her mother and Grandma Fanny. Gabriela had her hands wrapped around a mug of hot peppermint tea, and she was forcing herself to focus on the table talk.

Her mind kept drifting back to the conversation she'd just had with the New York lawyer who'd hired her to collect the amulet in Ecuador. The conversation hadn't gone well. Telling him that a panther ran off with the valuable amulet was the equivalent to telling her fourth-grade math teacher that the dog ate her homework.

"This developer is the devil," Fanny said. "He wants to build one of those awful couples resorts here. He's forcing the bank to foreclose on a whole passel of properties, and he's trying to buy houses on the cheap. That includes your mother's house and the houses of just about everyone you know."

"At least we have someone willing to buy the houses," Mae said. "The alternative is to just walk away and lose everything."

"I'm telling you we need to fix the wharf. We need to get the fishing business up and running again," Fanny said.

"How much would it cost to fix the wharf?" Gabriela asked.

"I figure around fifteen million," Fanny said.

Gabriela leaned forward a little. "Excuse me?"

"That includes some other stuff that would go along with the wharf," Fanny said. "I figure we'd want to rebuild Fred Grimlet's fish-and-chips hut that was right at the parking lot. It got washed away. And we could help some of the people who want to stay. We could give them a loan until they get back on their feet."

"How are you going to get fifteen million dollars?" Gabriela asked.

"That's where you come in," Fanny said. "I have a plan. Remember when you were a little girl, I used to tell you stories about a secret room in your Great Auntie Margareet's house on St. Vincent? Well, I just learned it's under the floorboards of Margareet's bedroom. And in that secret room, there's supposed to be all sorts of things that belonged to Blackbeard. Margareet used to talk about a chest that had maps and a diary. So, what I'm hoping is that you can go there and find the chest and maybe find a map that will lead to a treasure."

"How did you just find out about the room?"

"Annie told me."

"You aren't serious," Gabriela said. "Annie the ghost?"

"Yep. She dropped in the other night and told me about the room and that's when I got the idea about you finding the chest. That's what you do, right? You recover treasure."

"Yes, but this is different. This is fairy-tale treasure."

"I'm pretty sure it's real," Fanny said. "Margareet said it was real."

Margareet was Gabriela's great-grandmother's

sister. When most of Margareet's family migrated from the Caribbean to South Carolina, Margareet stayed on St. Vincent in the little house that had been passed to her from her grandmother. Margareet never married and when she died, she left the house to Gabriela.

"And besides, it's not just me. Annie wants you to find the treasure so you could save the town," Fanny said.

For as long as Gabriela could remember, her grandmother had told her stories about the tragic love affair between Blackbeard and a beautiful woman from Barbados named Annie. Sadly, Annie died while giving birth to their daughter. And according to Fanny's family legend, Gabriela was a descendant of Blackbeard and Annie.

Gabriela had never personally heard or seen Annie the ghost. Fanny often dragged Annie out during moments of minor crisis. *Annie is very upset that you didn't eat breakfast*, Fanny would tell Gabriela. *Annie is disappointed that you got a D in math. Annie is horrified that you smoked a cigarette.*

Fanny set a box of powdered-sugar donuts on the table. "So now all you have to do is hop over to St. Vincent and get the treasure chest."

"That's not going to happen," Gabriela said. "I

no longer own Margareet's house. Rafer got it in the divorce settlement. I haven't seen him or the house in seven years."

"I'm sure he'd let you get the treasure chest," Fanny said.

"It wasn't a friendly divorce," Gabriela said. "I gave him the St. Vincent house because I didn't want to see him every time I came back to Scoon."

"You two always fought like cats and dogs," Fanny said. "I never understood why you married him."

Gabriela had no good answer. She got into a fight with Rafer Jones on the first day of kindergarten and from that day on they argued about everything and yet they were inexplicably inseparable. They were also the scourge of the town. If a cow got painted red or an unoccupied car ended up submerged in the marshland behind town, the sheriff knew who to call on. They dated all through high school and got married while still in college. They fought over breakfast cereal, laundry detergent, which movie to watch, the temperature of the bedroom, and just about every other aspect of their lives. They had phenomenal makeup sex and then argued about its merits when they were done. They got divorced a week before their second wedding anniversary. The inhabitants of Scoon acknowledged that this was the loudest, most contentious, most fantastic divorce in the history of the town.

"I loved him," Gabriela said. "He was fun."

Plus, he was adorable and sexy from kindergarten straight through to the end of the marriage. Best not to share that part with her family, she thought. He was also a slob, lacked ambition, drank too much, and insisted on calling her Gabs.

"There's no way I can go to St. Vincent and search for a treasure chest stored under Rafer's bedroom," Gabriela said.

"Without the treasure it's hopeless," Fanny said. "I get that it sounds crazy, but I can't come up with anything else."

Gabriela looked at her mother.

Her mother gave up a sigh. "I'm afraid she's right about being hopeless. We're all scraping bottom on ideas and money."

"I'll think about it," Gabriela said. "I need to get back to New York first. I have some pending business commitments."

CHAPTER TWO

Gabriela paced in front of her Miele coffee machine. She needed coffee and she needed it *now*. She didn't have thirty-four seconds to waste waiting for the state-of-the-art machine to heat the water.

She'd taken an evening flight out of South Carolina and let herself into her condo a little after midnight. She'd crashed into bed, overslept, and now it was almost 9:00 a.m. That meant a late start to an overbooked day.

Deep breath, she told herself, watching the coffee dribble into her to-go cup. You're only a little behind schedule. It's not like this is world annihilation. Take a moment to enjoy your oasis of sanity.

Her oasis of sanity was 1,500 square feet of white walls and ceiling and a hand-scraped maple floor that was stained chocolate. The furnishings were clean-lined, comfortable, and contemporary. Two club chairs and a sofa in white chenille. Large flat-screen TV. Rectangular glass-topped dining table with six chairs. A home office in an alcove by a window. One bedroom, one and a half baths. And a chef's kitchen stocked with herbs and spices she'd collected from exotic job locations.

She screwed the cap on her coffee mug, hung her slim brown Fendi messenger bag on the shoulder of her designer suit, and took the elevator to the ground floor. She walked two blocks to the building that housed her single-room, fifth-floor office and paused when she got to the office door. The gold stenciled name on the door read G. R. McDuck. It always made her smile. The name was an homage to her comic book hero, Scrooge McDuck. He had humble beginnings, but he amassed a fortune by being "tougher than the toughies and sharper than the sharpies." He went on adventures all over the world and brought his treasures back home to Duckburg.

Gabriela didn't aspire to pushing her gold coins around with a bulldozer like McDuck, but she did like his risk-taking style and his drive to succeed. For as long as she could remember, she was envious of his adventures.

Gabriela entered the office and gave a smile and a hello to her personal assistant and sole employee, Marcella Lott. Marcella was at her desk multitasking between working on her computer and eating a bagel, heavy on the cream cheese. She was five years older and an inch shorter than Gabriela. Her skin was freckled, and her hair was red and curly. She looked like a thirtysomething Little Orphan Annie. And after a couple of glasses of wine she could belt out a pretty good rendition of "Tomorrow."

"Welcome back," Marcella said to Gabriela. "Sorry about the amulet. Did a panther really eat it?"

"Unfortunately, yes," Gabriela said. "My client wasn't pleased."

"I spoke to his lawyer this morning. They want their retainer back."

"We have a contract," Gabriela said. "I keep the retainer. Explain the facts of life to him, and then send him a gift box of Jacques Torres chocolates."

"The fifty-dollar box?"

"Twenty-five. He was a jerk when I talked to him last night. I don't think he believed me about the panther."

Marcella leaned forward and handed Gabriela

a large yellow envelope. "Here's your mail. Nothing that looks urgent. Your schedule for the next two weeks is also in there, including today."

Gabriela pulled out her schedule. "This is a blank piece of paper. What happened to my ten-million-dollar insurance fraud case in San Francisco?"

"They found the painting. I cancelled your plane and hotel arrangements."

"Do we have anything else to slot in there?"

"No. You blocked out two weeks. The only thing we have pending is that dot-com billionaire, what's-his-name. He said he's sorry he tried to kidnap you, and he really needs your help finding his high school yearbook. He says he's sure it was stolen. He's offering a big bag of money. Actually, it's a *huge* bag of money."

Gabriela drained her coffee mug. "Pass."

· · · ·

The next day, Gabriela boarded a plane to St. Vincent. This is ridiculous, she told herself, taking her seat. I'm going to break into my ex-husband's house because my grandmother talks to a ghost. Even more ridiculous, I'm supposed to come away from all this with $15 million. So why am I doing it if it's so ridiculous?

It was a rhetorical question. She already

knew the answer. She was intrigued by the idea that Margareet might have kept Blackbeard's chest hidden in a secret compartment under her bedroom's floorboards. If there was no chest anywhere under or in Margareet's house, the case was closed. But what if there *was* a chest with a diary or a treasure map? Her heart skipped a couple of beats at the thought.

. . . .

Gabriela landed at noon, and by one o'clock she was driving her rented Hyundai Accent through the downtown area of Kingstown. She'd been on the island several times with her family, and she was vaguely familiar with the roads. The most recent visits were ten years ago. Once to celebrate Margareet's ninety-fifth birthday. Two months later to lay Margareet to rest and settle her estate.

Gabriela headed west on Bay Street and eventually hooked up with the Leeward Highway. Twenty minutes later she rolled into the village of Layou and located Margareet's small bright blue cottage. The cottage clung to a hillside and looked out over the bay and beyond. The view was spectacular. The front porch ran the width of the house and held a hammock and two rocking chairs. The yard was packed with flowering shrubs, banana trees, dwarf palms, and ferns. There was a driveway but no garage. No sign of a car parked on the street in front of the house or in the driveway.

Rafer's at work, Gabriela thought. He owns a dive shop in Kingstown and there's a cruise ship docked in the harbor. The dive shop is probably packed with tourists.

She parked a short distance from the house, slung her Prada backpack onto her shoulder, and walked to the front door. She knocked twice and was relieved when no one answered. She was adept at picking locks, but it wasn't a skill she needed today. She still had a key that she'd found long after Rafer was gone.

She opened the door and called, "Hello. Anyone home?"

No answer.

The inside of the house had been painted white. The wood floors had been refinished. The furniture was mostly left from Margareet. Formal carved mahogany chairs and end tables. A tight-back couch upholstered in a wine-colored fabric. A small mahogany dining table.

Gabriela looked around and concluded that her divorce had been justified. There were sneakers under the cocktail table in front of the couch. Dive charts, pizza takeout boxes, and empty beer bottles littered the dining table. The man was still a slob and a drunk.

She did a quick walk-through to reacquaint herself with the floor plan. Formal living room looking out at the bay, small dining room, cozy kitchen with dated appliances, one bathroom that had been renovated to include a walk-in shower, two bedrooms. The larger bedroom that had been Margareet's was now an office. The smaller bedroom was fitted with a California King–sized bed that pretty much filled the room.

This was a lucky break, Gabriela thought. Fanny said the secret room could be found under the floorboards of Margareet's bedroom. That now held a surfboard, a mountain bike, a large brown leather club chair that had seen better days, a pair of metal file cabinets, a massive oak desk, and a boardroom-style leather desk chair. Most of the floor was exposed. No heavy bed to move.

Gabriela walked across the room, listening to the occasional creak of the old boards, looking for a seam that might indicate a trapdoor. She didn't find anything, so she checked out the smaller bedroom. She was on her stomach half under the bed with a flashlight when she heard the front door slam shut. Heavy footsteps made their way into the bedroom, and she saw two large sneaker-clad feet standing at the bedside. Hands wrapped around her ankles and she was pulled out from under the bed.

"Hello, darlin'," Rafer said. "I always knew you'd be back, but I always expected you to be in my bed, not under it."

Rafer Jones was six feet two inches tall and nicely muscled. He was wearing a T-shirt that advertised his dive shop, black-and-green camo board shorts, and Vans slip-on sneakers that were far from new. His sun-bleached hair was short and totally bed-head. He was beach-bum tan and had a five o'clock shadow at two in the afternoon. Gabriela thought he had aged better than she'd expected. In fact, he was disturbingly hot. None of this made up for the fact that she was sure he was still a jerk.

"I'm not back, and I have no intention of being *in* your bed," Gabriela said.

"What *were* your intentions?"

"Grandma just found out that there's something under the floor that shouldn't have been conveyed with the house. I came to retrieve it."

"Seems like the proper thing would have been for you to ask for my help."

"You weren't home." She got to her feet. "And I don't need your help."

"Good thing I'm an easygoing guy or I might

be inclined to report you to the police for illegal entry." Her Prada backpack was on the bed. He picked it up and looked inside. "A mini crowbar and a hammer? Are you serious?"

"I'll make sure that any damage I do gets repaired."

Rafer handed her the backpack. "You've got my attention. What's under the floor?"

This wasn't the way she wanted things to go down, Gabriela thought. She now had two choices. She could walk away to return at a better time, or she could involve Rafer. If she walked away, he would tear up the floor and possibly find Blackbeard's chest. She absolutely didn't want that to happen.

"Supposedly there's a chest hidden under the floor. Grandma Fanny says that it contains diaries and personal items from our relatives," Gabriela said. "I would like to have it. My grandmother would like to have it."

"Okay," Rafer said. "I get that. And you think it's under this room?"

"I was told it was under Margareet's bedroom. You're using it as an office now, but I didn't see anything that would indicate a trapdoor, so I thought I should check out this bedroom, too."

"I'd like to help you, but I'm not inclined to tear up all my floors," Rafer said.

"It shouldn't be necessary," Gabriela said. "I have a device that will allow us to see through the wood. This house doesn't have a cellar. It was built on a shallow crawl space. I'm hoping we can see something to indicate a room dug out of the dirt or maybe even the chest."

"You're using a stud finder."

"Yes, sort of. This one can see through four inches of concrete."

Rafer made a sweeping gesture with his hand. "Have at it."

Gabriela went back to the office and ran the sensor across the floor.

"I've got something dead center," she said. "There's an anomaly in the support beams. And I'm pretty sure I'm seeing metal hinges."

She'd been excited to see the hinges. Until that moment she'd had doubts. Truth is, she still had doubts, but they were now offset by *omigod, what if Margareet had been telling the truth?*

Gabriela rammed the crowbar between two boards, tapped it with the hammer, and pried the board up. The boards were wide and of varying lengths. The first board to come up was short. The second board was longer and more difficult.

"Do you want to help me with this?" she asked Rafer.

"Nope," he said. "You look like you can handle

it. I came home for a late lunch and maybe some afternoon hammock time."

He wandered off to the kitchen, returned with a sandwich and a soft drink, and looked down at the trapdoor that Gabriela had uncovered.

"Nice work, Gabs," he said.

Gabriela resisted hitting him with the hammer. "You know that annoys me. Why do you insist on calling me Gabs?"

"I like it. And it annoys you," he said, flashing her his killer smile. "It's a win-win."

She allowed herself a grunt of disgust and stared down at the trapdoor. The hinges and lock were substantial but rusted. The wooden door looked partially rotted. She gave it a good whack with the hammer, and it splintered. Another whack and it was off its hinges.

She lowered herself down through the gaping hole, pulled a flashlight out of her pocket, and switched it on. She was standing on packed dirt, and she judged the excavated area to be approximately the size of the room above her. It seemed to be sealed and rat-free. The spider population was thriving. A rusted kerosene lantern was tipped on its side close to where she stood. A lone chest sat in the darkness against a dirt wall. Even at a distance it was clear that this wasn't a jewel-encrusted Disney-style pirate chest. This was a sturdy, time-worn chest that might have been used to transport clothes, crockery, munitions, linens, or a man's personal effects. It was about three feet long and two feet wide and stood about two feet high with a barrel lid.

Clearance between the crude overhead cobwebbed joists and the dirt floor was barely four feet, making standing difficult. Gabriela stoop-walked to the chest and tried the lock, but it wouldn't budge. She grabbed one of the handles on the end of the chest and dragged the chest back to the trapdoor.

"How's it going?" Rafer asked, looking down at Gabriela. "It looks like you found a chest. Is there anything in it?"

"It's locked. I'm going to pass it up to you."

Rafer took the chest from Gabriela and set it aside. He reached down, grabbed Gabriela, and pulled her out.

"I can't believe this was actually down there," he said. "How did Grandma Fanny learn about it?"

"Margareet told her years ago." Gabriela paused for a beat. "And Grandma said Annie wanted me to retrieve it."

"Annie the ghost?"

"Yep."

That got another thousand-watt smile from

Rafer. "You were always a sucker for those ghost stories."

"So far, Margareet and the ghost are looking pretty reliable," she said. "Help me get this out to my car."

"Whoa, not so fast. Don't I get to see what's in the chest? I mean, it's in my house, so technically it's my chest."

"It's not your chest. It belongs to my family."

"That's not the way our divorce papers read. I got everything that was in Margareet's house."

"Yes, but this was *under* her house," Gabriela said. "And besides, there's nothing in this chest to interest you. Supposedly it's filled with things that would have sentimental value to Grandma."

"I'm a sentimental kind of guy," Rafer said. "Let's take a look."

"You're one of the least sentimental people I know."

"Second to you," Rafer said.

This was true, Gabriela thought. It was one of the few character traits they had in common. She examined the ancient padlock on the chest, took a slim set of tools from her pack, and picked the lock.

"I haven't kept up with your life," Rafer said. "I assume from what I've just seen that it includes breaking and entering and burglary. Maybe safe-cracking."

"I'm a recovery agent," Gabriela said. "I find lost treasures and people."

"Bounty hunter?"

"Not at all. I mostly deal with insurance fraud and high-end theft."

She lifted the lid and sucked in some air. The chest was filled with leather-bound books, bound rolls of paper that she assumed were maps, small suede drawstring pouches, assorted knives, and two eighteenth-century pistols.

Gabriela closed the chest and hung the pad-lock back in place. "Now that you've seen it, I'll be on my way."

"I thought the chest was supposed to contain diaries from your relatives," Rafer said. "I was thinking more along the lines of Margareet chron-icling a nooner. The stuff I'm seeing in the chest looks a lot older than Margareet." He removed the lock and lifted the lid. "Let's take a closer look."

Two hours later, they were done sifting through the contents of the chest.

"I've waded through a bunch of pirate scrib-blings and faded maps," Rafer said. "I suppose they could be authentic, but the line between fact and fiction seems blurry in a lot of what I've just read. Pirates were good at bending the truth."

He looked over at Gabriela. "You've been reading the same journal for a half hour. What's so interesting?"

"It's the journal of Sir Francis Drake, the first Englishman to sail around the world, the guy who helped Queen Elizabeth defeat the Spanish Armada. He was considered a war hero by the English and a vicious pirate by the Spanish."

"I'm sure you know every detail ever recorded about the man. You've been obsessed with pirates for as long as I've known you."

"I'm not *obsessed* with pirates. I find them interesting."

"Honey, you're obsessed."

"That's ridiculous. You're the one with obsessions."

"What are my obsessions?"

"Boobs and beer."

"Okay, maybe a little, but what else?"

Gabriela gave him a sideways glance. He was hopeless.

"So, tell me about Drake's journal," Rafer said.

"According to the journal, Drake was determined to find the Treasure of Lima. Specifically, he wanted the Seal of Solomon. He was never able to find the Seal, or at least he was never able to capture it, but he writes about it at length."

"You lost me at 'the Treasure of Lima.'"

"That's because you were obsessed with boobs while I was studying history. If you'd paid attention in Mr. Rachet's class, you would know that the Treasure of Lima originated with Pizarro."

"Rachet was a colossal bore. Tell me about this Seal of Solomon. I assume Rachet droned on about it while I was concentrating on not falling out of my seat in a mind-numbing stupor."

"In the interest of full disclosure, I don't remember Rachet talking about the Seal of Solomon. I just did a crash course on my iPhone. Supposedly the Seal is part of a signet ring made from brass and iron. Legend has it that the ring was engraved by God and given directly to King Solomon. The ring gave Solomon the power to command demons, genies, and spirits and to speak with animals."

"Yeah, that sounds like something God would do," Rafer said. "Just for giggles."

"The history of the ring gets fuzzy for a few centuries after Solomon, but in 1572, after four decades of fighting with the Incas and being close to losing the war, it's believed that Pizarro came into possession of the Seal of Solomon. You remember Pizarro, right?"

"He was a Spanish conquistador. Killed a bunch of Incas."

"He massacred the Incas and killed their king,"

Gabriela said. "It's said that he used the Seal of Solomon to conjure up dark forces to defeat the Incan emperor."

"The fact that Pizarro had guns and the Incas had slingshots might also have had something to do with their demise."

"You're ruining my story."

"Sorry," Rafer said. "Carry on."

"Pizarro acquired a massive treasure trove for the Spanish monarchy. It was known as the Treasure of Lima and it was kept in the city, guarded by Spanish soldiers and Catholic priests.

"After Pizarro's death, along came Drake, passing by Peru as he was sailing around the world. He learned of the treasure and of the Seal of Solomon. It was whispered that Pizarro hadn't entrusted the Seal to the care of the Lima priests. He'd hidden the Seal deep in the Peruvian jungle. Drake became obsessed with possessing the Seal but died before he actually got his hands on it. Some scholars think the Seal is in the lost Incan city of Paititi."

"You've got that look," Rafer said.

"What look?"

"The look that always got us into trouble. The Uncle Scrooge/ Indiana Jones look. You're thinking about going after the Seal, aren't you?"

"Maybe."

"Why the Seal?" Rafer asked. "If you're going off on a wild-goose chase, why not choose something local. This chest is filled with maps and diaries that are supposed to lead to treasure."

"None of those treasures can compare to the Seal of Solomon."

"If it even exists."

Gabriela shrugged. "There's no guarantee, but there's a lot of historical reference to it. And if it does exist, it would be priceless."

"Okay, so this seal is worth a lot of money. I get it. And you go all over the world finding valuable things that are lost. So, suppose you can find this seal. What's my cut?"

Gabriela narrowed her eyes. "You don't get a cut."

"Sweetie Pie, it's *my* journal."

"It's not your journal. It belongs to my family."

"Not anymore," Rafer said. "It came with the house. You gave it to me when *you* divorced *me*."

"The decision to end the marriage was mutual."

"You started it," Rafer said.

"And you ended it. You slept with Mary Jane Cooney."

"That was after the divorce."

"*It was an hour after!* Everyone knew. You did

it in your pickup truck in the courthouse parking lot."

Rafer grinned. "She ambushed me."

Gabriela rolled her eyes and grunted. "Ugh! Yuk!"

"Why is this invaluable seal so important to you? You look like you're doing okay. Do you really need more money?"

"The town needs it," Gabriela said. "Have you been back lately? They can't recover from the hurricane. People are being forced to sell their houses. The dock is gone. There's no fishing."

"You're going to get the Seal, sell it to some rich guy, and give the money to Scoon?"

"Yes."

Rafer slouched back in his chair and closed his eyes. "Crap." He opened his eyes and leaned forward. "Of all the lousy luck. I get a chance to really piss you off and make some money in the bargain and then you pull this on me."

"What? Do a good deed?"

"Yes. Good deeds suck. I hate good deeds. They always end up biting you in the ass."

"You have nothing to worry about. It's my good deed, not yours."

"Does the journal have a map in it with a big X marking the spot where the Seal is hidden?"

"Not exactly. There's a small map but it's vague. And there are some coded and cryptic clues to the Seal's suspected location."

"And are you thinking we should follow the cryptic clues?"

"There's no *we*. There's just *me*," Gabriela said. "I work alone."

"Not anymore, Pumpkin. My parents and my sister are still in Scoon, barely hanging on to their houses. I'm all about finding a magic ring."

"I can find the ring on my own."

"The hell you can. I'm not letting you or the journal out of my sight."

"You don't trust me?"

"Not even a little."

Gabriela thought about it for a beat and nodded. She couldn't fault his reasoning. She didn't trust him, either.

CHAPTER THREE

When the plane touched down in Lima, Gabriela had a "just been here, just did this" moment. She was back in South America. It was a different country with a higher-stakes cause, but there was still an element of déjà vu. The déjà vu moment was fleeting because she was with Rafer on this trip. He was sitting two rows in front of her. She couldn't actually see him, but she knew he was there. He was like a blister on her heel. A constant irritation. And it didn't help that he was smoking-hot and the flight attendant kept stopping to chat with him and at one point brought him warm chocolate chip cookies. Gabriela could smell them two rows away.

The next stop on their treasure hunt was Cusco.

It was the gateway city to Machu Picchu, but they weren't going to Machu Picchu. They were following Drake's map to the Wilkapampa Mountains in the La Convención Province. It would have been nice to breeze through immigration in Lima and catch the next flight to Cusco, but that wasn't practical. They would have to overnight in Cusco, and at 11,152 feet that would mean a crashing headache in the morning from lack of oxygen. So, they went with an alternate plan to catch a cab to the Wyndham Lima Airport hotel for a one-night stay.

"Tell me about our guide," Gabriela said to Rafer on the way to the hotel.

"His name is Pepe. He's meeting us at the Cusco airport when we get in tomorrow morning. We'll take off right away for La Convención Province. It's about a four-and-a-half-hour drive. He has his own car."

"You know him, right?"

"I know his cousin. Ralph Grinty. Ralph owns a bar on the island. He goes to Peru a couple times a year and hangs with this guy. Ralph says he's cool. His family owns a coffee plantation, but he doesn't have much to do with it."

"Can we trust him?"

"I don't think he'll kill us, if that's what you mean."

I'm stuck with a freaking moron for a partner, Gabriela thought. This is going to be a disaster.

• • • •

Pepe was waiting curbside for Gabriela and Rafer. He was in his early forties, short, rail thin, with close-set brown eyes and short-cropped wavy black hair. He was holding a sign that read PEPE. He rushed over to Rafer and Gabriela and introduced himself.

"I'm Pepe," he said. "Ralph told me to look for the biggest guy on the plane, so I'm thinking you are Rafer and Gabs."

Gabriela started to correct him on her name and gave it up. She could see where this was going. It was going to be Gabs all the way.

"Did Ralph explain our need for a guide?" Gabriela asked Pepe.

"Oh yes," Pepe said. "He was very clear. You are going to Convención Province to search for treasure. You have a map that is completely vague and beyond that you have no idea where you are going. Do not worry. This is right up my alleyway. I have taken other treasure hunters into the Valley of Secrets."

"Did they find any treasure?" Gabriela asked.

"No. So, you have an advantage because I know many places where there are no treasures."

Gabriela looked him up and down. He was wearing a short-sleeved button-down shirt, brown dress pants, and red sneakers. She and Rafer were wearing lightweight trail boots, cargo pants, T-shirts, and hooded sweatshirts. They each had a medium-sized backpack.

"My understanding is that we will be hiking in rugged terrain," Gabriela said, her eyes focusing on the red sneakers.

Pepe nodded. "This is true. It is why I'm such a good guide. I'm a fit, wiry little monkey. I see you travel light. That is a good thing because my Angelina has a big engine but a small luggage space."

"Angelina?"

Pepe pointed to a faded pea-soup-green Citroën that was parked at the curb. "This is Angelina. She is a 1970 DS 21 IE semiautomatic model. I keep her in tip-top shape. She is beautiful, yes?"

"She's missing a headlight," Gabriela said.

"An unfortunate accident," Pepe said. "I tell her not to fear. She is pretty anyway, and I have a new one ordered from Amazon."

Gabriela and Rafer stowed their packs in the trunk and squeezed themselves into the Citroën. Once they left the city limits the road narrowed, followed switchbacks, and clung to mountainsides.

Gabriela thought the scenery was spectacular and Pepe's driving was terrifying.

"My Angelina is like a mountain goat," Pepe said, using the wrong side of the road to navigate a hairpin turn. "She is very sure-footed. Once we get to Route 28B and we are in the Urubamba River valley she will fly like an eagle."

Rafer was in the front seat, smiling and looking relaxed. Gabriela was in the cramped backseat hoping Angelina didn't take flight ahead of time and send them soaring off the road on a switchback.

As it turned out, Angelina returned to mountain goat form when 28B left the river valley. The road once again climbed mountains and dropped down mind-numbing switchbacks with hairpin turns.

Five hours later they drove into Quillabamba.

"This is a very nice city," Pepe said. "We can stay here tonight and set off to find your treasure first thing in the morning. We are at 3,440 feet, so you will be comfortable here. It is high jungle. It grows excellent coffee and cacao and tea and coca. I spend much time here because my uncle owns cropland in one of the mountain valleys."

"Is this the coffee plantation?" Gabriela asked.

"Did my cousin Ralph tell you we had a coffee plantation?"

"Yes."

"Then it is a coffee plantation," Pepe said.

Gabriela did an internal eye roll. There was no coffee plantation. The cash crop was most likely coca that was turned into cocaine. Her idiot ex-husband had them hooked up with the nephew of a drug lord.

Pepe pulled to the curb in front of a small café. "We can have lunch here and discuss tomorrow's treasure search," he said. "Your hotel is next to the café. I have reserved rooms for you."

The inside of the café was painted bright yellow and blue. The tables and chairs were a mixture of odds and ends. A mouthwatering aroma was coming from the kitchen. They took a table for four by the window.

Pepe leaned forward. "I would much like to see the very vague map."

Gabriela took the small map from her pack and laid it out on the table. "The map is part of a journal that hasn't been authenticated but seems to have belonged to Sir Francis Drake," she said. "He was interested in the treasure trove that was acquired by Francisco Pizarro and stored in Lima. Supposedly an important item in that collection was removed from Lima and taken to a lost city."

"The Seal of Solomon!" Pepe said, eyes wide.

"You're looking for the Seal of Solomon, aren't you? I knew it! I have always been interested in this. When I was a child, I was told bedtime stories of Inca treasures and the Seal of Solomon."

"Gabs thinks it's in the lost city of Paititi," Rafer said.

"That has been debunked by many people," Pepe said. "Choquequirao, the sister city of Machu Picchu, was once thought to be Paititi. It is only partially excavated but it is no longer in the Paititi sweepstakes. The popular belief now is that Paititi doesn't exist. Or if it does exist, that it is deep in the national sanctuary of Megantoni and not accessible." Pepe lowered his voice. "I have never believed any of this to be true. I have always thought Pizarro followed an offshoot of the Urubamba River into one of the deep valleys to the northwest but not so far as Megantoni."

"Why do you believe that?" Rafer asked.

"It's where I would put my treasure if I was Pizarro," Pepe said, studying the map on the table. "It appears that this map follows the Urubamba River to an offshoot that is not named."

"The diary says to look for the serpent that runs backward and it will show you the way to the dragon head," Gabriela said. "I'm at a loss on this one."

A middle-aged woman set bowls of rice, vegetables, and heavily spiced pork on the table.

"This is my cousin Maria," Pepe said to Gabriela and Rafer. "She owns this café. She also knows much about this area. What do you think?" Pepe asked Maria. "Where do we find the serpent that runs backward?"

"The serpent is a river," Maria said. "We call it La Vibora because it can be deadly. It doesn't flow into the Urubamba like other waters. The source is high in the mountain and splits where it becomes La Vibora." She shook her finger at Pepe. "You would know La Vibora if you spent more time here with family."

"Someone has to be out in the world," Pepe said. "We can't all be in the fields. So, I am the worldly one."

"Heaven help us," Maria said.

She returned to the kitchen and everyone dug into the food.

"Do you know where La Vibora is located?" Gabriela asked Pepe.

"I do not," he said, "but I will find out from Maria when we are done eating."

"You and Maria speak English," Gabriela said.

"We are businesspeople," Pepe said. "English is useful for international dealings."

"Like coffee exportation?" Rafer asked.

Pepe gave a bark of laughter. "Yes. We export much coffee."

. . . .

Gabriela and Rafer were in front of the hotel, waiting for Pepe. The sky was light, but the sun hadn't completely risen above the mountains.

"Next time I get the guide," Gabriela said.

Rafer looked over at her. "You don't like Pepe?"

"He's a drug runner."

"You don't know that for sure."

"I'm pretty sure his family doesn't grow *coffee*."

"Sweet Pea, your grandfather had a still in his basement and supplied half the town with illegal hooch. That doesn't mean he wasn't a good fisherman."

"Illegal hooch doesn't equate to cocaine."

"Did you ever try any of that hooch? It was like liquid lightning. Two shots and your tongue went numb and you couldn't make a fist."

Pepe pulled to the curb in a black Jeep Wrangler. It had oversized tires, a KC LED light bar, and a yellow-and-black inflatable raft strapped to the roof. A man dressed in khaki camouflage fatigues was sitting in the backseat. He was small and muscular with skin the texture of cracked leather. His hair was black and pulled into a low ponytail. He was smiling brightly.

Gabriela thought he looked like a seventy-year-old kid who was getting taken to Dairy Queen for an Oreo Blizzard.

"Nice wheels," Rafer said to Pepe.

"The raft wouldn't fit on Angelina, so she has time off," Pepe said. "I borrowed the Jeep and Caballo from my uncle. Caballo will help carry supplies, and he knows the way to the dragon head. We will have to leave the river and go on foot through the high jungle when we see the dragon."

Gabriela took the seat next to Caballo. "Have you been to the dragon head?" she asked him.

"No," he said. "I have only seen it once from the river. It was many years ago. It is known to be a dangerous area. It is said to be the holy ground of Supay and to be guarded by the wizard El Dragón and his army of snakes. La Vibora is the boundary marking El Dragón's territory."

"Who's Supay?" Gabriela asked.

"Supay is the Incan God of Death," Pepe said. "He's the ruler of a race of demons. They are all very bad guys."

"Do you believe any of this?" Gabriela asked him.

"No," Pepe said, "but I have a small fear of it. Supay might not like people trespassing on his holy land."

"Way to go, Gabs," Rafer said. "First day on the job and you're going to piss off the God of Death."

"She is very pretty," Pepe said. "It might go in her favor, but we will be in trouble."

"And the wizard, El Dragón?" Gabriela asked. "Who is he?"

"He is a very mysterious fellow," Pepe said. "He is the high priest to Supay and he has many followers. Snakes and demons and humans who have lost their souls. I'm told he is to be feared."

"La Vibora is tricky," Caballo said. "We could always drown before we get to the land of Supay."

"Good to know," Rafer said. "I feel a lot better now."

CHAPTER FOUR

Two hours after leaving Quillabamba, Caballo leaned forward and told Pepe to turn at the next bend in the road.

"Are you sure?" Gabriela asked Caballo. "I don't see any rivers joining the Urubamba."

"You will see it when we turn," he said. "It is small. There will be a bridge. I have not been on the river in many years, but I have passed by this spot frequently, and it is on Google Earth."

Pepe stopped at the bridge. The stream meandered below them, and an overgrown dirt road turned off the pavement into the jungle.

"This is it," Caballo said. "This road will run beside the stream until the stream becomes La Vibora."

The Jeep bumped along the rutted road, plowing through scrubby shrubs for a little over a mile on a slight uphill climb. Pepe rounded a hairpin turn and La Vibora suddenly thundered in front of them. A hundred-foot waterfall rushed down the mountain and split into two falls just before crashing onto the rocks at the base. A fine mist of water sifted onto the Jeep even though they were a good distance away from the bottom of the falls.

"This is the serpent's forked tongue," Caballo said. "It is also the end of the road. We must travel on La Vibora from here."

Everyone got out of the Jeep, dragged the raft to the water's edge, and stowed the backpacks. La Vibora was moving away from the falls at a steady but gentle pace. The banks were gravel and sand sloping up the sides of the valley and then giving way to sheer rock.

"Tell us about the river," Rafer said to Caballo.

"As I remember, it flows between these sandy banks for a while and then the valley narrows and the current picks up. It is always twisting and turning like a snake and there are rapids before reaching the dragon's head."

"Do you remember it well enough to steer?" Rafer asked.

"No," Caballo said. "I know how to hold the paddle but not much else."

Rafer looked around. "Anyone?"

"I'm more a wheel guy," Pepe said.

"I'm good with a kayak and anything with a motor," Gabriela said. "My rafting experience is limited, but I'm willing to try."

"I've done some white-water rafting," Rafer said. "I'll steer."

Pepe sat in the bow, Caballo and Gabriela sat mid-raft. They all had paddles to help navigate the rapids. Rafer guided the raft downstream. The small electric motor wasn't needed and would be saved for the return trip. Traveling downstream they would let the current carry them.

Gabriela kept watch, enjoying the beauty, anticipating the worst and the best of the adventure. She'd traveled the world as a recovery agent and dealt with knife attacks, uncooperative officials, swarms of bats, snakes, and thieving monkeys. She'd suffered frostbite, altitude sickness, food poisoning, and several disappointing one-night stands. And while all these calamities were upon her, she was always propelled forward by the drip, drip, drip of adrenaline that accompanied the adventure of the chase and by the determination that she would capture the prize. Sometimes the prize eluded her but even then, she had the memory of the exhilaration of the chase. She expected this chase to be no different.

Rafer also kept watch. He watched Gabriela. She'd been his best friend, his first love, and if he was being truly honest, she was his only love. He wasn't sure what had happened to make things go so wrong. He suspected it was his fault. Not that it mattered now. What mattered now was that neither of them was the same person who suffered through those hellish two years of marriage. It was intriguing and annoying that Gabriela had many of the same personality traits and yet was so obviously different from the woman he'd married. Two things hadn't changed. She was still absurdly beautiful, and he was still getting sucked in by her harebrained schemes.

The valley narrowed and Rafer could feel the current picking up, pulling the raft forward. "White water ahead," he said.

Gabriela, Pepe, and Caballo took up their paddles. The raft entered the rapids and followed the swirling water around boulders and sudden stomach-churning dips in the riverbed. After a few minutes, La Vibora flattened out and everyone relaxed.

"That wasn't so bad," Pepe said. "I have traveled over worse roads with Angelina."

"Are there more rapids ahead?" Rafer asked Caballo.

"Oh yes," Caballo said. "As I remember the river drops several meters, and the rapids are very bad. Once we get through the rapids, we must begin to look for the dragon head."

"This boat didn't come with life jackets," Rafer said. "If things get rough, hang on to the rope attached to the raft. Don't let go of the rope. I'll get us through."

They floated around a bend in the river and heard the roar of the rapids ahead. Gabriela looked back at Rafer and thought he didn't look worried. This was classic Rafer. He wasn't a worrier. He'd be chill through a zombie apocalypse.

"Whoa," Pepe said, looking ahead. "This water is exploding. This is death water. We should turn back."

"There's no turning back," Rafer said. "Hang on to your paddle and do the best you can."

"My best isn't good here," Pepe said. "We're all going to die. I'm not ready. Angelina will get sold at auction for scrap metal. I have children and cats. What will become of them?"

"You're married?" Gabriela asked.

"No," Pepe said. "I just have children and cats."

"Heads up," Rafer said. "Here we go."

The raft instantly got sucked into the churning water, pitched nose down on a two-foot drop, and a wave hit Pepe with enough force to knock him off-balance. Gabriela back-paddled and the raft righted itself.

"This is hell on earth," Pepe yelled. "I am not liking this."

Gabriela and Caballo were working hard, helping Rafer to find the open water. Gabriela squinted against the spray, looking downstream, not seeing an end to the rapids. The raft took another plunge, hit a boulder, and flipped sideways, throwing Caballo across the raft and into Gabriela. Gabriela lost her grip on the rope and was tossed overboard.

She was underwater and disoriented. Her feet touched bottom, but she was swept away before she could respond. She slammed against a massive rock, hurtled downstream, brushed against another boulder, and was pushed to the surface by the velocity of the water. La Vibora dropped another four feet and Gabriela was pitched over the waterfall into a deep pool. The water churned around her and the current carried her to more rapids, more boulders, more tumbling water that barely gave her time to take a breath before going under. She popped up, gasped, and was about to go under again when she felt someone grab her and haul her back into the raft. Rafer. He whacked her on the back, she coughed up water and went down on all fours on the floor of the raft, still gasping for air.

Minutes later they floated out of the rapids. Caballo and Pepe sat hunched over in stupefied silence, breathing heavy, their hands still on their paddles.

Rafer scooped Gabriela up off the floor and sat her against the side of the raft. "Good God, woman," he said to her. "That was terrifying."

"Tell me about it," she said. "Those were serious rapids."

"I'm not talking about the rapids. I'm talking about you. I saw you disappear under the water and my heart stopped. I don't ever want to feel like that again. I can't believe fifty feet downriver you surfaced and I was able to grab you. Honest to God, Gabs, I thought you were gone. I thought I was going to be searching this river for your body."

"Really? You would have searched for my body?"

"I would have searched for eternity."

"Wow. Are those *tears* in your eyes?"

"River water," Rafer said. "Let's not get all gooey over this."

"Eternity is a long time to search."

"Okay, maybe not eternity but I'd put out a good effort. You have the diary strapped to your waist in a money belt. It ups the ante on your body."

Pepe made a clucking sound with his tongue. "That is not the way to make happy times tonight when you are tent mates. You should have stopped at looking for all eternity," he said to Rafer.

"We aren't tent mates," Gabriela said.

"I thought you were a couple," Pepe said. "You look like a couple."

"We used to be a couple," Rafer said. "She divorced me seven years ago. Kicked me to the curb. Slam bam thank you, sir."

Gabriela rolled her eyes, and Pepe's mouth dropped open.

"*Ay, Dios mio!*" Pepe said.

"We have a business relationship now," Gabriela told Pepe.

Pepe looked at Rafer. "How does this work? Will you sleep with a gun under your pillow? My last ex-girlfriend came after me with a knife. I have a scar on my arm." He shook his head. "You are a brave man to do this. There must be much at stake."

"She came to me and asked for help," Rafer said. "So of course, I said that I would. I'm just a big softy."

Gabriela's shirtsleeve was in shreds and her

arm was scraped raw. Blood was oozing from a gash in her forehead.

"We need to beach this thing," Rafer said to Caballo. "Gabs needs some medical help. How much further until we see the dragon head?"

"It should be just around the bend," Caballo said.

The raft drifted around a curve and Caballo pointed to a rock outcropping at the top of a hill. "The dragon's head," he said. "You can see the smoke coming out of his snout."

"How can that be?" Pepe asked. "How can a stone dragon breathe smoke?"

"I'm told it is steam from a hot spring," Caballo said. "There are many in this area."

Rafer got the raft to within ten feet of the shore. He slipped over the side, into the shallow water, and pulled the raft the rest of the way onto the sandbar. Caballo secured it, and Rafer got the first-aid kit out of his backpack.

"I need a big Band-Aid," Gabriela said.

"Sweet Pea, you need more than a Band-Aid."

"Just give me the kit."

"Relax. I've got this," Rafer said.

"No way. You faint at the sight of blood."

"Do not."

"Do too."

Rafer held the kit above Gabriela's head when she tried to grab it.

"Third grade," Gabriela said. "I punched you in the nose, and you spurted blood like a whale, and you fainted."

"It was *my* blood," Rafer said. "And it was *fourth* grade." He grinned. "You got sent to the principal's office. You were in big trouble."

"It was all your fault," Gabriela said. "You started it. Are you going to give me that first-aid kit, or what?"

"You're a mess. Just calm down and shut up and let me do this. I know what I'm doing. I had to take some EMT courses for the dive shop."

"Really?"

"Really. Swear to God. They're also helpful when you do your own cooking. I get a lot of burns. And once I cut the tip of my finger off slicing onions."

Gabriela smiled at that. Neither of them had been any good in the kitchen when they were married.

"Are you a good cook now that you're on your own?" she asked.

"No. I suck at cooking. Although I have some specialties. I can make grilled cheese and I can scramble an egg. I add Tabasco."

"Genius," Gabriela said.

"I need to clean this cut on your forehead," he said. "It's gonna sting."

"No problem," Gabriela said. "I have a high pain threshold."

"Since when?"

"Since forever."

"That's not the way I remember it."

"Just get on with it!"

He cleaned the cut and pulled it together with butterfly Band-Aids. He cleaned the scrape on her arm and wrapped it in gauze.

"If we were in civilization you wouldn't need the wrap," he said. "In the jungle I think you want to protect it until it scabs." He pulled her to her feet. "You're good to go. Try not to fall into any ravines or get eaten by wild pigs. I'm short on Band-Aids."

Caballo and Pepe stowed the raft out of sight from the river in case Supay sent El Dragón out to scout abandoned rafts. Rafer returned the first-aid kit to his backpack, and Gabriela changed her shirt and shrugged into her backpack.

"Let's move out," Gabriela said. "I'd like to get to the dragon head before we lose the light."

Pepe raised his hand.

"Yes?" Gabriela asked.

"I don't see a path," Pepe said.

"You're the guide," Gabriela said. "Make a path."

"This is very dense jungle and probably has many snakes," Pepe said. He looked at Caballo. "What do you think? Are there many snakes here?"

"Yes," Caballo said. "It is famous for snakes. And you will need a machete to hack through this jungle."

"Do we have a machete?" Pepe asked.

Caballo pulled a massive machete from his pack and handed it to Pepe.

"Whoa," Pepe said. "You brought the big boy!" He did a two-handed slash and decapitated a pigmy palm tree. He did another slash and took a chunk off the tip of his shoe.

"Nice work," Rafer said, taking the machete from Pepe. "In the interest of public safety, I'll lead this parade."

The vegetation was dense at the river's edge, where the forest floor was a mixture of ferns and moss-covered fallen and decaying trees. Bromeliads and immature banana trees and broad-leafed evergreens made up the understory. Above the new growth was a canopy of acai palms, fig, and kapok trees. As the land sloped up the hillside, there was more canopy and less sunlight filtering through. Less sunlight meant less vegetation on the forest floor, and the trek got easier.

"Are you sure we're going in the right direction?" Pepe asked Rafer after an hour of stumbling over tree roots and avoiding spiders the size of saucers.

"I'm wearing my dive watch and I'm following the compass reading," Rafer said. "We're going in the right direction."

Gabriela had to give him points for that. She was wearing the very same watch. It was heavy and clunky on her wrist, but it provided a wealth of information and it was solar. As long as there was sun, the watch kept working. She wore a diamond-encrusted bangle on the same wrist to offset the clunkiness of the watch.

She was second in line, watching for snakes and jungle predators. So far, the march had been uneventful. Birds fluttered in the canopy and small creatures rustled in the undergrowth. Occasionally there was monkey chatter in the distance. She heard something crash to the ground behind her and turned to see Pepe on the ground. He was flailing his arms and making desperate squeaking sounds. A twelve-foot constrictor was wrapped around his legs, moving up his body.

Rafer sauntered over and looked down at the snake. "Where did this come from?"

"It fell out of the sky," Pepe said. "It hit me on the head and knocked me over and now it is squeezing me."

"I guess I could whack its head off," Rafer said.

"Supay will not like that," Caballo said. "Unless you want to eat it. Then it might be justified. The meat can be tasty if you fry it and slice it thin."

"What happens if we don't want to eat it?" Rafer asked. "Do we sacrifice Pepe to Supay?"

"This snake is not large enough to eat Pepe," Caballo said. "You can most likely unwind it. Someone should hold its head and then someone else can take it by the tail and unwrap it."

"I'm game," Rafer said to Caballo. "Do you want the head or the tail?"

"I would throw up and mess myself if I touched it," Caballo said.

"I'll take the head," Gabriela said. "Do we have any rope?"

Caballo pulled a length of rope from his pack and handed the rope to Gabriela. She made a lasso, dropped the loop over the snake's head, and tightened it.

"I'll hold the head while you unwind," Gabriela said to Rafer.

"You should hurry faster," Pepe said. "This snake is moving to a part of my body I very much like and should not be unduly squeezed."

Minutes later, Pepe and the snake were set free.

"Something to add to my resume," Rafer said. "Snake unwinder."

"This might be a bad omen," Pepe said. "It might be a bad sign when snakes fall from the sky."

"He fell out of a tree," Rafer said. "Probably happens all the time."

"He could have been sent by Supay," Caballo said.

"That doesn't work for me," Rafer said. "The God of Death wouldn't drop a boa on someone's head. He'd send a bunch of vipers."

Pepe nodded. "You have to admit, Caballo, that makes more sense."

"Your snake was just clumsy," Rafer said to Pepe. "Probably not the pick of the litter. Everyone, saddle up. Party's over."

. . . .

It was late in the afternoon when they broke out of the forest. The last part of the climb would be over rock that wasn't steep enough to require climbing gear but was steep enough to be exhausting and require focus. The dragon head was within sight. Snakes were also in sight. Lots of them. They were sprawled on the rock, soaking in the last of the day's warmth from the setting sun.

"These are not good snakes," Pepe said. "These

are vipers. Pit vipers and coral snakes. And some evil black ones."

"They're just catching a few rays," Rafer said. "Don't disturb them."

And don't kick them in my direction, he thought. The thought of going eye to eye with a viper made his skin crawl.

"It will be good to get to the dragon head and find your treasure," Pepe said. "This is not my favorite place. I will be glad to leave it to El Dragón."

Rafer and Gabriela exchanged glances. The dragon head wasn't the end of the treasure hunt. It was the beginning. They'd read the diary from front to back and hadn't been able to make any sense of the many clues. They were hoping to have better luck on-site.

Caballo was last in line. He was steadily trudging along with a pack that would have been a burden to a mule, but he wasn't sweating or breathing hard. He occasionally looked down, threading his way around the snakes.

They reached the summit and looked down at the top of the canopy of trees and La Vibora. The river was a silver ribbon curling out of the steep canyon, visible for a short space, before getting lost behind a forested hill. The summit itself was relatively flat. The dragon head was a natural rock outcropping that faced La Vibora. A hot spring bubbled and steamed behind the outcropping. Snakes were everywhere.

"This is a freaking lot of snakes," Rafer said.

Gabriela shrugged out of her backpack. "They like the heat from the hot spring."

"Club Med in Supayville," Rafer said.

"It might not be good to joke about Supay," Pepe said. "Just in case these are his snakes."

Rafer dropped his pack on the ground. "I'll take my chances."

"The sun is setting, and the temperature is falling," Gabriela said. "Most of these snakes will hide for the night. It should be okay for us to set up camp here."

Pepe looked around. "This is an odd place for you to find the Seal of Solomon. There are no temples. No ruins. No caves."

"The treasure isn't here," Gabriela said. "The next clue is here. *Follow the candlelights that lead away from the dragon head*. We need to find the candlelights."

"When was this diary with the clues written?" Pepe asked.

"The sixteenth century," Gabriela said.

"Chances of those candles still being here aren't good," Pepe said. "The wild pigs would eat them."

"I don't think he was writing about candles," Gabriela said. "It's a riddle. Or maybe the inference was clear when Drake was writing in his journal, but it's obscure today."

"Whether I will wake up and be dead from snakebite is also obscure today," Pepe said. "My man nuts are already hiding inside my body."

CHAPTER FIVE

*G*abriela awoke at daybreak. Light was just beginning to filter through the ripstop nylon tent, and something was softly gliding over the outer fabric. She could see the outline of the object as it moved up one side and down the other. Snake, she thought. Long but not especially thick. Freaking creepy. And at the rate it was going it would be noon before it cleared the tent. Note to self—don't ever take another job that involves a jungle. She heard the scuff of shoes coming up to her tent; something scraped against the nylon and the object was removed.

"All clear, Gabs," Rafer said. "Rise and shine."

Gabriela crawled out and stood. "Snake?" she asked.

"Black racer," Rafer said.

"He flicked it off with a big stick," Pepe said. "It sailed clear over the dragon head."

"Another skill for your resume," Gabriela said. "Snake flicker. It can come right after cow painting."

"I was the best cow painter in the county," Rafer said. "I was a ninja cow painter."

Gabriela grinned. "I have to give it to you. You were the best."

"I have never painted a cow," Pepe said, "but I painted a lizard once. And then I got explosive poops from him."

Caballo nodded. "Many people get the poops from lizards."

"What are we doing today?" Pepe asked. "Do we know where we should go next?"

Gabriela peeled the wrapper off a protein bar and looked around. "Follow the candlelights that lead away from the dragon head," she said. "That's the clue."

"It is a very bad clue," Pepe said.

Gabriela nodded agreement. "I came out of my tent several times last night and I didn't see anything that remotely resembled a candlelight. There was no light at all."

Rafer shielded his eyes from the rising sun and looked out over the canopy. "Do you see the swath of light silvery-green leaves? I'm pretty sure they're kukui nut trees," he said. "They appear to start at the forest's edge and march in a broad line down the hillside and into the valley."

"And?" Gabriela asked.

"They're better known as candlenut trees. Maybe Drake took some liberties. Or maybe he remembered them as candlelight. The nuts have a high oil content. In ancient Hawaii they were lit and burned to provide light. A candlenut will burn for about fifteen minutes."

"How do you know this?" Pepe asked.

"It's the official state tree of Hawaii. I usually spend a couple months surfing there when business drops off during hurricane season in St. Vincent. Men get kukui nut leis at the airport. We have some kukui nut trees on St. Vincent. They grow slopeside."

"There are a lot of them here," Gabriela said. "They're spread out all over the place."

"They're an invasive species," Rafer said. "When Drake wrote in his diary, I imagine the trees provided a better-defined trail."

"What is the next clue?" Pepe asked. "Maybe it will help us find our way."

"Walk the gateway with caution and enter the house of many rooms," Gabriela said.

"I'm hoping this house does not belong to

Supay," Pepe said. "I'm thinking it would not be a good place. It would be filled with demons who are not usually nice people."

An hour later, they were packed up and moving downhill toward the valley. The kukui nut tree canopy was dense, and the ground was littered with the green globes that housed the nuts.

"We should spread out," Gabriela said. "Not so far apart that anyone will get lost, but far enough that we can all look for signs of a path and a gateway. The candlelights lead to a gateway."

"It is very dim in here," Pepe said. "And there are too many of these giant nut tree leaves on the ground on top of the disturbing nut balls. Who thought of such an arrangement? Where are the animals to eat the nut balls?"

They're here, Gabriela thought. They're staying away from us. She'd seen places where the rotting leaves had been disturbed. Probably by wild pigs and rodents.

Pepe went far right and Caballo went far left. Gabriela and Rafer took the middle. They reached the valley floor and the swath of kukui nut trees narrowed. Spider monkeys chattered out of sight in the canopy. There were rustlings in the ferns and the mulch that carpeted the forest floor.

"Do you think we missed the gateway?" Gabriela asked Rafer.

"Anything's possible," Rafer said. "Four hundred years of tree growth isn't helping us."

Gabriela stepped over a fallen tree trunk and onto the leg bone of a human skeleton. The bone snapped; Gabriela lost her balance and went facedown into the undergrowth.

Rafer pulled her to her feet by her backpack. "Nice find," he said to her. "Did you break anything besides his leg bone?"

"I'm okay," Gabriela said, staring down at the skeleton that was partially obscured by fallen leaves. A leather shoe was attached to one foot. Pieces of cloth clung to an arm. The other arm was missing. The skull was mostly intact. The rib cage had an elaborate sword stuck in it.

Pepe and Caballo came over to take a look.

"The bad news is that this man is dead," Pepe said. "The good news is that this isn't the work of Supay's demons. It is widely known that demons rip people apart and do nasty things with the pieces. This man is too much together."

Gabriela removed the sword and examined it. "I'm thinking this is eighteenth century and Spanish. The shoe is from a different time. High-top leather with laces. My guess is 1930 to 1945. Maybe as late as mid-1950s."

"We're like this dead man," Caballo said. "We don't belong here."

Gabriela wasn't spooked by the idea. She'd been in lots of places where she didn't belong. It seemed to her that this was one of the more benign. She slipped the sword through a loop on her pack and stepped away from the skeleton.

"How about his shoe?" Rafer said. "Don't you want to take his shoe, too?"

"Not my size," Gabriela said. "The sword might be useful. One can never have too many weapons. Let's keep moving. I'm going to think of this as a sign that we're in the right spot."

"Works for me," Rafer said. "This place has Pizarro written all over it."

The kukui trees ended after another hour of walking and the forest gave over to banana trees and orchids. The terrain began to slope uphill and suddenly the vegetation bordered a sheer rock face.

"Does anyone see a gateway?" Gabriela asked.

"I see a slot canyon," Rafer said. "The first twenty feet of it are hidden behind bamboo and giant white bird-of-paradise plants."

Gabriela scanned the rock face and found the crevice. "We're going to have to fight our way through the vegetation to get to it."

Twenty minutes later they were at the entrance of the canyon. It was approximately four feet wide and the walls were close to a hundred feet high. The floor of the canyon was sand.

"The clue said to walk the gateway with caution," Gabriela said. "That could be referring to flash floods or it could be that traps have been set to keep people like us out."

"Neither of those things are my favorite," Pepe said. "Perhaps I should stay here to guard the gateway."

"And miss discovering Paititi?" Gabriela asked.

"I can see it when they open it to tourists," he said.

"Caballo?" Gabriela asked.

"I will go with you," Caballo said.

"I'll take the lead," Gabriela said, moving into the canyon.

Rafer snagged her by her pack and pulled her back a couple of steps. "No so fast, missy. Who made you the boss? Why don't I get to lead if we're worried about dangerous traps? I'm big and strong and you're . . . you know."

Gabriela narrowed her eyes. "I'm what?"

"Not as big or as strong."

"I'm more observant than you are," Gabriela said.

"Since when?"

"Since always."

"Give me an example."

"This is ridiculous," Gabriela said. "Get out of the way. I'm leading."

"Not gonna happen."

"I have the solution," Pepe said. "We will let Caballo lead. He is expendable. And I will go, too, but I will be unhappy with you if I die."

"No one's going to die," Rafer said. "And no one is expendable. Gabs can lead."

"No. I'm sorry I got carried away. You can lead. You're right. You're bigger and stronger."

"Yes, but you're more observant."

"Just shoot me," Pepe said. "It will be less painful. Personally, I would like Rafer to go first because if a big ball rolls down the canyon like in the Indiana Jones movie, Rafer will be better at stopping it."

"Works for me," Gabriela said.

Rafer led the way. Gabriela followed Rafer. Pepe followed Gabriela and Caballo came last. Speaking was done in hushed whispers. It was unlikely that anyone else was in this remote area of high jungle, but they were following clues to what they hoped was the lost city of Paititi, and anything was possible.

The slot canyon curved several times and the width of the path constantly changed, but it was always manageable. Gabriela thought the canyon was beautiful but unusually barren. There were no footprints in the dirt. No snakes. No lizards. No vegetation. And so far, there had been no trip wires, snares, traps, or Indiana Jones–style giant rolling balls. There had also been nothing to indicate that this was the gateway.

"Uh-oh," Rafer said, stopping in the middle of the narrow path.

Gabriela moved next to him and stared ahead at a gaping hole in the canyon floor. She approached the hole and looked down into it. It was about three feet by three feet, taking up the entire path. It was maybe twenty feet deep with a jumble of bones and debris at the bottom.

"I see two skulls," Rafer said. "I see a machete but nothing else made of metal. No guns. No swords. I'm guessing they were natives."

"Most likely this trap was made of sand over young bamboo and banana or bird leaves," Pepe said. "We use something similar to protect our . . . coffee operation."

Rafer took his pack off, threw it to the other side, and jumped across. Gabriela and Pepe did the same. Caballo tossed his pack to Rafer, jumped short and fell into the pit.

Everyone rushed over and looked down at him. He was on all fours, attempting to stand.

"Are you okay?" Rafer called down.

"I will be okay when you get me out of here," Caballo said.

Gabriela found a length of rope in Caballo's pack and handed it to Rafer. Rafer fed the rope to Caballo, Caballo tied it around his waist, and Rafer hauled him up. Gabriela and Pepe grabbed Caballo's wrists when he was near the top and helped drag him out.

Caballo stood and brushed himself off. "I am going to be bruised. It is not good to fall onto skulls and bones."

"I knew you wouldn't make it," Pepe said to Caballo. "You have short legs like a beagle dog."

"This is true," Caballo said. "But I have length where it counts. I am well named. I am Caballo."

"Caballo is Spanish for 'horse'," Gabriela said.

Pepe clapped Caballo on the back. "Yes, and this man is hung like a Thoroughbred stud."

"From the day I was born I have been impressively large," Caballo said. "Huge in fact."

"We are all very proud of him," Pepe said.

Rafer was hands in pockets, rocked back on his heels, smiling. Gabriela was working hard not to stare.

"These bones have been in the pit for a very long time," Pepe said. "I think this path is not being looked after for many years."

. . . .

After forty-five minutes of walking, Rafer followed a curve and saw that the end of the slot canyon was in sight. He stopped and looked at the people behind him, making sure they understood the need for caution. They all slowly moved forward, staying in the shadow of the canyon wall. A vast wide-open space surrounded by towering limestone bluffs dotted with cave openings spread out in front of them. The remnants of stone buildings and perimeter walls were scattered across the valley floor.

"Paititi," Pepe whispered.

"Yeah, I'd know it anywhere," Rafer said.

"Maybe," Gabriela said.

"Maybe it has now become the Kingdom of El Dragón," Caballo said.

"It is believed by some people that El Dragón was drawn to this area by the Seal," Pepe said. "If El Dragón came into possession of the Seal of Solomon, he could unleash Supay on the world. Since we have not so far been involved in a demon apocalypse, I think we can assume El Dragón has not found the Seal."

"Great," Rafer said. "Anything else we should know?"

"The bedtime story goes that for centuries the Seal of Solomon has been hidden in a secret place, guarded by descendants of Spanish conquistadors. It is not clear if these guardians are still in place," Pepe said.

"It's a trifecta," Rafer said. "The God of Death, the Wizard of Odd, and the Guardians of the Seal. I feel like I'm in a Marvel comic book."

"This all may or may not be true," Pepe said. "Just in case, I will keep an eye out for demons and conquistadors. Of course, it might also be that El Dragón is here for the perfect conditions to grow coca. Even if it is only for personal recreational and religious use, one would be foolish not to tend a few thousand plants."

"So, this El Dragón guy could be a drug lord *and* a wizard?" Rafer asked.

"He is known as a high priest," Pepe said. "I don't know if he has achieved the status of drug lord, but I think he has a very nice lifestyle when he is not tending Supay's snakes."

"According to the journal, after we walk the gateway, we look for the house with many rooms," Gabriela said.

"Okay," Rafer said. "Everyone who wants to look for the house of many rooms with me, raise their hand."

Gabriela raised her hand. Pepe and Caballo halfway raised their hands.

"Let's do it," Rafer said, leaving the shelter of the slot canyon and walking into the sunshine.

The valley sat in an irregularly shaped bowl with towering limestone and rock cliffs that wind and water had carved out of the sides of conical-shaped mountains over millennia.

The floor of the bowl was rock and sand with minimal vegetation. About a quarter of a mile away from the slot canyon, a partially collapsed wall of stacked stone marked the boundary of what might have once been a village. Beyond the crumbled remains of multiple small structures, the floor of the bowl sloped up into a limestone cliff that was dotted with cave openings.

Gabriela walked beside Rafer. She was thinking that there was an eerie stillness to the valley. There were no sounds other than the ones they were making. The sky was a brilliant blue overhead. Two black dots rode the thermals. Large birds, she thought. Vultures, maybe. Looking for carrion. She hoped this wasn't going to be a fiasco. Her last two jobs hadn't been perfect recoveries. She wanted this one to succeed. This time it was personal.

They reached the outermost wall, climbed

it, and walked up a small rise. Gabriela sat on a large slab of stone and looked down at Caballo and Pepe as they picked their way through rubble, looking for small treasures.

Gabriela studied the remains of buildings and roads. "This was similar to Machu Picchu, but considerably smaller," she said to Rafer. "The brick construction is the same."

"Have you been to Machu Picchu?" Rafer asked her.

"Several years ago," she said. "I was looking for a man who'd stolen a priceless relic from my client. He was working at a restoration site there. It was a much easier trip than this one. I didn't have to tramp through jungles or camp out in a snake resort."

"Did you find him?" Rafer asked.

"Yes, and I was able to return the relic to its owner."

"I always thought you'd end up being a pirate and *stealing* relics."

"I thought about it," Gabriela said, "but I didn't think I'd get very far in my dad's fishing boat."

"When did you start doing this recovery stuff?"

"When we got divorced, Jenny Gooley got me a job with her uncle's company in Manhattan. He was in charge of a division that investigated insurance fraud. It turns out that I have an aptitude for searching and finding, and after a couple years with the company I went off on my own." Gabriela focused on what was once a brick roadway. "Some of these one-room buildings are almost intact, missing only a roof and a few bricks. From what I saw when we walked through, not much is left of the interiors." She turned and looked up the cliffside behind them. "I want to take a look at the caves."

She believed in Drake's diary. It had led her here. This was a lost city that had been abandoned for whatever reason. Perhaps it was always meant to be temporary. A safe place for workers who were building elsewhere. The ground was too rocky and sandy for growing crops. There was no good source of water that she could see. The buildings were simple and not intended for royalty or for storing treasure. She saw nothing intended for worship.

"I expected more from Paititi," Pepe said, trudging up to Gabriela and Rafer. "This is disappointing. And I do not see a house with many rooms."

It's here, Gabriela thought. I know it's here. I just have to find it.

. . . .

Three men stood in a dark cave and watched the intruders. The men were dressed in black fatigues, wore scimitars at their waist, and carried assault rifles. Their faces and arms were tattooed with black tribal and religious symbols.

The tallest of the three nodded to the man next to him and received a nod in return. The tall man smiled with tight lips and narrowed eyes. The smile was broken by a scar that ran from the middle of his cheek to his prominent jawbone.

"Patience," he said to his brethren. "We need to ask permission before we kill them."

CHAPTER SIX

The part of the bowl that contained the caves sloped up and away from the ruins. The entrances were of varying sizes and at varying altitudes. Steps had been chiseled into the limestone, making some of the caves more accessible.

Gabriela stood back and studied each cave entrance. "That one," she said, pointing to a small cave halfway up the hillside.

"Why that one?" Rafer asked.

"The steps leading up to it have been worn away from people walking on them. The cave next to it is also a possibility."

They hiked up to the cave and Gabriela stepped in first. The narrow entrance opened to a larger chamber that was the size of a small bedroom with a ceiling that sloped down to about two feet on the back side.

"Nothing here," she said. "Let's try the other cave."

The entrance to the second cave was slightly wider and opened to a similar-sized chamber with a domed roof. At the back of the chamber a three-foot-wide slot opened to a passageway.

Gabriela pulled a flashlight out of her pack and flashed light around the tunnel.

"I can't see the end of this tunnel," she said. "I want to explore it, but I think we should put it off until tomorrow. We're going to be losing light in another hour. We can use the first cave as shelter and take turns guarding the door." She looked at Pepe. "Are you packing a gun?"

"I do not have a license to buy a gun," Pepe said.

"That wasn't what I asked," Gabriela said.

Pepe pulled a Glock nine out of his pack. "I don't know how this got in there."

Gabriela looked at Caballo. "And you?"

Caballo pulled out a SIG Sauer MPX 9mm.

Rafer cracked a smile. "Nice. How many rounds can that hold?"

"Thirty," Caballo said. "And it has a laser dot for accuracy."

Gabriela looked at Rafer.

"I'm carrying," Rafer said.

Gabriela was also carrying. She had a black-market Glock .38 that Marcella had arranged to be delivered to Gabriela's Quillabamba hotel room.

"I'll take first watch," Gabriela said. "Caballo second. Rafer third. Pepe will take last."

· · · ·

Gabriela sat on a ledge and leaned her back against the front of the cave. The sun was setting. A howler monkey called in the distance. Nothing moved in the valley. She thought about her condo in New York with all the luxuries. A steamy shower and a comfortable bed with expensive linens. She could afford those luxuries because she did things like this. She looked out over the ruins on the valley floor and the sandstone cliffs that surrounded it and acknowledged that there were rewards to her job beyond the paycheck. It was uniquely beautiful here. Silent and alien. Food for the soul.

The sun dipped below the horizon and the sky darkened. The first stars appeared and two hours later the sky was blanketed with stars and a brilliant half-moon. The broken walls of the lost city were black against the moonstruck limestone.

Gabriela scanned the bowl from one side

to the next, and her heart skipped a beat when she saw something move on the valley floor. She leaned forward and concentrated, listening for the slightest sound, alert for more movement. She wondered if she'd imagined it. A moment later her eye caught a flash of black. A fleeting shadow. Something was definitely making its way through the ruins. The shadow moved between two buildings. A second black shadow followed. Two men, she thought. They were close to the outer wall that she'd climbed earlier in the day. She sat perfectly still, her senses sharpened by the adrenaline burning in her chest. No sound carried up to her. She remained vigilant, but the rest of her watch was uneventful. It was as if the two men had vanished.

. . . .

Daylight was softly creeping into the cave when Gabriela woke up. The floor was hard under her, but she was comfortably snug in her sleeping bag. Best of all, no one had raided the cave overnight. That was a good thing. She opened her eyes, and it took a couple of beats for reality to jolt her further awake. She was cuddled next to Rafer, with his arm wrapped around her. This was *not* a good thing. It was especially not a good thing because she'd been enjoying it. What the heck, she'd been enjoying it while she was still partially asleep, she told herself. It didn't count. Now that she was fully awake, she was horrified. *That's* what counted.

She eased away from Rafer and went to see how Pepe was doing on watch.

"Anything going on out here?" she asked him.

"Everything is quiet," Pepe said. "I understand you saw some movement, but there has been nothing as long as I have been on guard. Caballo and Rafer also did not see anything."

Rafer wandered out and joined Pepe and Gabriela.

"How's it going?" Rafer asked.

"There were no more sightings of the men I saw," Gabriela said.

"Do you want to go down and take a look this morning?"

"No," Gabriela said. "I want to follow the tunnel in the cave next to ours."

An hour later the sun was glaring against the limestone and everyone was packed up and ready to go. Gabriela switched her headlamp on and took the lead. The tunnel floor and walls were smooth natural stone. After five minutes of walking the smooth stone turned to hand chiseled. After ten minutes the tunnel forked.

"Left or right?" Gabriela asked. "Anyone have an opinion?"

"My opinion is that I'm freaking out," Pepe said. "This is like being in a grave. I smell Supay."

"That's just Caballo," Rafer said. "He hasn't smelled great ever since he fell in that pit with the bones."

Gabriela took the left fork and forged ahead. She'd been in lava tubes in Hawaii and in a coal mine in Pennsylvania. She wasn't claustrophobic. The air in the tunnel felt fresh, and she would have been more comfortable exploring if she hadn't seen the two men last night. The men worried her. They weren't simply out strolling in the night air. Their movements were stealthy. They were trying to stay hidden. And they vanished. There was still no sign of them in the morning.

The left tunnel began to slope downhill and the walls turned from limestone to dirt supported by timbers. There was another fork in the tunnel and Gabriela went left again because she saw light ahead. The tunnel ended with brick steps that led to an open doorway. Gabriela walked up the steps and into a small two-room structure. She turned her headlamp off and walked out into the ruins of the village that was below the caves. Everyone followed her.

"This is how the two men appeared and disappeared," Gabriela said. "There are probably tunnel entrances and exits scattered all around these ruins. We walked down the main street yesterday and glanced inside the buildings, but we didn't really do a thorough search."

"We should search all these buildings," Pepe said.

Gabriela shook her head. "No, the house with many rooms isn't out here. It's in the mountain. We need to retrace our steps and find the right tunnel."

"If we go back into the death tunnel, I will need a pill," Pepe said.

"Do you have any with you?" Gabriela asked.

"Yes," Pepe said. "I have many. Does anyone need a pill?"

"Do you have the red ones?" Caballo asked.

"No," Pepe said. "I have gray and orange and some gummy-bear vitamins. I also have some high-quality . . . coffee leaves."

Caballo signed up for the coffee leaves.

"Don't overdose on the *caffeine*," Gabriela said to Caballo. "We have a long day in front of us."

Rafer made a sweeping gesture toward the tunnel. "Ladies first."

"You don't want to be the leader?" Gabriela asked him.

"Gabs, you're the only one with a headlamp."

The beam from the headlamp was bright but not especially wide. When the tunnel widened, the sides were visible only in the distance. Okay by me, Gabriela thought. She didn't care about the sides. She wanted to see what was in front of her. There was a thrill attached to exploring the dark unknown. It started with curiosity and ended with a touch of fear. It was a ride on a brand-new roller coaster or zip line. It was the first time down a black diamond ski slope. Beyond the thrill was the determination to succeed. She was anxious to get back to the fork and move in the new direction. It would be another step closer to the Seal of Solomon.

She picked up the pace on the way back, reached the original tunnel, and took the right fork. After twenty minutes of following the winding pathway she saw a faint ray of light ahead and she heard the unmistakable sound of falling water.

Rafer grabbed her by the backpack and yanked her to a stop. "Let's not rush into this," he said.

"I never rush in," Gabriela said.

"You always rush in," Rafer said. "When we get a little closer, let's just hang back and make sure we're alone."

Gabriela paused at the end of the tunnel and looked out at a football-field-sized cavern with a high domed roof. A hundred-foot ribbon of water cascaded down the far side and splashed into a pool in the cavern floor. Sunshine poured through a massive opening near the source of the waterfall, and ferns and orchids grew in the sandy soil surrounding the pool. Caves of various sizes dotted the cavern walls. Some of the caves looked like natural rock formations and some appeared to have been excavated. Yellow brick pavers covered the cavern floor and led to the caves.

Gabriela was awestruck. "Amazing," she whispered.

"It looks like it was created by the *Avatar* guy," Rafer said. "All it needs is a flying dragon."

"It is also El Dragón's territory," Caballo said. "The Incan symbol for Supay is painted on this tunnel wall."

Gabriela looked at the line drawing of a horned devil. Another diablo was carved above the entrance to the large cave by the pond.

"I'm thinking that this could be the house with many rooms," Pepe said.

"El Dragón doesn't seem to be in residence," Rafer said.

"He is said to be a powerful sorcerer," Caballo said. "He could be watching even now, and we might not know. Who is to say where he travels?"

"I can easily believe someone is watching," Gabriela said. "More likely a drug lord than a sorcerer."

"You do not believe in magic?" Caballo asked.

"Magic, yes. Sorcery, no," Gabriela said.

Rafer adjusted his backpack. "Spoken by a woman who was sent here by a ghost."

They stood for a long moment, scanning the cavern before slowly walking along the outermost edge. Some of the caves contained pottery water jugs and remnants of small cook fires. Two caves appeared to have channels that went deeper into the mountain. None of the caves looked recently used.

Gabriela walked into the large cave with the Supay symbol carved over the entrance.

"This looks like some sort of temple," she said to Rafer. "There's an altar at the far end, and the walls are covered with symbols and storytelling drawings."

"Looks like the artist was big on snakes," Rafer said.

Pepe came in for a closer look. "These snakes are not doing nice things," he said.

"It reminds me of Kenny Chuchak and the duck," Rafer said to Gabriela.

"That was never authenticated," Gabriela said. "I put it into the category of urban legend."

They left the temple and Gabriela pointed across the pond to another cave with Supay carved over its entrance. "Let's check that out next," she said.

Rafer looked around. "Where's Caballo? He wasn't in the temple with us."

Everyone did a visual search around the cavern. No Caballo.

Gabriela had an uptick of adrenaline. "When did you see him last?" she asked Pepe.

"I don't know," Pepe said. "I was looking ahead, and he was behind me."

Rafer shouted for Caballo and the name echoed off the cavern walls.

"This is not good," Pepe said. "My uncle will be unhappy with me that I lose Caballo. And if El Dragón gives him to the snakes, he will be very uncomfortable."

"Let's retrace our steps and do a better search of the caves," Gabriela said.

An hour later all the caves had been searched and Caballo was still missing.

"Maybe he ran out of clean socks and went home," Rafer said.

"He would have left through the slot canyon," Gabriela said. "It's at least a hundred yards away. Even if he was running, we would have seen him. Either he decided to go exploring on his own, or else he was captured. There are three caves on this side of the cavern that have passageways leading into the mountain. One of those caves is the temple, and he never entered the temple, so Caballo has to be in one of those other passageways."

Gabriela stepped into a passageway and realized that it was actually another narrow slot canyon. She walked about twenty feet and the canyon curved. Another thirty or forty feet and she found an offshoot tunnel with light in the distance. She followed the offshoot and came to a dead end. She retraced her steps, walked for five minutes, and came to another offshoot. This one took her into the temple.

"It looks like everything attaches to the second slot canyon," she said to Rafer. She looked around him. "Where's Pepe?"

"He's moving slow. I think he tranqued out. Should have gone with the coffee leaves instead of the pills."

"Pills? As in multiple? How many did he take?"

"I don't know. I wasn't watching that close."

They returned to the second slot canyon and looked for Pepe.

"He isn't here," Gabriela said. "No sign of him." She looked down to the ground. "Except for his shoe."

Rafer nudged the shoe with his foot. "That's

his shoe, all right. With a bunch of scuff marks in the dirt around it."

"This isn't good," Gabriela said. "We've lost our guides, and I know they wouldn't desert us. Someone's cutting us down one at a time."

Rafer draped an arm around her shoulders. "Yep, now it's just you and me, Gabs. Like old times. Me following you to the brink of disaster."

"Excuse me?" Gabriela said. "I did not lead you to the brink of disaster. *You* were the troublemaker."

"Darlin', you've got a memory problem. You were the thrill junkie who wanted to ride old man Gustavson's prize bull in the middle of the night. You were the one who suggested we spray-paint the cows. I just did it better than you. And you were the one who dared the whole graduating class to skinny-dip in the mayor's swimming pool. I was the one who was always tagging along and saving your ass."

Gabriela blew out a sigh. "Whatever. Right now, we have a problem. We need to find Pepe and Caballo. We didn't hear gunshots and there's no blood, so that's encouraging."

Rafer picked the shoe up and tied it to his backpack. He retrieved his gun from his pack and shoved it under the waistband of his camo cargo pants. Gabriela did the same.

"You lead the way," Rafer said. "I want to keep my eyes on you. I don't want to turn around and find out you've become the latest victim of the phantom body snatcher."

Gabriela walked a short distance and came to an offshoot tunnel. She switched her headlamp on and took the offshoot. After another short distance she came to a T intersection with yet another new slot canyon, and she went to the right.

"Why did you choose to go right?" Rafer asked her.

"I've noticed small lines carved into the walls. There was a single line at the opening to the offshoot we just took. And now there were two lines on the right side of this canyon. The diary ended with the house with many rooms. I think that must have been as far as Drake got, but it wasn't far enough for him to find the Seal of Solomon. I think Pizarro hid the Seal deep in these canyons and tunnels and I'm hoping the scratches point the way."

Gabriela and Rafer walked past three more offshoots but there were no scratch marks, so they kept to the slot canyon. Moments after passing by the third offshoot Gabriela heard *thwap thwap*, and everything went black.

CHAPTER SEVEN

Gabriela saw light on the other side of her eyelids. She was struggling to move but her arms and legs weren't responding. The light got brighter, and she was able to open her eyes and see blurred images. The images became clearer, she had feeling in her fingers, and her brain kicked in. I've been drugged, she thought. I need to stay calm and work my way out of it. She was on her back on the floor, looking up at a high-domed limestone ceiling. She felt for her gun. Gone. Her last memory was walking through the slot canyon. She turned her head and focused on a tall man standing at a distance. He had high cheekbones, fierce black eyes, and black hair severely pulled back into a large knot. He was wearing slim black pants and a collared black shirt with a crimson-and-gold diablo emblem embroidered on his sleeve. He had more images of Supay tattooed in black ink on his face.

"She's awake. Get her on her feet," he said in English, with only a small trace of an accent.

Two men in black fatigues yanked Gabriela up. Their faces were tattooed with Supay symbols and their hair was pulled back into a single braid. Gabriela looked around the room and counted ten more braided and tattooed men in fatigues. They were all armed with sidearms and scimitars. Some of the men had automatic rifles.

Rafer was standing off to the side with Pepe and Caballo. Gabriela thought Rafer's body language was relaxed but she'd seen that expression on his face before and she knew he was waiting for his chance to act. Pepe and Caballo had less fight in them. Caballo had a bloody bandage on his finger. Gabriela hoped he wasn't missing part of it. Pepe had a cut on the side of his face that was beginning to bruise.

"Welcome to the party," Rafer said to Gabriela. "In case you're wondering, you got tagged with a dart. Turns out Dragón's hospitality skills are lacking."

One of the braided guards hit Rafer in the

head with his rifle butt, and Rafer went down to his knees.

"You are looking for the Seal of Solomon," El Dragón said to Gabriela. "I am also looking for it. Unfortunately, I have reached a dead end. So, I will need your assistance in completing my task. Your traveling companions have been very helpful. They tell me you've been following Drake's diary." He held the diary up for Gabriela to see. "I've paged through this and it's incomplete. Where are the rest of the clues?"

"That's all there is," Gabriela said.

"Perhaps you would like to see what's left of your friend's finger," El Dragón said. "Of course, we would be more inventive with a pretty woman."

"You have the diary," Gabriela said. "It stops with the house with many rooms."

"Yes, but you went further," El Dragón said. "You made all the correct turns to come this far. I'm sure you know how to proceed beyond here."

We'll all stay alive as long as he thinks we're useful, Gabriela thought. She cut her eyes to Rafer. Blood was staining the back of his collar, but he was on his feet, watching her, and she knew he was holding the same thought.

"Maybe you should tell him about Annie," Rafer said to Gabriela. "About how she helps you."

"Who is Annie?" El Dragón asked.

"She's a ghost," Gabriela said. "She gave birth to Blackbeard's child and I'm a direct descendant of that child. Now Annie is my spirit guide."

El Dragón looked at Pepe.

"I know this to be true," Pepe said. "Annie sent her to get the Seal."

"Why would your spirit guide want the Seal?" El Dragón asked Gabriela.

"I don't know," Gabriela said. "She didn't share that information."

"As a modern woman you do the bidding of your spirit guide without question?"

Gabriela shrugged. "You do the bidding of Supay without question."

"Supay is an all-powerful god. That is quite different from a ghost named Annie."

"Yes, but Annie seems to know the way to find the Seal."

El Dragón was still for a long moment. "I'll play along. Take me to the Seal. Your friends will stay here."

"No," Gabriela said. "We're a team. We all go."

El Dragón stared Gabriela down for a full minute and nodded. "Very well. We will all go."

Okay, Gabriela thought. Everyone's on board. We've bought some time.

"I need the diary," Gabriela said. "Annie won't

talk to me if I don't have the diary. It's her medium."

El Dragón gave Gabriela the diary. "This Annie had best be in a talkative mood."

Gabriela did a visual sweep of the area. She was in another cavern. It was much smaller than the previous one, and it had no natural light. Dim illumination was provided by a series of bulbs strung around the perimeter. She could hear a generator running in a distant location. Barrels and wood crates were stacked against a wall. A hand truck was leaning against the crates. Bales of what she suspected was marijuana were stacked near an exit tunnel. It seemed like a lot of pot for Dragón's personal recreational use. Of course, he was reputed to have an army to keep happy. Another exit tunnel was behind El Dragón.

Gabriela walked the perimeter and paused at the first exit tunnel. There were no lines carved into the limestone. The second exit tunnel had three lines.

"Do you have lighting in this tunnel?" she asked.

"No," El Dragón said. "It's not necessary. It is very short."

Gabriela was escorted by two guards and El Dragón. Caballo, Pepe, and Rafer were marched behind them at gunpoint. They all walked for a few minutes in the dark before coming out to a slot canyon. Gabriela instantly picked out four very faint lines on the canyon wall to her right. After twenty minutes in the narrow passage Gabriela saw five lines that were horizontal. All other lines had been vertical.

"This is the spot," Gabriela said. "Dig here."

El Dragón did another of the minute-long stare-downs as if he was reading her mind or communicating with Supay through mental telepathy. Finally he sent a runner out to get a pickaxe and shovels.

Rafer looked at Gabriela and raised his eyebrows. *Really?*

Gabriela's response was a shrug. Telling El Dragón to dig was an act of desperation on her part. Another stalling tactic. She was confident that the lines meant something. She had little confidence that they were telling her the Seal was buried beneath her feet. It was a thousand-to-one long shot. Still, sometimes a long shot paid off. If it didn't pay off after a couple of hours of digging, she'd blame it on Annie.

In the meantime, she'd watch for an opening to get the upper hand. They'd taken her gun and the sword she'd confiscated earlier, but they'd missed the knife she had strapped to her calf under her cargo pants.

• • • •

El Dragón's men had been working for almost two hours, taking turns with the pickaxe and shovels. After the first two feet of sand and gravel they hit solid sandstone and digging became more difficult. They now had a hole that was five feet across, spanning the width of the slot canyon, and almost five feet deep. There were two men in the hole. One of the men was chipping away at the sandstone and the other man was scooping it up in a bucket and passing it up to a man at the rim. Gabriela, Rafer, Caballo, and Pepe were huddled together at a distance, watched over by three guards with guns drawn.

Caballo was cradling his bandaged hand.

"Are you okay?" Gabriela asked him.

"I've been better, and I've been worse," Caballo said. "I only lost a fingernail. I told them what they wanted to hear before I lost a finger. El Dragón asked if we were seeking fortune and I said we were searching for Paititi. He said he knew I wasn't telling him everything. He cut an X in the top of my hand, and I was doing much bleeding. 'What else are you looking for?' he asked. That's when I told him we were looking for the Seal of Solomon. He was satisfied at that and one of his men wrapped my hand in this bandage."

Shouting carried back to them from the hole and several of El Dragón's men ran toward it. There was a lot of Spanish spoken, too rapid for Gabriela to catch. The three men guarding them were agitated, dividing their attention between what was happening at the dig site and keeping their prisoners at gunpoint.

"What is it?" Gabriela asked.

"The hole has caved in," Pepe said. "The men who were digging have fallen. It's not clear if they are okay. They are sending someone down by rope with a light."

Rafer and Gabriela looked at each other.

"Is it possible?" Rafer asked.

Gabriela shrugged again.

There was more shouting coming from the cave-in. El Dragón moved to the edge and looked in. His face was animated, and he was nodding and speaking rapid-fire Spanish to whoever was down in the hole.

"The men are dead," Pepe said. "It was a very long drop. El Dragón is excited because his man is saying he is in a cavern and it is filled with treasures."

"Holy crap," Rafer said. "Annie came through for us."

"Annie was your idea," Gabriela said. "I was following scratches on the tunnel walls."

"Yeah, pretty smart of me, right? I knew he'd get sucked in by something supernatural. And now here we are standing over the treasure Drake was looking for."

"Maybe," Gabriela said.

"What's with the always *maybe*," Rafer said. "There are treasures down there."

"Have you noticed we're at gunpoint?" Gabriela said.

"That's just a minor inconvenience. I'm sure you'll figure a way out."

"I'm working on it," Gabriela said.

El Dragón ordered that Gabriela be brought to him.

"You are going down to find the Seal," he said. "I now have two armed soldiers in place to ensure that you do your job. If you aren't back here with the Seal in thirty minutes, I will kill one of your friends. Another of your friends will be killed at the one-hour mark."

Gabriela stepped into the rope loop with one foot, wrapped one hand around the rope, and held a flashlight with her other hand. She was slowly lowered into the cavern while she swept the area with the beam from her flashlight. The two dead men were on the ground exactly where they'd landed. The two soldiers were waiting for her to step out of the loop. It was difficult to see the entire cavern by flashlight. Gabriela guessed that it was about the size of a two-story, three-bedroom house. The sides were dark and uneven. The air was damp and musty. The floor of the cavern was cluttered with collections of gold plates, ceramic urns, elaborately decorated silver helmets and swords, golden ornamental animals set with jewels, and baskets filled with jewelry.

She had a half hour to find the Seal and she had no idea where to begin. Not with the baskets of jewelry, she thought. The Seal would be hidden. Everything in the cavern was inconsequential compared to the Seal. She picked her way through the clutter of treasure, looking for a container that might be used to protect something beyond precious. She reached a sandstone wall and followed it to what appeared to be a small cave attached to the larger one. Two skeletons were sprawled in front of the cave entrance. They were nothing more than bones and two skulls. They each had pistols and elaborately decorated swords by their side.

Possibly tomb raiders who were trapped, Gabriela thought. Or conquistadors who were standing guard and for whatever reason died at their post. She was in favor of the conquistador theory. It allowed her to be mildly optimistic that there actually was a ring.

She carefully stepped over the bones and flashed her light around the small cave that was about the size of a couple of Cadillac Escalades set side by side. The walls had been scraped smooth and inset with tiles depicting demons, snakes, and Incan gods. Gabriela ran her hand over the tiles and found one that wasn't perfectly in line. She tapped the tile with the butt of her flashlight and thought the irregular tile sounded different from the others.

She used her knife to chip the grout. She pried the tile off the wall of the cave and exposed a niche that was as big as a shoebox. The niche held a small silver box with a clasp shaped like a cross. She thought the niche itself seemed benign. No obvious booby traps. No venomous snakes or spiders. The soldiers were at her back, watching from a distance. She pulled the box out and held it in the palm of her hand. She took a breath, opened the lid, and looked down at a man's signet ring. Her heart skipped a couple of beats. The ring looked as if it might have been forged from brass and iron, and the symbols on the ring matched the symbols she'd seen in her research.

She checked her watch. She'd been searching for the ring for twenty-five minutes. She returned to the rope and called up to El Dragón.

"I've got it," Gabriela shouted. "Pull me up."

"Send the ring up first," El Dragón said.

"That doesn't work for me," Gabriela said. She shoved the silver chest into her cargo pants pocket, tugged on the rope to make sure it was secure, and went up Navy SEAL style, leaving the loop behind.

Two soldiers helped her to her feet when she reached the rim.

"I'll take that box," El Dragón said to Gabriela.

"And then what?" she asked. "Are we free to go?"

"Of course not," he said. "You will all be killed. I can't risk you returning. Although, it might not matter once I slip the ring on my finger. I'll be able to unleash the power of Supay on the world, and only his loyal followers will survive and prosper."

Gabriela took the box from her pocket and handed it to El Dragón. "It's all yours."

"At last," he said. "Supay will be pleased." He opened the box and glared at Gabriela. "This box is empty."

"The box is yours, but the ring is mine," Gabriela said. "I'm wearing the ring and I have the power of Supay."

They were standing close to the edge of the cave-in. Gabriela whirled around and landed a perfectly executed kick to El Dragón's chest that knocked him off-balance. A second kick sent him tumbling through the gaping hole in the slot canyon floor. He landed with a sickening thud, and everyone hurried over to look down at him. He slowly struggled to his feet, there was a flash of light, and the cave was filled with phosphorescent green smoke. When the smoke cleared, El Dragón was gone.

"You don't see that every day," Rafer said.

"He was lucky to have fallen on the dead men," Pepe said. "They made a good landing for him."

One of El Dragón's men aimed his gun at Gabriela.

She raised her hand in a fist, showing him the ring. "I have the power of Supay," she said. "Do you dare to shoot the ring bearer?"

The six remaining men all backed away from her.

"Go," she said. "Drop your weapons and leave my sight."

Pepe translated the command into Spanish, and they all turned and ran.

"Nice work," Rafer said to Gabriela. "You sounded a little like Tarzan, King of the Jungle, but you got the job done. Do you have a direct line to Supay now that you're wearing the ring?"

"I haven't heard from him," Gabriela said.

"It looks like it's too big on your finger," Rafer said. "It would fit better on my finger."

"It will fit better in my pocket," Gabriela said, taking the ring off and putting it in a zippered pocket.

"What's next, Supreme Leader?" Rafer asked. "Do we bury the dead? Retrieve some treasure? Try to find the Wizard stumbling around in the green fog?"

"We take the guns and get out of here," Gabriela said. "We came for the ring and we're leaving with the ring. I would like to take more of the treasure, but I don't want to risk El Dragón somehow mustering his men and engaging us in a firefight. Our position is complicated by the gaping hole in front of us. We're going to have to move forward and hope the canyon leads us to a safe exit."

CHAPTER EIGHT

*G*abriela was the first to step out of the canyon and into jungle. The canopy overhead was thick but there was no undergrowth. The ground was dappled with sunshine where the trees had been deliberately thinned, and gardens grew in those sunny spaces. A cluster of small, single-story houses sat beyond the gardens. Chickens were wandering everywhere.

Rafer came to stand alongside Gabriela. "I think we found El Dragónland."

"Very cleverly hidden under the canopy," Pepe said. "You would not necessarily see this from the air."

"This backs up to either a road or a river," Rafer said. "I hear generators working and the houses are prefab. This is all relatively new, and it was all carted in."

Two uniformed men came out of one of the houses and walked down a wide path that led to more houses.

"We need to find the road or the river without being seen," Gabriela said. "We can't just walk down Main Street."

"They haven't cleared to the north," Caballo said. "We can lose ourselves in the jungle there."

The two soldiers disappeared in the village and there was no other movement.

"Go for it," Gabriela said. "Run!"

They reached the dense jungle without being seen and pushed forward, skirting the village, keeping it in sight. It was larger than Gabriela had originally thought. There was a temple dedicated to Supay and a large house beside it. She assumed this was El Dragón's residence. It was set apart from the village and there appeared to be a helipad behind the temple. There were some large sheds in the distance, by the river. Hard to tell if they were for assembly or storage. Something that looked like an open kitchen. No people. The village ended and an open field led to the river. A rope stretched across the river with a large box that served as a ferry attached to it. The land across the river sloped up the side of a mountain. Acres of green shrubs were planted in slope-side rows. Men were working in the green fields.

"Coca plants," Caballo said. "Big operation."

"This is why there was no one in the village," Rafer said. "They're all working in the fields."

A shallow-draft boat with an oversized outboard motor was beached a short distance downriver from the ferry. No roads or vehicles were visible.

"It looks like it's all about the river," Gabriela said. "We might have to wait for night to steal a boat. If we do it now, they'll be on top of us."

A soldier standing just short of the coca field answered a walkie-talkie and looked beyond the village to the slot canyon mountain. He shook his head and his hand instinctively went to his holstered revolver.

"What's he saying?" Rafer asked Pepe. "He's talking too fast for me to get it."

"I can only get snatches," Pepe said. "He's too far away. There was some swearing. I think he might be talking to the men from the slot canyon. There's probably more than one way to exit it."

"He's agreeing with something," Gabriela said. "He's nodding his head *yes*."

The soldier snapped the walkie-talkie back onto his belt and called to the workers in the field.

"They're going to rescue El Dragón," Pepe said.

"I guess in hindsight, they didn't buy the power of the ring on your skinny finger," Rafer said to Gabriela.

The field workers crammed themselves into the ferry and pulled themselves across the river. One of the soldiers from the slot canyon ran through the village and into the clump of field workers. He was gasping for air, trying to talk, gesturing toward the mountain. The field workers went to a nearby shed and came out with arms and rescue equipment.

"When they all leave to rescue El Dragón, we can steal the boat," Rafer said.

"They aren't all going to rescue El Dragón," Pepe said. "Most of them are going to be combing the jungle looking for us."

"Plan B," Gabriela said. "When we no longer see anyone in the area, we very quietly get the boat in the water and drift away with the current."

Ten minutes ticked by and the sounds that carried back to them were from the far edge of the village. El Dragón's men were starting their search close to the slot canyon.

"Now or never," Gabriela said, running for the river.

They got the boat in the water, lowered the outboard, and a man exited a shed.

"Alto!" he shouted.

Gabriela was at the helm. She cranked the engine over, yelled for everyone to hang on, pushed the throttle forward, and they roared away.

Three more men ran out of the shed, raised rifles, and shot at the boat. A bullet zinged off the starboard side and ripped away some fiberglass. Nothing else got hit. Gabriela maneuvered around a bend in the river and the village was left behind.

"So much for stealth," Rafer said.

Gabriela powered back to get the boat to plane. "I don't want to go full throttle here and all of a sudden throw us into rapids. We're traveling with the current, so I'm hoping this is taking us to a larger river that we recognize."

"We might still be on La Vibora," Caballo said. "It curls around the mountain. It is why La Vibora appears to run backwards. I have been on the section that empties into the Urubamba upstream from where we began. The family has fields on that part of La Vibora." He looked at Pepe. "You have been there many times. It is some of your uncle's plantation. You would have always come in by road."

"I never knew the name of the river," Pepe said.

"It seems it is a shortcut to the slot canyons," Caballo said. "I'm sure the conquistadors did not know of it. In fact, I did not know of the slot canyons or the El Dragón village until today. Uncle's plantation has no need to extend that far and the river traffic has not been of any consequence."

"Uh-oh," Rafer said. "I hear a boat coming up fast behind us."

Gabriela pushed the single lever forward and the boat rocketed through the water. Pepe, Rafer, and Caballo grabbed the confiscated rifles and positioned themselves to shoot. A larger boat came into view and a uniformed soldier fired a shot that pinged off Gabriela's outboard motor. Rafer returned fire and shattered the larger boat's windshield. He got off another shot and the soldier fell into the water.

"One down," Rafer said.

The larger boat dropped back.

"If this is La Vibora, how far is it before we reach the plantation?" Gabriela asked Caballo.

"I don't know that answer," Caballo said.

Twenty minutes later they motored through another valley with rows of coca plants.

"Is this family property?" Gabriela asked.

"No," Caballo said, "but we might be getting close. There are smaller operations in the area that sell their leaves to the family. El Dragón might even be one of them."

The winding river narrowed, and the sides turned to steep sandstone where no vegetation grew.

"Listen," Rafer said. "Boats behind us."

"It sounds like more than one," Gabriela said.

The boats came into view. Three boats moving at fast speed.

Gabriela throttled up.

Caballo was on his walkie-talkie, speaking in rapid-fire Spanish. Rafer and Pepe were on their bellies, rifles aimed at the lead boat that was closing the distance and almost within range.

"The plantation might be around the next bend," Caballo shouted to Gabriela. "I told them we are approaching."

The lead boat fired off a shot.

"It fell short but not by much," Rafer yelled to Gabriela. "Can we go faster?"

"I have it full open," she yelled back.

Rafer and Pepe fired a couple of warning shots, but the lead boat didn't fall back. A second boat came alongside the lead boat and opened fire.

Gabriela swerved and steered in line with the curve in the river. She rounded the bend and the plantation appeared. Coca plants clung to the mountainside for as far as she could see; there were several large buildings with corrugated roofs, a village of small huts, and an assortment of trucks and Jeeps and chickens and goats. There was also a large dock lined with armed men.

Gabriela looked over at Caballo.

He was smiling. "Welcoming committee," he said to Gabriela. "Don't shoot them," he said to Rafer and Pepe.

Gabriela roared up to the dock, and the three boats chasing them slowed to an idle and held at a distance. The men on the dock fired off some warning shots at the boats, a flock of macaws took to the air, and the three boats turned and left.

"You have good boat skills," Pepe said to Gabriela.

"I was raised on a boat," she said. "I thought it was odd that there would be two Mercury V8s on this flats boat, but I think I'm understanding its value."

"There are times when you need to go fast in Peru," Pepe said.

"This is quite the operation you have here," Gabriela said, scanning the plantation.

Pepe nodded. "We produce a lot of coffee."

"I know it's not coffee," Gabriela said.

"Too bad," Pepe said. "I have to kill you now."

"You're kidding, right?"

Pepe smiled wide. "Yes, of course I am kidding. I am a big kidder."

"What are the large buildings used for?"

"One is for storage of the leaves and the finished product. Two more are factory buildings where we process. The smaller one to the side is for living supplies and a kitchen. There are tables outside and showers. We can get something to eat and then we can leave."

. . . .

Pepe finished his food and went in search of a ride back to his uncle's Wrangler. Gabriela and Rafer stayed at the table.

"You have to admit that he turned out to be a great guide," Rafer said.

"*Caballo* was a great guide," Gabriela said.

"Yes, but Pepe was smart enough to bring him along. And even better, Pepe has an uncle who's a drug lord, and his men saved us from the crazy wizard people."

"True. He gets points for that one."

"Now that we have the ring, what comes next?" Rafer asked.

"I'm taking it back to New York to get it authenticated."

"And after that?"

"We see if anyone claims ownership. If someone claims ownership, we should get a finder's fee. If no one claims ownership, we sell it."

"You've done this before," Rafer said.

"Every now and then I find something on my own. Mostly I find things for other people. It's a better guarantee of income."

"We lost our backpacks when we were captured," Rafer said. "Do you have your passport on you?"

"Yes. It's in my cargo pants pocket. My wallet and cell phone are also in a pocket. Fortunately, I packed them in waterproof baggies. And you?"

"Same. Do you want to try to fly out of Quillabamba tonight or wait for tomorrow?"

"I want to get out as fast as possible. I'll have Marcella make arrangements when we get cell service in Quillabamba."

"How long do you think I'll need to be in New York?"

"You don't need to be in New York at all. There are several experts that I've worked with in the past, and I'm sure they'll help me. Authentication shouldn't be a problem."

"Gabs, babe, we're in this together. I'm not going to bail on you for this last step."

Gabriela raised an eyebrow at him. "Still don't trust me?"

"Nope. Besides, we're a team. Just like the old days when we were painting cows."

"It's not just like the old days. We're different people. We have different lives now."

"We *had* different lives. And we will again when this is resolved. And as far as being different people, that's the problem. Sometimes I'm with Gabs, and sometimes I'm with killer ninja. You took out El Dragón like a pro. I've only seen moves like that on television."

"I've acquired some skills in the past few years. And you have a lot of nerve calling me killer ninja. You shot a man!"

"Yep," Rafer said. "I've still got the eye. You should see me take down a row of beer bottles. And I'm the island dart champ."

"You always sucked at darts."

"Not anymore. You're not the only one with some new skills. I've learned a few tricks in other areas, too, but you wouldn't be interested in that."

"Spare me."

Pepe trotted over. "Are you quarreling again? It's as if you were still married."

"She started it," Rafer said.

"I absolutely did not," Gabriela said.

"Just between you and me," Rafer said to Pepe, "she's a bit of a control freak."

"I would not say things like that about a woman when she has a knife in her hand," Pepe said.

"It's a butter knife," Rafer said. "I'm not worried."

"I could gouge your eye out with this," Gabriela said.

Pepe gently took the knife from her. "The kitchen workers would not like to have to clean that off their utensil," he said. "We should go now. My cousin Raymond is going to give us a ride back to my uncle's Jeep. It is a long drive, but it is better than taking the river. There are very bad rapids ahead and there is no easy way to portage around them."

CHAPTER NINE

Marcella was idling at the curb when Gabriela and Rafer walked out of the airport.

"Where's the rest of your luggage?" Marcella asked. "Where's your backpack?"

"That's a long, complicated story," Gabriela said.

Gabriela slid onto the front passenger seat of Marcella's Honda CRV and Rafer got into the back.

"Is he with us?" Marcella asked.

"Rafer Jones," Gabriela said.

Marcella adjusted her rearview mirror so she could see him. "He looks like Surfer Thor," she whispered to Gabriela. "Is he staying with you?"

"Yes," Rafer said.

"No," Gabriela said.

Marcella pulled out into traffic. "Okeydokey, then. I'm just going to head into the city."

"You can't stay with me," Gabriela said to Rafer. "I have a small one-bedroom condo."

"I can manage," Rafer said.

"I can't," Gabriela said. "I'm looking forward to having some privacy."

Rafer smiled. It was his full-on smile that showed off his perfect white teeth and brought out the crinkles at the corners of his eyes. "Afraid to stay alone with me?"

"Yes. You might provoke me when I have something more lethal than a butter knife in my hand and there would be no Pepe to save you."

Rafer leaned forward toward Marcella. "She talks a tough game, but deep down she actually likes me. Especially since I'm her hero. I saved her life."

Marcella made eye contact with him via the rearview mirror. "Really?"

"Yep," Rafer said. "Cross my heart. She would have drowned in the La Vibora River if I hadn't saved her."

Marcella looked over at Gabriela. "Is that true?"

Gabriela blew out a sigh. "Yes."

"Wow," Marcella said. "That's heavy."

. . . .

Gabriela always had a few moments of culture shock when she returned to New York after spending time in a foreign country. She had to re-acclimate to the concrete, the noise, and the pace of the people. The adjustment didn't usually take long, but it was complicated this time by Rafer. He wouldn't go away, and he wasn't part of her normal city rhythm.

She stood on the sidewalk in front of her condo building and waved goodbye to Marcella as she drove off.

"She's nice," Rafer said. "What does she do?"

"Everything."

Gabriela let herself into the building and took the elevator to the seventh floor. There were four units to a floor. Gabriela lived in one of the units that faced the street. She unlocked her door and Rafer followed her in.

"Gabs," he said, looking around. "You've gone classy on me."

"It's a little bare-bones but it's comfortable and I like the location. I wish I could spend more time here, but my work has me on the road a lot."

"Do you like all the travel?"

"Sometimes. Getting shot with a tranquil-izer dart wasn't my favorite part of Peru, and the

Jungle Jane outfit I'm wearing is getting old. I'm looking forward to taking a shower and getting into clean clothes."

"I haven't got any clothes," Rafer said. "Everything was in my backpack."

"Go out of my building, turn right, walk half a block, and you'll be in shopping heaven."

"If I go out, will you let me back in?"

"Only if you come back with a fresh loaf of bakery bread."

. . . .

Gabriela was in her kitchen when Rafer returned with bags of clothes, a bunch of sunflowers wrapped in cellophane, and a loaf of sourdough. He put the bread and the flowers next to the prep sink on the large black granite island and turned to Gabriela. Her hair was still damp and tucked behind her ears. She was wearing black Pilates pants and a white T-shirt, and she was working at the cooktop.

"What have you got in the skillet?" he asked. "It smells amazing."

"Chicken marsala. I had some frozen chicken cutlets, and I found a pack of mushrooms in the fridge."

"You mean you made this? You didn't have it delivered?"

"I enjoy cooking."

"Since when?"

"Since I got divorced," Gabriela said. She put her spoon down and tended to the flowers. "I love sunflowers. Thank you."

"Do I get to eat this chicken marsala?"

Gabriela set the vase of flowers on the island, poured two glasses of pinot noir, and handed one to Rafer. "Yes, you get to eat it. And then you're leaving. Marcella got a room for you at a boutique hotel a block away." She put the sourdough and a bread knife on a cutting board and took it to the table.

"A less secure person might think you didn't want him hanging around."

"He'd be right," Gabriela said. "I'm glad we reconnected and are able to work together for a good cause. That doesn't mean I want to live with you. Living with you was a disaster."

She brought the skillet and a serving spoon to the table and set the skillet on a black wrought-iron trivet. She took a seat across from Rafer and admitted to herself that there was an even more compelling reason to get him out of her condo. She was liking him. A lot. And she was finding him to be way too attractive. The unruly sun-bleached hair, the three-day beard, the hard-muscled tanned body. She gave herself a mental face slap. Stop it! No more thinking about his body. And for God's sake, no more wine. Another glass of wine and she might not want to send him to a hotel. Get him fed and get him out of here, she told herself.

. . . .

Rafer rang Gabriela's doorbell at 8:00 a.m. He was freshly shaved, and his hair was mostly tamed. He was wearing Allbirds high-tops, perfectly fitting jeans, a blue button-down shirt, and a black blazer.

Gabriela opened the door and stared at him. She was speechless. Not because there were no words. She was speechless because she didn't want to say what she was thinking. She was thinking *wow*.

"I figure you're going to see your expert appraiser today," he said. "Thought I'd get here before you could sneak out on me." He wandered toward the kitchen area. "I need coffee."

He was right about the sneaking out, Gabriela thought. She just didn't sneak out soon enough. She'd been counting on him sleeping late. She followed him to the kitchen, tapped the touch pad on the Miele, and put a mug under the spout.

"Marcella set up a ten o'clock appointment. My

historian is uptown by the Met Museum, so we should leave here around nine."

Rafer took his coffee and slouched in a chair. "Tell me about your expert."

"Simon Gitten. He teaches antiquities at Columbia, and he works with restorations at the Met. He specializes in medieval Jewish tradition and Islamic occultism. I retrieved a coin collection for a client last year and Simon was able to verify its authenticity."

"And he knows about the Seal of Solomon?"

"He's the leading authority in this country."

"How do you know what to look for with something that only exists in legends? I googled it and there are lots of different versions of the Seal."

"You're right," Gabriela said. "It's a problem, but Simon should be able to establish a date. And a lot more information is available to him than to us. He has access to documents dating back to the time of Solomon."

. . . .

Simon Gitten had a home office on the fourth floor of a venerable and slightly shabby building on East 86th Street. Gabriela and Rafer crossed the small lobby, took the ancient elevator to the fourth floor, and walked the length of the narrow, dimly lit hallway to Gitten's condo. Gabriela rang the bell and Gitten answered immediately.

"Come in," he said. "This is very exciting."

He was seventy years old with Albert Einstein gray hair. He was five feet, five inches tall and had an average build for a potbellied seventy-year-old. The front room of the condo contained a cramped sitting area with a brown leather rolled-arm couch, a straight-back chair, and two mismatched overstuffed chairs arranged around a coffee table. The coffee table was stacked with folders, books, and scholarly manuscripts. There was a large desk on the other side of the cramped room. A laptop computer was open on the desk. It was surrounded by more books, papers, and folders.

Gabriela introduced Rafer and handed Gitten a little velvet sack.

"Here it is," she said. "The ring's original chest was lost in the struggle to get the ring."

Gitten took the sack to his desk. "There's been so much written about the ring throughout history that I always suspected there had to be some truth to it. I never thought it would be placed in my hand."

"Do you think it has supernatural powers?" Rafer asked him.

"I would doubt that part of it," Gitten said. "These ancient artifacts frequently have elaborate stories attached to them. Although, I have to say that the Seal of Solomon ranks right up there with the Holy Grail when it comes to the consistent and widespread belief in its powers. Unlike the Grail, the Seal has appeared and disappeared throughout its history. And many times, the Seal's appearance has been associated with extraordinary events."

"Like Pizarro defeating the Incans," Rafer said.

Gitten sat at his desk and pulled on white gloves. "Precisely!" He opened the sack and held the ring in his gloved hand. "Amazing," he said. "It's just as I thought it would be. Legend has it that these symbols were engraved by God."

"How do we know if this is the real thing?" Rafer asked. "Can you carbon-date it?"

"It's not usually possible to carbon-date metal. We can date metal objects by analyzing the metals, alloys, and impurities present and comparing their composition percentages to known periods in time. We can also use this analysis to determine origin. Testing is performed using metallography and energy-dispersive X-ray spectrometry. I'll look at it under magnification as a preliminary inspection. If it looks good, I'll take it to the lab for further testing."

"Sounds good," Gabriela said. "When do you think you'll get back to me on this?"

"It depends on equipment availability," Gitten said. "Fortunately, there's not much going on right now, so we could know as early as tomorrow."

"I'm surprised that you left the ring with him," Rafer said when they left Gitten's apartment.

"I've been through this process before, and I trust Gitten."

"Okay, now what?"

"I'm getting a manicure and then I'm having lunch with a prospective client. After lunch I'll go to my office to see if Marcella has anything for me."

"You have an office?"

"Yes. It makes me look legitimate and Marcella can't work from her home. She has two kids, three cats, and she lives in Brooklyn with her mother."

"A manicure sounds exciting, but I think I'll go off on my own. I'll make dinner reservations for us."

CHAPTER TEN

*G*abriela and Rafer left the restaurant at nine thirty and walked the four blocks back to Gabriela's condo.

"I really liked that restaurant," Gabriela said to Rafer. "It's relatively new and I've been wanting to try it."

"The concierge at my hotel recommended it."

They reached Gabriela's street, turned the corner, and their attention was caught by the scene halfway down the block. Several police cars and an EMT truck were angle parked in front of Gabriela's condo building. A uniformed cop was at the door.

"We're restricting entrance to the building," he said to Gabriela. "Residents only."

"I'm a resident," she said, showing him her key. "What's going on?"

A CSI van pulled up and two men got out.

"Homicide," the cop said. "Seventh floor."

"That's horrible," Gabriela said. "Are we in any danger?"

"We swept the building, and it looks okay. Lock your door just in case and don't go wandering around."

Gabriela and Rafer stepped into the elevator and looked up at the security camera. It seemed to be in working order.

"Are there security cameras on the stairs?" Rafer asked.

"Not sure," Gabriela said. "There's also a service elevator that may or may not have a camera."

The elevator doors opened to the seventh floor and Gabriela and Rafer stepped out. A section of the foyer was cordoned off with yellow tape. Two EMTs stood by a stretcher. Several men in wrinkled suits were inside the crime scene tape. A photographer was working. The door to 7C was open.

Gabriela approached the EMTs. "What happened?"

"The older gentleman who lives in 7D was stabbed," one of the EMTs said.

"Here in the hallway?" Gabriela asked.

"Yeah. His door was closed, and he had his keys in his hand. Looked like he was going in and someone stabbed him."

"In the back?" Gabriela asked.

"No. He was facing the perp. His cell phone was on the floor. I heard one of the cops say he'd punched the panic button."

"Any suspects?"

"Don't know," he said. "We're just waiting around for the ME to release the body. Did you know 7D?"

"Not really," Gabriela said. "I live across the hall, and we would say hello, but that was the extent of it."

Gabriela unlocked her door and she and Rafer stepped inside. She locked and bolted her door, opened the middle drawer of the credenza in her foyer, and withdrew a 35mm Beretta.

Rafer did a small, raised-eyebrows grimace. "Who are you?"

"Everyone has a gun in their credenza in New York," Gabriela said. "Stay here while I make sure no one is hiding in a closet."

"I can't stay here while you go all badass on me. I'd feel like a wuss."

"Just stand back while I do this walk-through," Gabriela said.

"See, there you go again, ordering me around.

We're never going to have a successful relationship this way. Maybe you need counseling."

"I don't need counseling. And I don't want to have a relationship."

"Apple Dumpling, there's all kinds of relationships. We're in business together. We have joint ownership of a spooky ring. Not to mention a whole pirate chest full of assorted junk."

Gabriela looked in the coat closet and powder room. She moved from the foyer to the open-concept kitchen and living room.

"If the bolt isn't thrown from the inside, I have an easy lock to pick," Gabriela said. "It's one of those things I always meant to change but never did."

"Okay, but your front door was locked."

"That doesn't mean someone isn't in here. The door locks automatically when it's closed. There are three drawers in my credenza. One of them wasn't pushed in all the way, and the cushions on the couch aren't exactly as I left them. Someone has searched my condo."

"You should tell the police."

"Not unless I find another dead body. Maybe not even then. They'll bring CSI in here and make a mess. And I have things I'd rather not share with the police."

"Drugs?"

"Weapons. Files and trinkets from past jobs. Expensive lingerie."

"You don't have any bomb-making stuff, do you?"

"Nothing heavy-duty. A small amount of C-4."

"Other weapons?"

"The usual. Knives and guns."

"Hidden around your condo?" Rafer asked.

"In a gun safe."

"Do you keep the expensive lingerie in the safe, too?"

Gabriela went to her bedroom and looked under her bed and in her closet. She checked the en suite bathroom. She opened her dresser drawers.

"Someone has gone through my things and tried to make it not obvious," Gabriela said.

She went to the closet that contained the gun safe and a document safe. Both were still secure.

"I guess they didn't bring their own C-4," Rafer said.

"I know this is a stretch, but I think it's possible this is the work of El Dragón. I had a luggage tag on my backpack. He would have my name and address."

"So, they broke in, searched for the ring, and

didn't find it. Your neighbor caught them coming out of your condo and hit the panic button," Rafer said.

Gabriela nodded. "And they killed him."

"If it was El Dragón, he'll be back," Rafer said. "He'll want to get into the safe. He'll be hanging out across the street with his locksmith tools and dart gun and crazy Supay worshippers. Are you sure you don't want to get the police involved?"

"I doubt they would even believe me. It's a ridiculous story. *I* even have a hard time believing it. Plus, there might be a small issue with the ring and how it happened to leave Peru," Gabriela said.

"And it would come up in the investigation."

"Yes."

"So, you're a criminal?"

"It's up for debate. The ring falls into a gray area because it isn't actually an Incan relic. It was just sort of visiting. Still, it could make things complicated."

"Personally, I find it hot that you smuggled a priceless voodoo ring onto a plane and flew it to New York."

"You find everything hot."

"Not everything."

"And it's not a voodoo ring," Gabriela said. "It predates voodoo."

"A mere technicality. The ring conjures up demon armies."

Rafer did his thirty-second impression of a demon zombie.

Rafer humor, Gabriela thought. Next thing he would be talking about eating brains and taking over the world. Not a place she wanted to go right now since her neighbor just bled out in the hall . . . possibly at the hands of Supay worshippers.

"Gosh, look at the time," Gabriela said. "You need to get back to your hotel."

"I'm not going back to my hotel. I'm staying here."

"You are *not* staying here."

"Of course I'm staying here. What happens if you're all alone and El Dragón returns?"

"The only way into this condo is through a steel fire door that is impenetrable once I throw the bolt. And if he does manage to get in, I'll shoot him."

"Okay, then what about me? I don't have a gun. I could walk outside and get darted. You would have to put yourself in danger by rescuing me."

"You're assuming I would rescue you."

Rafer walked to the couch and stretched out. "It's a little tight squeeze lengthwise but I can manage. Don't suppose you want to share the bed?"

"I don't want to share the condo."

"You have an extra pillow? A couple blankets?"

"You can't stay here tonight."

"You don't mind if I use your toothbrush, do you?" Rafer asked.

. . . .

Gabriela woke up to the smell of coffee brewing. It took her a moment to put it together. Rafer was in the kitchen. He insisted on spending the night, and truth is, while she made a lot of noise about him going back to his hotel, she was glad he didn't. Having a homicide victim just outside her door had been unnerving and sad. Especially since she suspected she was partially to blame for his death.

She made her way to the kitchen and found Rafer holding a mug of coffee. He was staring into the fridge and he was naked.

This is not a good way to start my day, Gabriela thought. On the other hand, he had a great ass. And she knew that when he turned around to face her the view would get even better.

"What are you doing?" she asked him.

"Looking for breakfast. I was hoping to find a bagel."

"In the freezer," she said. "Why are you naked?"

"I got gravy on my shirt last night. Since my

other shirts are at my hotel, I had to wash the one with the gravy. And then I decided I might as well wash everything. I like your washer. It has one of those small-load attachments."

Gabriela got coffee and returned to her bedroom. I'm living in a television sitcom, she told herself. I'm being stalked by a guy who worships the God of the Dead and my ex-husband is naked and in my kitchen. I never aspired to being normal, but this is too weird even for me.

. . . .

Rafer and Gabriela were finishing lunch when Gabriela got a text from Simon Gitten. His tests were complete, and he'd be home for the rest of the afternoon if Gabriela wanted to get her ring and the test results.

Twenty minutes later Gabriela turned the key on her new door lock. She also had a newly installed security system that was monitored and a doorbell that had both video and audio. Marcella was a genius at getting a job accomplished in record time. Her success, to a large extent, was due to a very large petty cash account earmarked for bribery. The hall carpet was still wet from being professionally scrubbed. The door to 7D was partially open. CSI was still working inside.

Gabriela paused at the open door, debating

if she should tell the men about El Dragón. It seemed less of a possibility today. A pillow slightly out of place. A sweater not perfectly aligned with the one below it. Lingerie that was a little messy. Not exactly damning evidence.

Wait and see if anything else develops, she decided. Chances were good that she'd been affected by the drama of the moment last night. She took the elevator with Rafer, crossed the small lobby, and went out to the street.

"Looks okay," Rafer said. "I don't see anyone with a dart gun."

Gabriela lived on a narrow cross street. Cars were parked on either side with barely two lanes open for traffic.

"Do you want me to text Uber?" Rafer asked.

"No," she said, stepping around the CSI van. "I see a cab at the corner."

She raised her hand to hail the cab and a black SUV pulled out of a parking space behind the van. It swerved to a stop in front of Gabriela and two tattooed men got out and wrangled her into the backseat. Rafer grabbed one of the men, dragged him out of the car, smashed his head against the CSI van, and left him lying in the road. The second man had Gabriela by the hair. He reached inside his jacket with his other hand and pulled out a gun. Gabriela twisted around to face him and punched him in the throat. His eyes bulged, he dropped the gun and clutched his throat. Gabriela hit him again in the face and blood spurted from his nose.

Rafer reached in and hauled her out of the SUV. "Time to go, Rocky," he said. "You can kill him next time."

The driver jumped from behind the wheel, gun drawn, but Rafer and Gabriela were already running down the street. They turned a corner, flagged down a cab, and jumped in.

"I guess that answers a bunch of questions," Rafer said. "Don't imagine there are a lot of people in New York with Supay symbols tattooed on their face."

"El Dragón wasn't in the car."

"I noticed. I'm sure he wasn't far away. I can't imagine three soldiers doing this on their own."

Gabriela told the driver to drop them at 84th Street.

"I'm sure we aren't being followed, but it doesn't hurt to be extra careful," Gabriela said. "I don't want to put Simon in harm's way."

· · · ·

Gabriela and Rafer left the cab and walked the two blocks to 86th Street. It was a sunny day with a chill in the air. Gabriela was wearing a cream-colored Loro Piana cashmere jacket with a matching scarf, and Rafer had the collar to his blazer turned up. They entered Gitten's building and took the elevator to his floor. Minutes later they were in Simon Gitten's condo, waiting for him to locate the ring and his notes on his cluttered desk.

"Here it is," he said, finding a little white box, handing it over to Gabriela. "My findings were disappointing. The ring is a fake, but it's a very good one. That's the bad news. The more interesting news is that every detail seems to be correct. At least from what my research over the years tells me. It's possible that whoever made this ring had the real thing to copy."

"If it's so good, how do you know it's a fake?" Rafer asked.

Gitten handed him a folder with the paperwork. "I was able to get a date from the metal. I placed it at early to mid-1800s."

Gabriela opened the little white box and looked at the ring. "I would have guessed it was authentic."

"Yeah, but we should have suspected. When we were in trouble it didn't conjure up an army of demons," Rafer said.

"I have high hopes that you'll find the real one," Gitten said. "I know it's out there. Perhaps this was left to protect it. When this copy was made there was no way to tell it wasn't authentic."

. . . .

Rafer draped an arm over Gabriela's shoulders and leaned into her when they got to the sidewalk. "Tell me about it," he said.

"About what?"

"I've known you for most of my life. I've played poker with you. I know your *ah hah!* look."

"That's ridiculous. I don't have an *ah hah* look."

"Gabs, you got one in spades. I could see the synapses firing in your brain. I could hear the wheels turning when he told you the date."

"Gitten said the ring was made in the early 1800s. I've done some research on the Treasure of Lima. In 1820, Lima was politically unstable and the Viceroy of Lima decided he needed to move the city's fabulous wealth for safekeeping. Captain William Thompson, commander of the *Mary Dear*, was put in charge of transporting the riches. Thompson loaded the treasure onto his ship and then turned pirate, sailing away with the treasure and burying it on an island off the coast of Costa Rica. So, suppose the Viceroy knew of the ring hidden away in the mountains and decided to put it on the *Mary Dear* with the rest of the treasure?"

"That's a lot of supposing," Rafer said. "Suppose your journal is a fake that takes people on a doomsday adventure?"

Gabriela stopped in mid-stride and turned around. "We need to go back to talk to Gitten."

· · · ·

Rafer was slouched in one of Gitten's overstuffed chairs, and Gabriela had pulled a chair up to Gitten's desk. He'd examined the journal and for the past hour he'd been silently scrolling through digital archives on his computer.

"The journal seems to be authentic," Gitten said, handing the book back to Gabriela. "I can do further testing on the paper but I'm ninety percent sure it will date to the late 1500s. Speech patterns, script, materials used are all consistent with the late sixteenth century."

"And what about my theory that the ring ended up on the *Mary Dear*?"

"There are enough mentions of the Seal of Solomon being part of the Treasure of Lima for us to consider the possibility," Gitten said. "If Pizarro hid the ring in the mountains and it was guarded by conquistadors, it's possible for its location to be known by a select few and passed on to new generations. It was widely rumored that the vast treasure Pizarro accumulated had been kept in different locations. And there's a good amount written about the rush to collect the treasure and unite it in 1820." Gitten's face became more animated, and he sat forward in his chair. "I just pulled something interesting up. It's a photo of a scrap of paper housed in the National Library in Lima. It's a letter written by a senior officer in the Viceroy of Lima's special brigade to his wife. He tells her he's on a treacherous mission to retrieve a priceless relic that must be returned to Lima. 'Dear wife,' he says, 'this mission is fraught with intrigue and deception, and I worry for the safety of all concerned. These are fearsome times.'

"A second letter follows. 'Dear wife, the metal worker has finished his task and we will soon close this chapter and take leave.'

"It's possible he was speaking of the ring. The last letter is dated March 1820. Months later, the bulk of the Treasure of Lima was loaded onto the *Mary Dear*."

"So, the ring might have sat in the cave for two hundred years and change," Gabriela said. "And then in 1820 it was replaced with a fake and moved to Lima."

"Why the fake ring?" Rafer asked.

"In the 1800s it was fairly common practice to

replicate incredibly valuable pieces," Gitten said. "If the fake is believed to be real, it stops the quest for the original."

"It's still common practice," Gabriela said. "I find it in my recovery work all the time."

"Do we know where this treasure island is located?" Rafer asked Gabriela.

"Not exactly," Gabriela said. "I need to go home and do some research."

CHAPTER ELEVEN

Gabriela answered her new video doorbell a little after six o'clock and opened the door to Rafer.

"Pizza delivery," he said. "I brought dinner." He dropped his duffle bag on the floor and set the pizza box on the kitchen island.

"Why the duffle?" Gabriela asked.

"I moved out of the hotel."

"Are you returning to St. Vincent?"

"No. I'm moving in with you."

"No, you aren't moving in with me. We're no longer married. We don't live together."

"We lived together in the jungle. We can live together in New York. Not much difference."

"There's a big difference. There were no options in the jungle."

"There's safety in numbers right now," Rafer said. "We can watch each other's back if we stay together. And most important, you have all the guns. So here I am." He looked toward the door. "I see the CSI guys have packed up."

"They left shortly after I got home."

"No sign of demons or El Dragón?"

"No. It's been quiet."

Rafer helped himself to a piece of pizza. "How's the research going?"

Gabriela uncorked a bottle of pinot noir, poured out two glasses of wine, and took a piece of pizza.

"William Thompson was a known and respected trader. He was supposed to safeguard the treasure that had been loaded onto his ship and sail around with it until the political situation in Lima improved. This was a huge mistake on the part of the Viceroy. As soon as the *Mary Dear* was out of sight of land, Thompson and his men cut the throats of the Viceroy's appointed guards and tossed their bodies overboard. Thompson sailed to Cocos, buried the treasure, and left the island. The plan was for Thompson and his men to split up and return to divide the riches when it was safe, but before they were able to reach another port, they were picked up by a Spanish man-of-war. The crew of the *Mary Dear* was put on trial for piracy, convicted, and hanged. William Thompson and his first mate, James Alexander Forbes, made a deal. To avoid the noose, they agreed to lead the Spanish to the stolen treasure.

"Thompson took the Spaniards to Cocos, but after landing, Thompson and Forbes escaped into the jungle and were never recaptured. The treasure was never recovered, either."

"So, is this where we're going next? Cocos Island?"

"I don't know. Over the years, everyone and their cousin has searched for treasure on Cocos and none was found. No one is allowed to search now because Cocos is designated as a national marine park."

"I've been to Cocos," Rafer said. "It's famous for its dive sites."

"You were on the island?"

"Not on the island. I stayed in a live-on-board dive boat. Only a few Rangers are allowed to stay on the island. The diving is amazing. The water is filled with scalloped hammerhead sharks, Galapagos sharks, tiger sharks, marble rays, and orcas. I was there once on my own and last year I guided a group of divers. It's fairly inaccessible. You fly into San Jose and then it's a two-hour van ride to Puntarenas, where you pick up the dive boat.

After that it's about thirty-six hours on the water before you get to Cocos."

"Do you think Thompson buried his treasure there?"

"I think it's doubtful. The island is beautiful but small. It's got a couple of sand beaches but mostly the coastline consists of steep cliffs. The interior is dense mountain jungle. And it's been thoroughly searched by early treasure hunters." Rafer topped off his wine. "Did you ask Annie about Cocos?"

"I tried but Annie doesn't talk to me. She only talks to Grandma. I called Grandma and she said she'd try to contact her."

Rafer gave a bark of laughter. "In the meantime?"

"I'm looking into other islands."

"As I remember, there aren't a lot of other islands. A few that are small enough not to have names. The Catalina Islands are to the north. Another mecca for divers. I have a couple friends in the area. I can see if they know anything."

"I've also done some research on El Dragón. His real name is Leon Nadali. He was born in Peru, but his parents moved to San Francisco when he was ten. His father is Peruvian, and his mother is Haitian."

"Voodoo," Rafer said.

"That didn't come up in my research. Leon attended Berkeley but dropped out in his junior year. He surfaces a year later in an article on satanic cults. He's just a goofy-looking goth kid in a group photo. No mention of him other than the photo caption. After that there's an arrest for drug possession and low-level dealing. He made bail and skipped out, probably went back to Peru, because he was never captured. There's a twenty-year gap in his history and then he reappears in Peru as a spiritual leader known as El Dragón the Sorcerer. An article was written about him because his temple of worship was visited by a local rock band and one of the band members mysteriously died during a cleansing ceremony. After that there were several mentions of him in an alternative paper connecting him to Supay. There are more recent internet posts on several social platforms that speak of his supernatural powers and dedicated followers. I found a blog that referred to his followers as Soldiers of Supay. When I do a real estate search, I come up with a condo in Lima and an estate in Santa Barbara County. Both carried big price tags, so Leon is doing okay."

"No mention of his coca farm in the mountains?"

"No, but it might have been under another

name or a holding company. Or he might be squatting."

"I'm impressed that you were able to find all that information."

"I have several very good search engines," Gabriela said. "A large part of my work is done through computer searches."

"Do you think this guy is a true believer?"

Gabriela shrugged. "The Supay thing gives him control over an indoctrinated workforce. So, it seems to be effective from a business point of view. On a more emotional level, being the high priest of a demon god gives the dropout goth kid an ego boost. What I know firsthand is that there are times when his pupils shrink to pinpoints, he looks scary crazy, and the cruel, all-powerful fanatic cult leader emerges."

"Yeah, I saw that look," Rafer said. "It almost had me believing in Supay."

"I guess my answer is yes, I think he's a true believer. I also think he's crazy smart in his quest to build an empire."

"I think what you're saying is that he's effectively insane. He's a high-functioning whack case."

"That would be one way to put it," Gabriela said.

Rafer took another piece of pizza and pulled

his iPhone out of his pocket. "I have a friend with a dive shop in Puntarenas. He's been there for years and dives the entire coast of Costa Rica. If there's a treasure island, he'll know about it."

"I'm going back to my searching," Gabriela said. "You aren't planning on doing laundry tomorrow morning, are you?"

"Do you want me to do laundry?"

"I want you to leave your clothes on."

"You have a lot of rules, Gabs. Leave your clothes on. Don't sleep in my bed. Don't use my toothbrush."

Gabriela looked over at him. He was smiling. He was being playful. Nice, she thought, but he still couldn't sleep in her bed.

. . . .

Rafer was at the dining room table, working on an iPad, when Gabriela emerged from her bedroom. Her hair was swept back into a loose knot at the nape of her neck, and she was dressed in black Pilates pants and a white T-shirt. She had Graff diamond butterflies at her ears.

She got coffee and joined Rafer at the table. "Any news from your dive friend in Costa Rica?"

"Yeah. I got a text from Evan late last night. He said there's a guy in Drake Bay who claims to be a descendant of the treasure-stealing William Thompson. The guy is always talking about the treasure and how when he finds it, he's going to be a billionaire. Claims it was never on Cocos but won't tell anybody where it is. General opinion is that he's a nut."

"Anything else?"

"I did a little more searching this morning and there's a history of some Thompsons living in Drake Bay," Rafer said. "Not a lot of information given about them. Just a couple sentences in reference to William Thompson and the *Mary Dear*."

"Did your friend give you a name?"

"Dan Thompson. Evan said Thompson runs a day boat for fishing and diving. I couldn't find any mention of him. You might have better luck."

"Have you had breakfast?"

"Just coffee."

"I'm in the mood for an omelet," Gabriela said. "I'll see if I can find Dan Thompson after breakfast."

She chopped peppers, onions, and Italian sausage and sautéed them in her omelet pan. She set them aside and whisked up six eggs. When the eggs were perfectly set she added the peppers, onions, sausage, shredded cheddar, and Gruyère cheese, folded the omelet, divided it in half, and slid it onto two plates. She ground fresh pepper across the omelet, added a sprig of parsley, and took the plates to the table.

Rafer looked at the omelet. "Do you have ketchup?"

"It would be a criminal act to put ketchup on this omelet," Gabriela said.

"I like ketchup."

Gabriela went to the fridge and returned with a small bottle of Tabasco. "I don't have ketchup. This is as close as I can come."

Rafer ate the omelet and pushed back from the table. "I have to give it to you. That was a great omelet. Maybe we should get remarried."

"Because I can make an omelet?"

"Yeah, what do you think?"

"I think that's a dumb reason to marry someone."

"I don't think it's so dumb. It was a damn good omelet."

Gabriela stacked the plates in the dishwasher and went to her desk. After an hour at her computer, she concluded that even in an advanced search there wasn't much on Dan Thompson. He was fifty-six years old. Divorced. His daughter lived in San Diego. He owned his boat but not his truck.

Gabriela got a second cup of coffee and called her mother.

"How's the town doing?" Gabriela asked.

"Not good. Eddie and Margie Dugan are gone. Eddie closed up his auto body shop and they moved in with Margie's sister in Atlanta."

"Have you heard any more from Annie?"

"You don't really believe in Annie, do you?"

"No, of course not. Just wondering if Grandma Fanny said anything."

"She said that Annie's been quiet lately."

Gabriela called Marcella.

"I'm working at home today," Gabriela said. "Do we have anything new to discuss?"

"Two potential clients. You got a card from your dentist that you're due for a checkup. Your aunt Sofie enrolled you in the fruit-of-the-month club for your birthday and I've got a case of pears sitting here for you. And I just got a bill from a locksmith."

"Pay the locksmith. Make a dental appointment for me at the end of the month. Eat the pears."

"What about the clients?"

"We can talk about them over lunch. Would you stop at the deli and get me a chef salad and get a meatball sub for Rafer?"

"Sounds like a plan. Anything else?"

"Book Rafer and me on a flight to San Jose, Costa Rica. Ultimate destination is Drake Bay. You probably need to get us on a small plane for that hop."

"Hotel arrangements?"

"Two rooms in Drake Bay. Make the reservations for three nights."

Gabriela hung up and Rafer ambled over.

"It sounds like we're going treasure hunting," Rafer said.

"This trip could very easily turn out to be a complete bust, but right now Dan Thompson is all we've got, and time is running out for Scoon."

"This isn't just about Scoon anymore, is it? You're hooked. You can't give up the chase."

He's right, Gabriela thought. Damn. Part of it was her father's work ethic. Don't be a quitter. When coupled with an unhealthy amount of curiosity it made it impossible for her to walk away from an unsolved problem. Especially if the unsolved problem involved pirates or ancient treasure.

"Are you going to try to get onto Cocos?" Rafer asked.

"It depends on Dan Thompson. I want to start with him. It sounds like he's actively looking for the treasure."

"For forty years, according to Evan."

"That's a long time."

"Without finding anything," Rafer said.

Admit it, Gabriela said to herself. This is stupid. You want the ring to be buried in a chest in Costa Rica, but that doesn't mean it is. Chances are better that it's in a private collection in Lima or New York. And chances are even better that it's a myth.

"You're thinking," Rafer said.

"I'm thinking this trip is probably a waste of time and money, but I have to follow through on the lead, as skimpy as it is."

"That's my girl," Rafer said. "Pigheaded to the end."

• • • •

Marcella staggered into Gabriela's condo a little after noon with her arms wrapped around a large cardboard carton. A grocery bag was perched on top of the carton. Her tote bag was hitched on her shoulder.

Rafer took the carton from her and set it on the kitchen island.

"I brought your pears," Marcella said to Gabriela. "I sent a thank-you note to Aunt Sofie." She took three plastic containers from the grocery bag. "Lunch."

Gabriela and Marcella sat at one end of the dining table, eating out of their plastic boxes, and Rafer sat at the other.

"Here's the first job," Marcella said, handing Gabriela a folder. "Baker Fidelity. Suspected insurance fraud. Two million dollars, give or take a couple thousand, worth of jewelry stolen from Nan and Bill Wisneski's Connecticut house while they were at their second home in Naples, Florida. A week after the theft, Mrs. was photographed at a charity gala in Naples wearing diamond studs that resembled the ones supposedly stolen. She claims all diamond studs look alike."

"Not if they're Graff," Gabriela said.

"The Baker Fidelity folder contains a photo of Mrs. at the gala, plus a list with photos of all the stolen jewelry."

"What's their history?"

"Mr. was president of Consolidated Construction. The company took a nosedive and Mr. got fired without compensation. He's currently with another firm but he suffered some losses."

"Negotiate a contract. See if Jimmy is available to do surveillance. He was great on the last job he did for us."

Marcella scribbled some notes in her iPad and gave Gabriela the second folder. "Vincent Krauss in South Africa. Billionaire. Owns a bunch of safari resorts and some vineyards. He collects ladies' shoes and he's convinced two of the ruby-red slippers worn by Judy Garland in *The Wizard of Oz* are in the wind. He wants you to find them."

"Any merit to this? Could there be a lost pair of Dorothy's shoes?"

"None I could find. There were several pairs, and they all seem to be accounted for."

"Decline on the shoes."

Marcella looked down the table at Rafer. "His meatball sandwich looks better than my salad."

Rafer smiled at her. "You want one of my meatballs?"

"That's the best offer I've had in a long time," Marcella said.

Rafer rolled a meatball down to her, and Marcella speared it with her fork.

"That's gross," Gabriela said, staring at the mess of red sauce on her table.

"Yeah," Rafer said, "but it would have been a strike."

"In your dreams," Gabriela said, getting up to snag a Lysol wipe from the kitchen. "That wasn't even a spare."

Rafer leaned back in his chair. "I guess I know a strike when I see one. Who won the Scooner

Bowl Championship three years in a row? Me, that's who. And I would have won more if the Scooner Bowl hadn't burned down."

"How did it burn down?" Marcella asked.

"Grease fire in the snack bar," Rafer said. "Got out of hand and, *vooomph*, the whole place went up in flames. All that was left were a bunch of charred bowling shoes and some scorched balls."

Gabriela wiped up the meatball mess on the table and thought she didn't want to reminisce too much about Scoon because she might decide it wasn't worth saving. The Scooner Bowl was a cow barn before it was a bowling alley and it never lost the cow smell. Probably it burned so fast because it was wood clear up to the rafters, where the bats and flying squirrels lived.

"The third folder is for your Drake Bay trip," Marcella said to Gabriela. "Transportation, hotel, and climate information. The town looks a little primitive. I'd pack a roll of TP, just in case. And you want to leave your Manolo stilettos at home."

By four o'clock Gabriela had done enough Drake Bay research to decide she probably didn't need to bring her own toilet paper, but Marcella had been right about the Manolo Blahnik shoes. So far as she could see there was no paving in Drake Bay beyond the landing strip.

Marcella had arranged for a van pickup at the

airport but no rental car. Her cryptic message was *be prepared to walk.*

Gabriela was going through a mental checklist of things destined for her suitcase when her phone rang. The caller was unidentified.

"Yes?" she said into the phone.

"Is this Gabriela Rose?"

"Yes."

She recognized the voice. It was El Dragón.

"I have something that belongs to you," he said. "And you have something that belongs to me."

"That's a little vague," Gabriela said. "Would you clarify that for me?"

There was some rustling and a woman screamed. More rustling and Marcella came on the line. "I'm sorry," she said, her voice shaking. "I didn't think. I just opened the door."

Marcella went away and El Dragón returned. "I want the ring."

"It's worthless," Gabriela said. "It's supposed to give you the ability to talk to animals and I tried to talk to a chicken but it was a bust."

"That's because you're not a believer," he said. "I have the power of Supay in me. The ring was meant to be mine."

"Finders keepers," Gabriela said.

"Your friend's life is in your hands. We will

torture her. She will die slowly and painfully. You will have to live with that."

"I want to talk to Marcella."

Marcella came back on the line.

"Are you okay?" Gabriela asked.

"Y-y-yes," Marcella said.

"Do you have all of your fingernails?"

"Y-y-yes."

"Put El Dragón back on."

"Well?" he asked. "How is this going to play out?"

"You can have the ring."

"There will be no police involved, and you will come alone, and you will follow my directions precisely. Once we have the ring, I will release your employee."

"It must be a simultaneous swap."

"Of course. The exchange will take place at nine o'clock at 416 East Meek Street."

"I'm not familiar with Meek Street," Gabriela said.

"The building is under renovation. We will be waiting for you on the fifth floor."

The line went dead.

"And?" Rafer asked.

"El Dragón wants the fake ring. He's going to trade Marcella for it."

"Sounds like you got the good end of that one."

"The trade is going to take place at nine o'clock at 416 East Meek Street. I have no idea where Meek Street is located."

Rafer pulled it up in satellite view on his iPad. It was on the Lower East Side and appeared to be a one-way street. They could see attached brownstones on one side and a collection of large buildings on the other. Some of the brownstones had small yards behind them and then backed up to more brownstones. The building El Dragón had chosen was in the middle of the block and in street view, looked like it was in sorry condition. The brownstones all looked like four- or five-story tenement-era constructions with metal fire escapes crisscrossing their facades.

"He said the building was under renovation."

"Smart," Rafer said. "It's Saturday. The building will probably be empty."

"He also said no police, and I'm supposed to come alone. I'm not comfortable with either of those conditions, but I don't want them to start ripping Marcella's fingernails off because I didn't pay attention."

"Can you delay the rescue?"

"I don't have any way to contact El Dragón. His number didn't show up on my phone. He was probably using a burner."

"If you go into that building alone, there's no guarantee that *psycho sorcerer* won't kill both of you."

"I have to take that chance. Marcella is in this predicament because of me."

"Understood. We have a couple of hours. Let's take a look at the area. And I wouldn't mind borrowing a gun and a knife."

CHAPTER TWELVE

Gabriela and Rafer strolled down Meek Street. Scaffolding covered the front of 416 and plastic sheeting covered the scaffolding. A small construction dumpster was parked in front of the building. There were no pedestrians on the sidewalk and no car traffic on the street. Streetlights were lit in the housing complex across the street, but none in front of the brownstones. The houses were dark, their facades lit only by an occasional window square. The door to 416 was ajar.

They continued walking to the cross street. There was a Korean grocery on the corner and moderate activity on the cross street. They circled the block, looking for an entrance to the backyards, and found none.

"I guess this would account for the fire escapes in the front of the buildings," Rafer said. "There's no street access from the backs of the buildings."

"That makes this building an odd choice for a hostage situation," Gabriela said. "There's only one way in and one way out. If I brought police, El Dragón would be trapped inside."

"He's crazy, but I don't think he's stupid," Rafer said. "I'm sure he has a plan."

Gabriela checked her watch. "It's almost nine. I'm going in."

"This doesn't make me happy," Rafer said. "I'm going to be really pissed if you get killed."

"I'm not planning on getting killed, but feel free to jump in if you hear gunfire."

Gabriela pushed the door open and stepped into the small foyer. There were five mailboxes on one wall. A door on the other wall. Stairs started just past the door. The stairwell was dimly lit by wall sconces at each floor.

Gabriela reached the second-floor landing and paused. She didn't see anyone on the stairs above her or below her. No sounds carried down to her from the fifth floor. She suspected someone was there because she could see multiple footprints in the construction dust on the stair treads. She took a moment to breathe. Stay calm, she told herself. Stay alert. She went up another flight of stairs and paused again. The door to the third-floor apartment was open and one of El Dragón's tattooed soldiers was standing in the doorway. He nodded at Gabriela and she continued up the stairs.

The door to the fourth-floor apartment was closed. Only one sentry in the stairwell, Gabriela thought. She moved slowly on the last set of stairs. She would make El Dragón wait a little. She would be composed when she entered the apartment. She wouldn't let El Dragón feed off her fear. And she did have fear. It was throbbing in her throat and it was sitting in her chest like a fireball.

She reached the last step, crossed the hall, and pushed the door open. Marcella was facedown on the floor with her hands bound behind her in zip-tie cuffs. El Dragón and two soldiers were standing over her.

Gabriela crossed the room and went down to one knee beside Marcella. "Are you okay?" Gabriela asked.

"Yes," Marcella whispered.

Gabriela stood and faced El Dragón. "Cut the zip-ties and help her to her feet."

"Not until I see the ring," he said.

Gabriela took the ring from her pocket and held it in the palm of her hand. "Cut her loose."

"Give me the ring."

Gabriela went steely-eyed. She had to play the

role, she thought. Make it look like she was upset about giving him the ring. "Cut her loose," she said.

El Dragón reached out for the ring and Gabriela closed her fist over it and snatched her hand away.

El Dragón drew his gun. "I want the ring."

Gabriela handed it to him. "Wear it in good health," she said.

El Dragón stared at the ring. "I've pursued this for so long. I've searched for this ring in three other lives. My lord Supay will be pleased."

"Are you going to remove Marcella's cuffs, or are we leaving like this?" Gabriela asked.

"You aren't leaving," El Dragón said. "I have other plans. Supay will be further honored today. We will cut out your beating hearts as an offering to him. And then we will burn this building to purify our offering."

"And to hide your atrocity," Gabriela said.

"Yes. It will serve a dual purpose," El Dragón said.

He nodded to one of his soldiers. "Cuff her."

The soldier approached Gabriela and she kicked him hard in the crotch. He staggered back, cupping himself, and El Dragón fired off a warning shot that sent a chunk of ceiling plaster crashing to the floor.

"Supay likes a live, unblemished sacrifice," he said to Gabriela, "but I'll shoot you if I have to. Supay will have to make do with one live heart and one dead heart."

A shot was fired from the stairwell. Three more shots followed. El Dragón cut his eyes to Gabriela.

"Police," Gabriela said. "And FBI."

A couple of uncapped gallon cans of gasoline were on the floor by Marcella. El Dragón kicked them over and the gas sloshed out, soaking Marcella and spreading across the floor. He flicked a lighter, dropped it onto the floor, and fire exploded in front of him. He waved his hand and there was a flash of green light, followed by a smoke cloud. The building smoke detector kicked in and the alarm went off.

Gabriela grabbed Marcella by the arm, yanked her to her feet and away from the flames. "Fire escape," Gabriela yelled, pushing Marcella toward the front of the apartment.

Rafer burst into the room and a beat later the doorway was obscured by a wall of fire that raced up the wall and along the floor.

"We need to get Marcella out of here," Gabriela said. "She's soaked with gasoline."

Rafer smashed through the glass and the window's protective covering. He cut the zip-ties off

Marcella and she went through the window first. Gabriela and Rafer followed. They scrambled down the metal grid and dropped to the ground.

Gabriela looked up and saw smoke and flames pouring out of the fifth-floor window. A few people were gathering on the street, drawn there by the wailing fire alarm. A siren could be heard several blocks away.

Gabriela, Rafer, and Marcella kept to the shadows and quickly walked to the cross street.

"I thought I was going to die," Marcella said. "Those men are insane." She held her hand out. "Look at me. I'm shaking. I can't stop shaking."

"I took a quick look around the room before I went onto the fire escape," Gabriela said. "El Dragón and his soldiers weren't there."

"They didn't go down the stairs," Rafer said. "I would have run into them. There are probably stairs to the roof. These buildings are attached. If they got onto the roof, they would be able to go building by building until they were on another street and could go down a fire escape unnoticed."

"What was the shooting about in the stairwell?" Gabriela asked.

"I heard gunfire, so I jumped in. I got to the third floor and one of El Dragón's soldiers stepped out of a doorway and shot at me. The bullet nicked me in the arm, I shot back, and he went down and didn't get up. I didn't stop to check him out."

"I didn't realize you were shot," Gabriela said. "Are you okay?"

"Yeah, I'm okay, but my shirt looks like it was in a war zone."

Gabriela flagged a taxi and they all got in.

"Do they have the ring?" Rafer asked Gabriela.

"Yes. Hopefully they'll take it back to Peru, give it to Supay, and live unhappily ever after."

"I'm getting high from the fumes coming off Marcella," Rafer said. "Open the windows."

"The fumes are making my eyes water," Marcella said. "Or maybe I'm crying. I'm still so rattled I don't know what I'm doing."

Gabriela had her arm around Marcella, hugging Marcella tight against her. "I'm so sorry this happened to you, but it's okay now. You're safe."

Marcella nodded. "I knew you'd find a way to rescue me, but I was still scared."

"Me, too," Gabriela said. "And then I was angry. Give yourself hazard pay from petty cash and go shopping for new clothes tomorrow." Gabriela paused for a beat. "You're coming back to work, right?"

"Right," Marcella said. "Maybe we should have one of those security peepholes installed in the door."

Twenty minutes later, they dropped Marcella off at her mother's house in Brooklyn and doubled back to Gabriela's condo.

"I smell like gasoline and campfire," Gabriela said, unlocking her door. "I'm taking a shower and then I'm doing laundry. I'll wash your clothes, too; just leave them by the washer-dryer. We leave for Costa Rica first thing in the morning."

She went straight to her bedroom and stripped. She wanted to rid herself of more than the smoky clothes. She wanted to clear her head. Her job frequently involved an element of danger. She accepted that part of the job and dealt with it. This time it was different. The danger had followed her home. An innocent man was murdered. Marcella was kidnapped and almost killed. Rafer was shot, although thankfully not seriously. A building was set on fire. All because she'd been talked into doing a good deed. Now she was hooked into not only the good deed but the adventure as well. And it wasn't done. Tomorrow she would take off for Costa Rica. More time and money spent. At least she would be free of El Dragón, she thought. That would be big.

She stepped into the steaming shower and let the hot water beat on the back of her neck. She pumped her favorite Jo Malone shower gel onto a nylon scrubby and the scent of mimosa and cardamom washed away the odor of gasoline. She was enjoying the luxury of the moment when Rafer stepped into the shower.

"Hey," he said. "You don't mind if I join you, do you?" He closed his eyes and put a hand to his heart. "Oh man, what is that smell. I love it."

"It's my shower gel."

He pumped some into his hand and lathered up. "This is great. Just like old times."

"It better not be," Gabriela said.

"Nothing personal, Gabs, but you know how I get in a nice steamy shower."

"It will be a lonely experience if you get steamy in my shower."

"No problem. I'm good at lonely experiences. Over the years I've pretty much perfected them."

Gabriela was pretty sure he was talking about sex, but then maybe not. She supposed he could be making a statement about his life in general. That would be sad. She turned and took a head-to-toe, slow look at him. Nope. He wasn't talking about life in general. He was talking about sex.

"Move over," she said. "You're hogging the hot water."

Five minutes later Gabriela stepped out of the shower, wrapped herself in a towel, and handed one to Rafer. "Do you think El Dragón will have the ring tested?" she asked Rafer.

"Yes. Once he realizes he can't conjure a demon army, he'll be back on the hunt. Hopefully we have enough of a head start. If we can find the ring and pass it on fast enough, he'll be someone else's problem. The sticking point is, finding the ring. We aren't even sure it exists."

Blood was seeping through the extra-large Band-Aid that covered the three-inch-long slash on Rafer's left bicep.

"Are you sure you don't need stitches on that bullet wound?" Gabriela asked him.

"It's not deep," Rafer said. "It was scabbed over until it was doused with the hot water."

Gabriela dabbed at the cut with a paper towel and applied a new Band-Aid. "Let me know if you change your mind and want to go to a clinic."

"For sure." Rafer grinned. "Let me know if you change your mind about . . . you know."

CHAPTER THIRTEEN

*G*abriela had always heard that San Jose, in the middle of Costa Rica, was very beautiful and very safe, but she had never experienced it firsthand. She'd flown into Juan Santamaria International Airport on several occasions, but she'd never left the airport to explore the city. It was always a stopover. And today it would be another stopover. She'd packed light. A single carry-on suitcase and a small daypack. Rafer had done the same.

"I couldn't get an address or a phone number for Dan Thompson," Gabriela said to Rafer as they walked the short distance to their connecting flight. "I found an ad for his dayboat, but it said to inquire at any hotel."

The flight from San Jose to Drake Bay was

forty-five minutes long on a single-prop plane. Gabriela watched the rain forest stretch out below her and realized it had become a familiar sight. The carpet of green was occasionally broken by a river or a village. The sky was a cloudless, brilliant blue. The Pacific Ocean came into view and the plane skimmed over treetops, found the short landing strip, and stopped inches from the van sent by Gabriela and Rafer's hotel.

Fifteen minutes later, Gabriela and Rafer stepped into the small hotel lobby and picked up their room keys.

"I'm looking for Dan Thompson," Gabriela told the hotel manager. "I believe he runs a day-boat for fishing and diving. Do you know where I can find him?"

"If you take the road to town, he's the pink-and-blue house flying a Jolly Roger," the woman said. "It's hard to miss. It's about a ten-minute walk."

"Does he have a phone?" Gabriela asked.

"I don't have a number," she said. "We just send people down the road to talk to him. He's a real character."

"Works for me," Rafer said. "It's a nice day to go for a walk." He draped an arm around Gabriela's shoulders. "As long as I've got my sweetie with me."

"I didn't realize you were a couple," the manager said. "Would you like to change out your two rooms for a suite?"

"Thanks, but two rooms are better," Rafer said. "I can't sleep with her. She's a cutie pie, but she snores and drools."

"Of course," the manager said. "I understand completely. My cat is a bit of a drooler."

Gabriela dropped her luggage off in her room and met Rafer on the front porch of the hotel.

"You're a dead man," she said to him. "Live in fear."

"Now what?"

"I do not snore. Nor do I drool."

"I know, but I had to say something. Here I am traveling with a total hottie and we're in separate rooms. How does that look?"

"It looks better than the way you're going to look if you ever tell anyone else that I snore."

"A broken nose and a black eye?"

"At the very least," Gabriela said, leaving the hotel. "We're supposed to go out to the road and turn left. Then we walk for ten minutes."

The road was two lanes of packed-down dirt and gravel. There was dense vegetation on both sides with occasional openings showing spectacular views of the Pacific.

"Not a lot of traffic on this road," Gabriela said after five minutes.

"None, unless you count chickens and goats," Rafer said. "This is my kind of living. I even have a hammock in front of my room."

"Did Evan tell you anything helpful about Dan Thompson?"

"He said he knew all the good dive spots."

"That's it?"

"That's pretty much all Evan is interested in."

They walked past several small bungalows with cars parked in driveways.

"Civilization," Rafer said. "We must be getting close to the village."

The road curved slightly and a blue house with pink trim appeared on the right-hand side. A Jolly Roger flag was waving in the wind and a Jeep Wrangler was parked on the front lawn.

Rafer and Gabriela went to the door and Rafer knocked. A weathered fiftysomething man answered the door and squinted out at them. He was short and chunky with gray hair pulled back into a ponytail.

"Buenos," he said.

"Howdy," Rafer said. "Do you speak English?"

"English, Spanish, and Portuguese," he said. "Take your pick."

"We're looking for Dan Thompson," Gabriela said.

"Well, you found him. I'm Thompson. Are you interested in diving?"

"I hear diving is good here," Rafer said.

"It's the best. You want to see sharks? We got 'em. We got sharks'll eat you alive if you don't know what you're doing."

"I'd love to see some sharks," Rafer said, "but we have other business. We're on a treasure hunt. We were told you might be able to help us."

"Who told you that?"

"My dive buddy, Evan."

"Evan from Puntarenas?"

"Yep. Crazy Evan."

"He's a good man. Knows his stuff," Thompson said. "I saw him stare down a white-tipped reef shark once. Nose to nose. Makes my heart beat faster just remembering it."

"Evan said you've been hunting for treasure for as long as he can remember."

"That's the truth. I'm a direct descendant of William Thompson and I come from a long line of Thompsons who have been trying to find William's treasure." He leaned forward. "Most people think us Thompsons are a bunch of crackpots chasing rainbows."

"Gabriela is a direct descendant of Black-beard," Rafer said. "She's an even bigger crackpot than you are."

Thompson's face lit. "Is that true?"

"That's what they tell me," Gabriela said.

"Her blood is a little tainted by illegitimacy," Rafer said, "but it's Blackbeard's blood all the same."

"Impressive," Thompson said. "Since you came to me, I assume you're insterested in the Treasure of Lima."

"Right," Rafer said.

"Two things wrong with that," Thompson said. "First, I've dug up just about the whole island and I haven't been able to find the treasure. Second is, why should I share any of it with you?"

"I have Drake's diary," Gabriela said, pulling it out of her daypack. "It took us to La Convención Province in Peru, where we found a replica Seal of Solomon ring. We think the real ring was in-cluded in the Treasure of Lima."

"Do you have the replica ring?" Thompson asked.

"No," Gabriela said. "We lost the ring."

"This all sounds fishy," Thompson said. "It's not my first rodeo, you know. You're not the first ones to try to find my secret island. And I haven't given up any information to anyone, except of course Mickey."

"Who's Mickey?" Rafer asked.

"I'm not telling you," Thompson said. "At the risk of being inhospitable, you gotta go now. I got things to do."

"Like what?" Gabriela asked.

"Things," Thompson said.

"I think that's a big fib," Gabriela said. "I don't think you have anything to do. I think you're sitting around here bummed out because you can't find the treasure. Thompsons have been looking for it for generations and haven't been able to find it. So, here's my deal. We'll help you find it and all we want is the Seal of Solomon ring."

"If generations of Thompsons haven't been able to find it, why do you think you can find it?" Thompson asked.

"Because that's what I do," Gabriela said. "I find things. I'm good at it. And what have you got to lose . . . a couple days that you would waste anyway?"

Thompson was back on his heels, hands in his pants pockets. "Hunh," he said.

Gabriela smiled at him.

"What the hell," Thompson said. "Do you want a cold brewski?"

"Sure," Rafer said.

"I'm in," Gabriela said.

They followed Thompson into his kitchen and

took a seat at the table. Thompson gave them a beer and joined them.

"In the beginning everyone thought the treasure was buried on Cocos Island," he said. "Folks wasted a lot of time searching there. It wasn't until my grandfather found the map that the Thompsons stopped searching Cocos."

"You have a map?" Gabriela asked.

"It was stuck in a drawer with a lot of old papers. I don't know what made my grandfather look in the drawer but there it was."

"Can we see it?" Gabriela asked.

"I gotta ask Mickey. It's partly his. We made a deal. Whatever we find I get sixty percent and Mickey gets forty percent on account of his relative was only the first mate on the *Mary Dear* and mine was the captain."

"James Alexander Forbes," Gabriela said.

"That's right," Thompson said. "You know your history."

"Our deal is that we'll help you find the treasure, but we want the Seal of Solomon," Gabriela said.

Thompson leaned forward. "Let me get this straight. You're going to help me find the treasure, and Mickey and I get to keep it all except for the ring?"

"Yes," Gabriela said.

"Deal," Thompson said. "You're right. I haven't got anything better to do."

Ten minutes later, Mickey Forbes joined them at the table. He was in his fifties, red-haired and freckled, tall and thin with eyes and a nose like an eagle's. He took his beer, chugged half a bottle, and turned his attention to Gabriela.

"So, you're the lady who finds stuff," Mickey said.

"They want to see the map," Thompson said to Mickey.

"I guess it's okay, so long as we have a deal," Mickey said. "In the absence of a pirate code, which doesn't totally apply here, I propose we swear to be hearty fellas and abide by the agreement."

"I swear," Thompson said.

"I swear," Rafer said.

"I swear," Gabriela said.

"I swear," Mickey said. "Done deal."

Thompson left the table and returned with a yellowed piece of folded paper. He spread it on the table, and everyone looked at the map.

"This doesn't mean much unless you know the area," Thompson said. "The island is small and kind of gets lost in a cluster of islands that are just offshore. My grandfather recognized it right away because it's shaped like a heart. He bought it for fifty dollars and named it Juliet Island."

Gabriela read the inscription at the bottom of the map. "Herein lies the Treasure of Lima and all that the fair *Mary Dear* bears."

"Problem is, this tells us about the island, but it doesn't tell us where the treasure is buried," Thompson said. "My dad found a small chest twenty-two years ago, and we haven't found anything else since."

"What was in the chest?" Gabriela asked.

"Gold coins and silver jewelry. Some of the jewelry had gemstones in it. I remember it like it was yesterday. Real exciting."

"No Seal of Solomon?" Rafer asked.

"No. Nothing like that. No rings at all."

"I'd like to see the island," Gabriela said.

"It's a two-hour boat ride," Thompson said. "We can set off first thing in the morning. They make good sandwiches at the grocery in town if you want to pack yourself some lunch. Where are you staying?"

"Gracie's Place."

"That's a good choice of hotel. Gracie will pack you a real nice lunch if you ask her."

Gabriela and Rafer left Thompson's house and

continued down the road to town. They passed a couple more houses and a two-pump gas station.

"What do you think about Thompson and Mickey?" Gabriela asked Rafer.

"They seemed okay. A little off the bubble with the pirate stuff, but I'm used to that."

"Are you referring to me?"

"Yeah. Is that an issue?"

A pack of assorted-sized dogs ran up to them, tails wagging, eyes bright. Happy to see visitors.

"This must be the welcoming committee," Rafer said. "It looks like we found the town."

The buildings were mostly single story with tin roofs and a colorful patchwork of siding materials. There were several small restaurants, a couple of municipal buildings, a grocery, and a hardware store advertising fishing supplies. Gabriela and Rafer went into the grocery and got bread, peanut butter, and a bag of cookies. They walked up and down the street and stopped at an outdoor café for tacos and beer.

"Do we have a plan?" Rafer asked Gabriela.

"I thought we'd take a look at the island and see if something jumps out at us. It didn't show up on any of my searches, so it has to be small."

"What if nothing jumps out at us?"

"I guess we just start digging."

CHAPTER FOURTEEN

*G*abriela was pacing on the front porch when Rafer strolled out of his room.

"Anxious to get going?" he asked. "It's barely sunrise."

"Anxious to get coffee and pick up our lunch," she said. "Gracie isn't an early riser. She's getting everything together now."

"You're on hammock time here, Gabs. You need to chill. Do you ever check your blood pressure?"

"My blood pressure is perfect. And this isn't a vacation."

"Do you ever take a vacation?"

"Yes."

"When? When was the last vacation?"

"I take mini vacations."

"What's a mini vacation?"

"A massage. Barre class. A pedicure. Meditation."

"Boy, you really know how to have fun."

"When was your last vacation?"

"Three months ago. I bicycled around the Big Island of Hawaii with a couple friends. And then we surfed the north shore of Oahu."

"Who runs your business when you're away on vacation?"

"My staff. Jaimie, Victoria, and Fluffy."

"Is Fluffy a cat?"

"No. Fluffy is a guy with fluffy hair. He looks like a big dandelion-puff ball."

Gracie stepped out of the lobby and waved at them. "Coffee's ready," she said.

Rafer and Gabriela got coffee and pastries to go. Gracie handed them brown bag lunches, and they set off on the road to Thompson's house. Four feral piglets ran across the road in front of them and roosters crowed in the distance. The sky was blue and cloudless. Gabriela was wearing an olive-drab T-shirt with a camo shirt as a jacket. She had the diary zipped into a waterproof money belt. The vegetation parted on the side of the road and Gabriela caught sight of the Pacific. Another five minutes and the Jolly Roger whipped in the wind in front of them.

Thompson was loading the Jeep when Rafer and Gabriela approached.

"I've got water and beer, and bait in case we feel like fishing," Thompson said. "Mickey's in the house making a last pit stop. He has a prostate the size of a watermelon."

Mickey came out and everyone got into the Jeep.

"I keep the boat a couple miles down the coast," Thompson said. "Got a better harbor there."

Twenty minutes later they boarded the *Julie Dear*. It was a twenty-eight-foot Parker 2820 XLD with a sport cabin and twin Yamaha F300s. The boat suited Thompson perfectly. They both looked like they'd been left in the sun and the rain too long.

"You named the boat after the island and the *Mary Dear*," Gabriela said to Thompson.

"The name of your boat's gotta mean something," Thompson said. "It's gotta say something about your past and it's gotta look to the future."

Gabriela's dad named his boat *Mugs* because he got a discount when it came time to paint the name on the stern since it was only four letters.

The *Julie Dear* had a closed wheelhouse that seated four. Two people were comfortable in the mate's chair and the captain's chair and two were cramped in the side chairs. Rafer chose to ride outside, and Gabriela took the mate's chair next to Thompson.

"Tell me about the island," she said to Thompson. "It didn't show up on any of my maps."

"It probably did but you didn't recognize it," Thompson said. "It's in a cluster of rocks and small lava cones that join up underwater."

"Vegetation?"

"Lots. Tropical. Got a couple waterfalls that are real pretty."

"Animals?"

"Only birds so far as I know," Thompson said. "And Mickey."

Mickey was sitting on one of the side seats. "Haw," Mickey said. "Good one."

There was a two-hour stretch of silence after that with the boat on autopilot and Mickey and Thompson nodding off, waking up with a snort and nodding off again.

An alarm went off on Thompson's watch and he went to full alert.

"It's either time for lunch or else we're closing in on Juliet," he said.

Mickey was also awake. "If we're getting close. Maybe we should blindfold them so they can't find their way back."

"They're partners now," Thompson said. "We

all took the oath. And besides, there's no land-marks. Water is water."

That was all true, Gabriela thought, but she was wearing a watch that told her their exact lo-cation. She could return to the island at any time.

A couple of dots appeared on the horizon. The dots got larger, and Gabriela could see that there were two good-sized islands and several smaller ones. Beyond the islands she could see the coast-line in the distance.

"Do the other islands have names?" Gabriela asked Thompson.

"Not officially," he said. "People call them whatever they want. Juliet is the only privately owned island, and her name isn't official."

Thompson circled the island so Gabriela could see the shoreline.

"It's looks like there are two sandy beaches and the rest of the island is lava rock and cliff," Gabriela said. "I didn't see a dock."

"I anchor in this small cove," Thompson said. "You have to wade to the beach area. The lack of a dock keeps people from thinking they could come ashore. That and the signs I've posted tell-ing everyone to keep out. Hope you don't mind getting your feet wet."

"No problem," Gabriela said. "I expected the

island to be smaller. From a distance the two lava cones appear to be on separate islands, but they're connected by a bridge of barely submerged land."

"Actually, they're connected by a lava flow," Thompson said, dropping anchor.

Gabriela stepped off the rear swim platform and sloshed her way to the beach. Thompson followed her.

"My first thought, and for that matter my grandfather's and my father's first thought, was that William also chose this cove," Thompson said. "It's the logical place to drop anchor. It's protected from rough seas. It has a sand beach. And beyond the beach is a good stretch of fairly flat land that would be perfect for burying treasure."

Gabriela, Rafer, Mickey, and Thompson stood in the middle of the beach and looked around. The edge of the beach and the land beyond were pocked with holes. Scrubby plants and grasses grew in the holes and surrounding area.

"Looks like you've been doing some digging," Rafer said to Thompson.

"Years ago," Thompson said. "This was the first dig site. Three generations of Thompsons have dug up this ground and found only one chest. The faded orange flag marks the spot."

"I'd like to see the other dig sites," Gabriela said.

Thompson pulled a map out of his pack. "They're all marked on the map. We can work our way around the island at the lower level. We tried some slopeside that proved to be difficult digging in shallow soil. I'll point them out as we go."

An alarm went off on Mickey's phone. "Hold on," he said. "I gotta take my meds."

"Are you sick?" Rafer asked.

"I had some clots so I'm on one of them blood thinners," Mickey said. "Those are the pink pills I take twice a day. And then I got a tranq that keeps me from worrying too much about the blood thinner."

"It all started when Mickey fell off a cliff taking a shortcut from a dig," Thompson said.

"It was because of my cataracts," Mickey said. "The edge of the cliff was fuzzy."

"They had to drill a hole in his head to drain out some fluid and for a while he was barking like a dog," Thompson said.

"I wasn't barking like a dog," Mickey said. "That was a cough I got."

"Sounded just like a dog barking," Thompson said. "We all expected him to lift his leg against a tree."

"I tried that once and I fell over," Mickey said. "It was before they drilled the hole in my head."

"Moving on with the map," Gabriela said. "It looks like you have a path."

"We always anchor here, so over the years we've worn a path that pretty much circles the island," Thompson said.

After two hours of fording streams and avoiding pits that were six feet deep, Gabriela reached another sandy beach.

"Was there any logic to where you chose to dig for treasure?" she asked Thompson.

"Nope. Mostly we just dig on instinct. Mickey and me would walk along and Mickey would say, 'Let's dig here,' and that's where we'd dig."

"It would have to look like a good spot to put a treasure chest," Mickey said. "We tried using metal detectors, but they never detected anything."

Gabriela walked to the water's edge and looked up at the lava cone. She estimated it went to about four thousand feet. It was heavily forested and stripped with canyons and waterfalls. She couldn't imagine a pirate choosing the sloped side of a minor volcano for buried treasure.

"Not a chance," Rafer said to Gabriela.

"You're reading my mind," she said.

"It's not hard. You're staring up at the volcano and thinking, 'If I was a pirate, would I want to carry a stupid treasure chest up there to bury it in solid lava?' No way."

The sun was low on the horizon when Rafer, Gabriela, Mickey, and Thompson returned to the boat and pulled up the anchor.

Gabriela chose to sit outside with Rafer, leaning her back against the side of the boat.

"I thought the island would be smaller and easier to explore," she said. "It didn't occur to me that it would be volcanic."

"It didn't occur to me that Thompson and Mickey would be dumb enough to excavate the entire perimeter," Rafer said. "They've been digging holes for forty freaking years."

"Thompson told me that he had some items in the treasure chest authenticated, and they appeared to be part of the Treasure of Lima. He lied to authorities about the location of the find to protect what he considers his legitimate inheritance."

"Let me guess. He told them the pieces were found on Cocos."

"Yep. From way back when Cocos was fair game to treasure hunters," Gabriela said.

"I get the feeling that these two guys are reaching desperation on finding the mother lode. They've dug up every square inch worth digging."

Gabriela leaned her head back against the gunwale and closed her eyes. "I think there's a good possibility that the Treasure of Lima is on Juliet Island and we missed seeing something important. William Thompson had a lot of valuable things to hide. One of those things was a solid-gold life-sized statue of the Virgin Mary. Where would he put it? And if he left a map to the island, why didn't he also mark the treasure locations?"

"We need a better understanding of the geography," Rafer said. "Maybe William didn't bury the treasure one chest at a time. Maybe he kept it together in a cave or a lava tube."

"We have the island coordinates from our watches," Gabriela said. "We might be able to get some data on the island formation. And I'd like to see it from the air."

"It shouldn't be too hard to schedule a helicopter. They do tourist runs along this coast all the time."

CHAPTER FIFTEEN

Gabriela sat on the hotel's front porch and looked out at the Pacific. She was nursing her second cup of coffee and planning her morning. Rafer strolled out of the lobby and sat beside her.

"You were up late last night," he said. "I was doing hammock time and your light was on until one in the morning."

"I was looking for information on Juliet Island."

"Did you find any?"

"Just the basics. It's not significant in any way. It's a privately owned unexplored island with tropical vegetation and a 2,025-foot cone. The cone is high for the size of the island. It makes the slope especially steep and undesirable for burying treasure."

"What about the second cone?"

"Technically it's on the same island, joined by a submerged land bridge. Elevation is 1,304 feet with a collapsed caldera. It's clear on Google Earth if you know where to look."

"We didn't get to explore that part," Rafer said.

"It's inaccessible. Steep cliffs of jagged lava and no beach. It's unlikely that William would have scaled the cliffs with the Holy Mother tucked under his arm."

"Is the helicopter ride still scheduled for this morning?"

"Yes," Gabriela said. "Gracie made the arrangements. Thompson is going to pick us up and take us to the airport."

"Is he riding with us?"

"Probably," Gabriela said. "He has a lot of his life invested in this venture. I can't see him letting us go off unchaperoned."

Twenty minutes later the Jeep rolled to a stop in front of the hotel and Gabriela and Rafer got in.

"Good day for flying," Thompson said, turning out of the parking area and onto the road. "No fog and no wind. You should be able to get a good look at the island."

"Have you looked at it from the air?" Gabriela asked him.

"Yep," he said. "Lots of times. In my younger days I'd climb to the top and look around, but not so much lately. Easier to do a flyover."

"Have you ever used a drone?"

"I tried, but the damn things are tricky. Lost a couple of them in the jungle and gave up on the idea. I imagine you're looking for level spots on the mountain where someone could bury a chest. I have to tell you there's only a few and we dug all of them. Still, it's good to have new eyes looking around. You could see something Mickey and me missed."

"What about caves?" Rafer asked.

"We haven't found any," Thompson said. "That don't mean there aren't any. It just means we haven't found them."

The rest of the ride was quiet while Thompson dodged chickens and potholes. He parked at the end of the landing strip and pointed at a small red helicopter.

"There she is," Thompson said. "The best bird on the whole coast."

Mickey was standing beside the helicopter. He waved at everyone, and they all waved back.

"Looks like Mickey is going with us," Gabriela said.

"Wouldn't be much of a trip without him," Thompson said. "He's the pilot."

"Omigod," Gabriela said. "He has cataracts and a hole in his head."

"The one eye is pretty good," Thompson said. "He doesn't seem to have a problem unless it's foggy, and he's not real good at night. Aside from those times he can hold his own with the best of them, drunk or sober."

"Gracie said she would get me the top-rated helicopter in the area," Gabriela said.

"Yep," Thompson said. "That would be Mickey. Of course, he's also got the *only* helicopter in the area."

Gabriela cut her eyes to Rafer, and Rafer grinned back at her.

"Gabs, sometimes you just gotta go with God," Rafer said.

"Welcome to the Red Bird," Mickey said. "Make yourself comfortable and we'll be off. There's a headset for each of you."

"How long have you been flying helicopters?" Gabriela asked Mickey.

"About thirty years," Mickey said.

"Have you ever had a crash?"

"Sure," Mickey said. "Everyone who flies helicopters crashes. There's about a couple thousand moving parts in this contraption. I never had a *serious* crash, though. Once I took out a weather balloon. That was a mess. And once I caught a rogue gust of wind and crashed into Manny Ortega's henhouse."

"That was something," Thompson said. "There were mangled birds all over the place. The whole town came out to scoop them up."

"They were good eating," Mickey said.

Thompson nodded agreement. "Almost as good as when you hit the goat on the runway."

Rafer and Thompson climbed into the two backseats and Gabriela took the copilot seat.

Gabriela looked down at the empty jelly jar that was on the floor between the seats.

"That's mine," Mickey said. "I take it everywhere. You get an enlarged prostate and you never want to be too far away from a jelly jar."

"Maybe this isn't a good idea," Gabriela said.

"Hang on," Mickey said. "Here we go. Everyone buckled in?"

The Red Bird rose a few inches off the runway and glided forward. Mickey leaned in and squinted.

"Are we close to the trees yet?" he asked.

Gabriela closed her eyes, felt the bird lift, and when she opened her eyes, they were skimming the treetops.

"You might want to pick her up a little," Gabriela said. "You've got a high canopy ahead."

"She sounds just like Adele, doesn't she?" Mickey said to Thompson. "Brings back memories."

"Who's Adele?" Gabriela asked.

"Adele is his ex-wife," Thompson said. "She was real bossy."

"She wasn't bossy," Mickey said. "She just liked giving directions. It was a talent she had."

"Some talent," Thompson said. "Now she's giving directions to Gloria."

Gabriela looked over her shoulder at Thompson. "Who's Gloria?"

"My ex-wife," Thompson said. "Adele and Gloria left Mickey and me and moved in together."

"Could have knocked me over with a feather," Mickey said. "We were married for twenty-two years and I never knew she liked girls."

"Everybody knew but you," Thompson said. "She wore your clothes and smoked cigars."

"They weren't cigars," Mickey said. "They were blunts. They were cigar wrappers filled with pot."

"I didn't know that," Thompson said. "I guess that's okay, then."

The Red Bird was over the ocean. A pod of whales appeared below them and was soon left behind. The shoreline was visible in the distance. Gabriela checked her watch and knew the island would soon come into view.

"Can you land the helicopter on the island?" she asked.

"Negative," Mickey said. "I tried setting down on the beach once, but there was too much slope and it was too narrow."

"There she is," Thompson said. "There's Juliet on the horizon."

In minutes they closed the distance and were next to the twin cones.

"I'll go around her real slow," Mickey said. "Let me know if you want me to zero in on anything."

"Take Red Bird over the submerged land bridge," Rafer said. "I want to see it from both directions."

"That's the diver in you," Thompson said. "You're thinking underwater cave entrance. I don't want to discourage you, but I've been down there many times and never found anything."

"Does the island have tides?" Rafer asked.

"Minimal," Thompson said.

After an hour they left Juliet and returned to the airstrip.

"I'd like to go back tomorrow and do some diving," Rafer said to Thompson.

"I'll dive with him," Gabriela said to Thompson. "I assume you have equipment."

"Yep," Thompson said. "I can get you fixed up."

Thompson dropped Gabriela and Rafer at their hotel and left for home. Rafer and Gabriela got takeout lunches of arroz con pollo and french fries from Gracie and ate at a picnic table in front of Gabriela's room.

"We're finally alone," Rafer said to Gabriela. "Tell me what you really think about Juliet Island."

"I saw several places today that looked like they had potential for William's treasure stash. They were all shot down by Thompson. It doesn't surprise me. He's spent years combing the island, and he saw all the same things that I just saw. Waterfalls that could have caves hidden behind them. Flat, diggable areas on the side of the mountain. Cave-ins that might indicate the presence of a lava tube. I want to believe that the Seal of Solomon is somewhere on this island, but I'm having doubts."

"I hear you," Rafer said. "Do you have plans for this afternoon?"

"I have a call scheduled with Marcella," Gabriela said. "Life goes on in New York. I have clients that are being ignored."

"Anything I can do to help?"

"No, but thanks."

"In that case, I'm going to the village," Rafer said. "I thought I'd poke around a little."

· · · ·

Leon Nadali had his black hair pulled back and neatly knotted at the nape of his neck. His custom Brioni suit and Breitling watch suggested money and taste. His Supay facial tattoos suggested a preoccupation with things dark and evil. The preoccupation was consistent and not dependent on his wardrobe or his location. El Dragón and Leon Nadali were one man. And that man was on a holy mission.

The four men with Nadali were wearing Brioni off-the-rack. The jackets were altered to hide the weapons they carried. Their facial tattoos were similar to Nadali's. The men were soldiers in service to Supay and El Dragón. New York and the suits felt alien to them. They preferred their black fatigues. They were uncomfortable without a scimitar resting against their leg. Nevertheless, they were proud that they were chosen for this assignment, that they were part of El Dragón's elite team.

Simon Gitten was on the floor of his cluttered condo. He was naked and hog-tied and bleeding from a cut on his cheek. Nadali stood over him.

"This is tiresome," Nadali said to Gitten. "I've already wasted too much time. I'm in possession of a ring that I suspect is a fake. I've been told that you are the leading authority on such things. I've also learned that a previous owner of the ring has visited you. I want to know what you told her."

"This ridiculous display of macho force is entirely unnecessary," Gitten said. "You could simply have hired me to research the ring. I'm a scientist and a businessman."

"Yes," Nadali said. "But you have loyalties and professional ethics. My original request for your assistance was rejected. So here you are in this unfortunate position, which we can make considerably more uncomfortable. In fact, I might even decide to kill you."

"The ring is a very good replica," Gitten said.

"And?" Nadali asked.

"And that's all. I was hired to test the ring for authenticity."

"I want to see the assay report."

"It's filed under Rose."

"We've been through your file cabinet and there's nothing under Rose."

"It's not in the standing file cabinet. It's in the file drawer of my desk."

One of the men brought the file to Nadali.

"Of course," Nadali said, paging through the report. "This is helpful. The assay traces the replica ring to the early 1800s. William Thompson was entrusted with the Treasure of Lima in 1820. He stole it and sailed for Costa Rica. The crew of the *Mary Dear* were captured. Thompson and his first mate, James Alexander Forbes, escaped into the jungle on Cocos Island. And the Treasure of Lima was never recovered."

"You can untie me now," Gitten said.

"My master Supay will release you from your earthly bonds," Nadali said. "Marco will stay behind to help with your journey."

CHAPTER SIXTEEN

I have a good feeling about today," Gabriela said to Rafer. "I did some phone work and solved some client issues yesterday, and this morning I woke up thinking everything was right with the world."

"Gabs, the world is a mess. It's always been a mess. It was designed to be a mess. Everything has never been, nor will it ever be, right with the world. Basically, we're all supposed to eat each other to survive."

"What about vegetarians?"

"You have a point," Rafer said. "No one wants to eat a vegetarian. Maybe with bacon and gravy."

They were halfway down the road to Thompson's house. They were carrying bags of food and a large thermos of coffee from Gracie. They were wearing bathing suits under their clothes in anticipation of diving.

"Hold on," Rafer said. "Why are you in such a good mood? Did you hear from Annie?"

"No. However, I've been going over the maps and the geological information. As you know, a lava tube is a natural conduit formed by flowing lava that moves beneath the hardened surface of a previous lava flow. If lava in the tube empties, it leaves a cave that can be miles long. I think we should look for a lava tube."

"I'll buy that."

"There are two areas I'd like to explore today," Gabriela said. "One is on the collapsed side of the smaller cone. The other is directly opposite it on the larger island. Two hundred years ago both those areas would have looked different due to fresh lava flows. It's possible that a lava tube entrance was exposed when William was snooping around."

"And now it's underwater," Rafer said. "I had the same thought. I've actually been in some underwater lava tubes in Hawaii. Spectacular diving in North Kohala close to Kawaihae Harbor."

"I've never been in a lava tube, but I'm looking forward to it."

Rafer nodded. "When was the last time you were diving?"

"Last year. I was investigating a shipwreck in the Maldives."

"Did you find the treasure?"

"It wasn't treasure I was looking for," Gabriela said. "It was proof of fraud. And yes, I found it."

Ten more minutes of walking and they came on Thompson loading the Jeep with scuba gear.

"I've got a good feeling about today," Thompson said. "I think today is the day."

Rafer looked around. "Where's Mickey?"

"He's flying today. Some big-shot tourist coming in. Wants to see whales. They always want to see the whales."

. . . .

When Nadali and his soldiers boarded the small plane that would take them to Drake Bay, the pilot wasn't alarmed by the facial tattoos. He'd flown his share of crazies from California, and he was used to seeing tribal body art. He was also used to not looking too closely at the contents of the locked containers that were stored as luggage.

Nadali gave a curt nod to the pilot on entrance and silently walked to the back of the plane. He sat alone. His men knew not to disturb him. He was Supay's high priest, he was a powerful sorcerer, and he could be cruel if he was displeased.

He sat in his seat with his hands tightly clasped. His eyes were dilated to solid black, and his lips moved as he silently, feverishly chanted to his lord. He had Supay's voice in his ear. It wouldn't be silenced by his prayers. The God of Death was angry. He had been promised the Seal of Solomon and the promise had not been fulfilled. Retribution would be terrible if Nadali failed again.

It was a short, uneventful flight. The plane touched down and taxied to inches from where Mickey Forbes was waiting. Mickey knew the drill. He would load the tourists into the van and take them to their lodging. They would have a traditional lunch of chicken and rice; they would get dressed in colorful shirts, hang their expensive cameras around their necks, and he would helicopter them out to see the whales.

"Howdy," Mickey said to the somber men as they filed into his van. "Hope you had an enjoyable flight."

No one spoke. Nadali was not in a good place. His eyes were black, and he was pale under his facial tattoos. His men suspected he was in Supay's grip. They had seen him in this state before and it always led to pain for some unfortunate soul.

· · · ·

The *Julie Dear* was anchored in a small cove, east of the submerged land bridge that connected the two parts of Juliet Island.

"Watch for the sharks. They like this side of the island," Thompson said, helping Rafer and Gabriela secure their tanks over their wet suits. "You've got Aqualung Argonaut knives and Tovatec Fusion 530 headlamps. That's as fancy as I can get. You're probably used to carrying two tanks and a rebreather, but I don't have much call for that pro stuff."

"No problem," Rafer said. "We aren't going deep or far from the boat." He went through a last check of his equipment, gave a thumbs-up, and went over the side. Gabriela followed him. Once in the water she adjusted her mask and oriented herself. The water was clear with good visibility, making it easy to keep Rafer in sight. They'd already decided on the route they would take. Explore the east side of the smaller landmass first, cross to the larger part of the island, and work their way around to the sand beach.

They swam through a school of ladyfish and paused to watch a large hammerhead shark cruise past them. They were following the contour of the land in a shallow dive, looking for crevices and shelves that might lead to a lava tube.

After an hour they returned to the *Julie Dear* for fresh tanks.

"Did you find anything?" Thompson asked.

"Just the usual lava formation," Gabriela said. "Nothing worth investigating."

"Some good-size spiny lobsters down there," Rafer said. "If we don't find a lava tube we should at least go back and get dinner."

"Too bad Mickey had to miss this trip," Thompson said. "He's all about lobster. Probably only thing he likes better than lobster is flying his helicopter. I imagine he's rushing everybody through lunch so he can take off and look for whales."

· · · ·

Mickey squinted through his cataracts and watched as the tattooed man in the black T-shirt and black military-style cargo pants heated the fireplace poker in the gas cooktop flame. Mickey had been on his way, delivering the tourists to their hotel, when he'd been ordered at gunpoint to drive to Thompson's house. Now he was bound to one of Thompson's kitchen chairs and he was confused.

"This is a little crude," a man in an expensive black suit and black shirt said, "but we needed to improvise."

"Who are you?" Mickey asked.

"I'm El Dragón," the man said. "I'm a high priest and supreme worshipper of the Lord God Supay. I am also a sorcerer with powers you can only imagine. When I obtain the Seal of Solomon, I will rule the world."

"I'm being punked, right?" Mickey said. "Who put you up to this? My ex-wife? Thompson?"

"Burn him," El Dragón said to his soldier.

The soldier took the glowing red poker and held it against Mickey's neck while Mickey screamed, his clouded eyes bulged in their sockets, and he peed his pants.

"So now you see that we're serious," El Dragón said. "If you continue to be uncooperative our next move will be to gouge your eye out with the fireplace poker."

Mickey hoped it would be the left one, with the worse cataract. It was basically useless anyway.

"We know that you are in partnership with Dan Thompson to find the Treasure of Lima," El Dragón said.

"How do you know that?"

"It's not a secret. Every bartender, fishing captain, dive shopkeeper, and street addict knows that you and your pathetic relatives have been searching for the treasure for generations."

"Yes, but we've never found it."

"We know this is Dan Thompson's house and he is obviously missing. Where is he?"

"He's diving," Mickey said.

"Where?"

"I don't know."

The soldier brought the poker close enough to Mickey's eye that he could feel the heat.

"Okay," Mickey said. "I might know. I think I might know. There's this island that some people wanted to dive."

"What people?" El Dragón asked. "What island?"

"Two treasure hunters. One of them is related to a pirate like Dan and me."

"Her name?" El Dragón asked.

"Gabriela Rose."

"I knew when I woke up this morning that this would be a wonderful day," El Dragón said. "It turned bad for some moments, but now I can feel Supay smiling again."

* * * *

"These are the last two tanks," Thompson told Rafer and Gabriela. "It's almost four o'clock. You have one more hour to dive. And don't forget the lobsters."

Rafer and Gabriela wasted no time returning to the last spot they visited. It was a twelve-foot ledge jutting into the ocean. The ledge was a mere fifteen feet below the surface of the water, and under the ledge was an opening large enough to accommodate a VW Bug. A lava tube stretched away from the opening. The opening was obscured by kelp, but Gabriela had stumbled on it in an effort to avoid a shark.

They switched their headlamps on and followed the tube for ten minutes, occasionally encountering schools of fry. The tube turned, slanted uphill slightly, and almost immediately went dry.

Rafer removed his mask and mouthpiece. "I can breathe," he said. "This tube has an exit somewhere that's not underwater."

After five minutes of awkward walking over sometimes rough and sometimes slick lava rock, Rafer and Gabriela were stopped by a partial cave-in.

"If we can't get through here, do we have enough in the tank to go out the way we came in?" Gabriela asked.

"We should be okay," Rafer said. "If for whatever reason we can't get to the boat, we can definitely make it to the sand beach."

Gabriela switched her handheld flashlight on and aimed it at the opening in the cave-in. "It looks clear after about three feet. If we can clear more of the rock away, we might be able to crawl through."

They removed their tanks and worked at enlarging the opening.

"I'm sweating in this wet suit," Rafer said, "but I don't want to take it off. It'll give some protection going through the cave-in."

"Do you think you can fit?"

He removed his headlamp and handed it to Gabriela. "Piece of cake."

Gabriela watched Rafer's feet disappear as he pulled himself through the three-foot tunnel. There was a thud and a grunt. The flashlight beam made a sweeping motion and Rafer gave a low whistle.

"What?" Gabriela asked. "What's the whistle about? What do you see?"

"Come see for yourself."

Gabriela fed him their tanks and lights and climbed over the rubble and through the opening. She stood next to Rafer and swept her light around the large domed cave. Her heart skipped a beat and she reached out to Rafer, taking his hand. "It's the Treasure of Lima," she said.

Rafer was smiling. "We'll have to send a thank-you note to Annie."

The cave was filled with chests. Some were

elaborately carved and decorated with silver and others were sturdy and without ornament. Mixed with the chests were barrels that Gabriela thought most likely held provisions. A cache of nineteenth-century weapons was stacked beside one of the chests.

"Shine your light past the weapons," Rafer said to Gabriela.

She directed the beam past the weapons and the light caught on the life-sized, golden statue of the Virgin Mary.

Gabriela's breath caught in her throat. "She's beautiful," Gabriela said on a whisper.

"Are those tears in your eyes?" Rafer asked.

"Sweat," Gabriela said, dabbing at her eyes. "She's smiling. It's as if she's happy to see us."

"The feeling is mutual," Rafer said. "Moving on to a harsher reality, we have no natural light in here, and we have limited battery life on our devices. We have two headsets, two flashlights, two iPhones. We have no idea how long it will take us to find our way out of here and it will be difficult without light. If we're going to look for the ring, we need to limit the time. We can come back tomorrow with Thompson and Mickey and more equipment."

"I don't think the ring would be packed away

in one of the large chests," Gabriela said. "It would be in its own special box. It would be in a very safe place."

"I'll walk the perimeter of the cave," Rafer said. "You search the interior."

Gabriela picked her way through the chests and barrels. Think like William Thompson, she told herself. Listen to your instincts. He went to special pains to hide a fake ring. Why would he do that? Because he feared its power? No. Because he revered it as a religious relic. Just as he revered the statue of Mary. He'd placed her in the very center of the chamber on a slight rise in the floor.

Gabriela approached the Virgin. She was shorter than Gabriela. The contours of her face were softer. Her enigmatic smile reminded Gabriela of the *Mona Lisa*, and Gabriela thought there was an inner peace that transformed both women. She thought they must hold secrets that were both wonderful and sad.

That was at least true of the golden Mary. She had a beautiful little ring box cradled in her hands. Gabriela asked permission before taking the box. She opened the lid and looked in at the Seal of Solomon.

"We'll find a better home for you and the Seal," Gabriela said to the Virgin.

She tucked the ring into a pocket inside her

wet suit and flashed her light at Rafer. "I have it," she said.

"I've walked the entire perimeter and found three exits," Rafer said.

"How will we know which one to take?"

Rafer clapped his hands and shouted. Hundreds of bats detached from the ceiling and flew out one of the tunnels.

"We follow the bats," Rafer said.

After five minutes of walking, they felt the air change. Another minute and they saw a glimmer of light ahead. They came to the end of the lava tube, pushed through dense foliage, and looked out at the ocean. They were directly above the sand beach, and they were at an elevation that was just high enough to be overlooked for hidden treasure.

Gabriela thought William Thompson found the perfect repository for the *Mary Dear*'s cargo. Cargo he'd obviously never cashed in.

"We have to find our way down to the beach," Gabriela said. "We're losing light and it's going to be tricky in the dark."

"Stay close to my back and I'll bludgeon us through the scrub."

"I couldn't raise Thompson on my walkie-talkie," Gabriela said.

"I can see the boat," Rafer said. "It's still

anchored in the same spot. He's probably napping."

Minutes later, Gabriela lost her footing, crashed into Rafer, and took him down. They went into a twenty-foot skid, dropped ten feet off a ledge, and landed in a patch of a'a lava.

"I don't like to complain," Rafer said, "but *ouch*!"

"I tore a hole in Thompson's wet suit," Gabriela said. "He's not going to be happy."

"On the positive side. We just covered a lot of ground."

By the time they reached the beach Gabriela had three more chunks taken out of her wet suit and Rafer was limping.

"Try the walkie-talkie again," Rafer said. "Tell Thompson to put the running lights on."

"He's not picking up," Gabriela said.

"Equipment failure," Rafer said. "We rolled halfway down the mountain. The walkie-talkie looks like it was run over by a truck."

"More like it was run over by an air tank," Gabriela said.

Rafer rapped his knuckles on his tank. "It's still half-full. Are you up for a swim?"

"Will we be able to find the boat in the dark?"

"Gabs, there's beer on that boat. I could find it in the dark with my eyes closed."

They waded into the water and the *Juliet*'s running lights blinked on.

"Thompson woke up," Gabriela said.

"This is prime feeding time for sharks," Rafer said. "Stay close to me."

When they reached the swim platform of the *Juliet*, Gabriela went up first. "That was creepy," she said to Rafer. "I'm not a fan of night diving."

Thompson was in the cockpit, in his captain's chair. "Did you find it?" he asked.

Gabriela shucked her tank. "Yes," she said. "We found it. We found the Treasure of Lima. And I have the ring."

Thompson didn't move from the chair. "Can I see it?"

"Are you okay?" Gabriela asked. "You don't sound right."

"I'm okay," he said. "I'm just . . . I'm okay."

Gabriela was standing outside the cockpit, but she could see Thompson sweating and trembling. The door to the cabin was open and El Dragón stepped into it. Gabriela could see two men behind him. They all had guns drawn.

"I would like the ring," El Dragón said. "We have one more captive. He's not feeling up to talking, so we're leaving him in the bunk."

El Dragón stepped aside so Gabriela could see Mickey, bound and gagged.

"As you can see, he's also rigged with explosives," El Dragón said. "Our friend Dan Thompson is wearing a similar suicide vest. If you do something stupid, I'll detonate the vests and we will be nothing but bloody dust."

"You would kill yourself?"

"I have no fear of death. My lord Supay will ensure that I have a place in the kingdom."

"Maybe," Rafer said. "I'm guessing Supay will be pissed that you sent the ring to Davey Jones' locker."

"There is that risk," El Dragón said. "So, I would very much appreciate it if you would give me the ring, Miss Rose."

"What's in it for me?" Gabriela asked.

"Your life," El Dragón said. "You give me the ring and tell me where I can find the rest of the Treasure of Lima and I will have no reason to kill you."

"Why should I trust you?"

"What is the alternative?"

"I could call your bluff," Gabriela said.

El Dragón turned and shot Thompson in the foot. Thompson screamed and slumped in his chair.

"How many bullets would you like me to put into this man?" El Dragón asked Gabriela.

Gabriela took the ring from the pocket in her wet suit and tossed it to El Dragón.

He snatched the ring out of the air and in that instant Rafer grabbed Gabriela, threw her overboard, and dived in after her.

Gabriela surfaced, saw El Dragón and his men shooting into the water. She filled her lungs with air, went under, and swam for shore. She surfaced a second time and saw a boat pull up alongside the *Juliet*. Rafer surfaced beside her.

"You threw me off the boat!" Gabriela said. "What the hell?"

"Was there an alternative?"

"Yes. You could have yelled *jump*."

A searchlight swept across the water.

"They're looking for us," Rafer said. "Don't go for the beach. Swim for the lava tube."

After what seemed like an eternity to Gabriela, she reached the submerged land bridge and was able to cling to the rocky outcropping above the lava tube. Rafer was next to her.

"I'm exhausted," she said to Rafer. "Now what?"

"They're going to come after us. They're going to want the rest of the treasure."

"I'm sure you're right. And when we lead them to the treasure, they'll kill us."

"We need to go into the tube. We'll be safe in the cave," Rafer said.

"I can't go into the tube. I haven't got air."

"I have half a tank. We can buddy breathe."

There was a sliver of moon in the sky. It threw enough light for Gabriela to see a small tender leave the side of the large boat that was next to the *Juliet*. The tender motored to the beach and four armed men got out and waded ashore. The tender went to deeper water and slowly made its way around the island, flashing the searchlight beam across the shoreline.

"I'm convinced," Gabriela said. "Let's do it."

They went through the tube much faster than they did the first time. They reached the curve and upward slant and burst out of the water sucking in air.

"I've had instruction on buddy breathing," Gabriela said. "That's the first time I've had to put it to use."

"You're a good diver. You don't panic. And you have good endurance."

"Thanks. I think it comes from all those years working on my dad's boat. Still, I have to be honest, I get a heart flutter when a shark gets too close."

"No shame there," Rafer said. "They're freaking scary."

They shucked their equipment when they reached the treasure cave, took the exit tunnel, and pushed through the brush that was shielding the tunnel opening. They could hear the men searching the beach and surrounding jungle below them. The tender was still sweeping the island with its searchlight. Lights were on in the *Juliet* and the larger vessel.

Rafer and Gabriela sat huddled together and silently watched the search.

"They don't know if we're dead or alive," Gabriela whispered. "They were shooting into the water, and now they can't find us."

"I'm guessing they'll stay until daylight and do one last island sweep. When they can't find us and Thompson can't tell them where the treasure is hidden, I'm hoping they'll leave. El Dragón has the Seal of Solomon. He'll be anxious to get it authenticated or at least try it out."

"Demon armies?"

"Yeah, and he can have meaningful conversations with the wild goats."

They hunkered down so they couldn't be seen and took turns sleeping. The two boats were still anchored at sunrise. The tender was tied up to the *Juliet*.

Gabriela stood and stretched. "I'm hungry and thirsty and unhappy."

"I'm not looking forward to spending the rest of the day with you," Rafer said. "I've seen you when you haven't had coffee and it isn't pretty."

"Someone is walking around on the *Juliet*," Gabriela said. "Looks like a soldier."

"Probably guarding Mickey and Thompson."

"Two soldiers," Gabriela said. "They're dragging Mickey and Thompson out to the deck."

Thirty minutes ticked by and El Dragón appeared on the deck of the bigger boat. He stepped onto the swim platform and crossed to the *Juliet*. He was followed by a third soldier. Mickey and Thompson were on the floor propped against the side of the boat. Their hands were cuffed in front of them. El Dragón stood over them.

"I can't hear," Gabriela said, "but I imagine he's grilling them on the treasure."

"I hate sitting here watching this," Rafer said. "I'd like to go down there and beat the crap out of Mr. Asshole Sorcerer."

"Whatever he's saying to them, they aren't responding. They both look completely out of it."

El Dragón turned from Mickey and Thompson and looked out at the island. He gave orders to two of the soldiers. They got into the tender and roared off.

"Search and recover," Rafer said.

The third soldier dragged Mickey and Thompson back into the cabin. El Dragón returned to the larger boat.

"I have to give it to him," Rafer said. "El Dragón's got a nice boat."

"He's probably having a relaxing breakfast of coffee and pastries on his nice boat."

"Another reason to dislike him," Rafer said.

Gabriela went into the cave and returned with a large silver jug that was decorated with precious stones.

"One of us should sneak out and get some drinking water," she said. "I can hear a waterfall that might not be too far away."

"I'll go," Rafer said, taking the jug. "Maybe I can score us some fruit. I saw a lot of mango and breadfruit trees when we were hiking with Thompson and Mickey."

Gabriela sat alone on the hillside and choked back emotion. Her stomach felt hollow, and her heart felt small and sad. They'd found the treasure but at a terrible expense.

CHAPTER SEVENTEEN

*A*t midday Rafer and Gabriela were slouched against the outer edge of the lava tube. Gabriela was on watch and Rafer was napping.

"The tender just returned," she said, nudging Rafer awake. "They're hoisting it up onto El Dragón's boat."

Minutes later, the soldier left *Juliet*'s pilothouse, walked to the swim platform, and crossed over to the big boat.

Rafer fell asleep again and Gabriela gave him a shove. "How can you sleep?" she said. "Don't you want to see what's happening?"

"Nothing is happening. When something happens let me know and I'll get all excited."

"Something *is* happening. They're leaving."

Rafer sat up a little straighter and squinted out at the ocean.

"You're right," Rafer said. "They're under power. And it looks like they're leaving the *Juliet* behind. That would be good. We'd have a way to get off this island. It's a far swim in shark-infested waters but what the hell, we haven't got anything else to do today."

"I'm pretty sure Mickey and Thompson are still on the boat."

"Yeah, and I'm pretty sure they wouldn't leave them behind if they were still alive."

El Dragón's boat idled at a distance.

"What are they waiting for?" Gabriela asked. "They're just sitting in the water."

"I have a bad feeling about this," Rafer said.

"I have the same bad feeling," Gabriela said.

KABLAM! The *Juliet* exploded.

"Oh my God," Gabriela said in a whisper. "Crap, Mickey and Thompson were on that boat."

"I shouldn't have left them behind," Rafer said.

"You had no choice."

"There's always a choice. I really liked them. They were good men who were resolute in their search for the treasure. They shouldn't have died like this."

Gabriela choked back down her own emotion

at the loss of Mickey and Thompson and doggedly stared at the wreck. Big chunks of the boat shot up into the air and splashed down into the water. There was some fire and black smoke, the *Juliet* sank, and the fire went out.

"Guess that's one swim we don't have to take," Rafer said.

"Do you have a plan B?"

"Not at the moment." He looked at Gabriela. "You're doing that thing with your mouth."

"What thing?"

"You have this way of squinching your lips together and screwing your mouth up to one side."

"I do not."

"It's your totally pissed-off face."

"Since when?"

"Since always. You looked like that in first grade when I ate your cupcake. And then you punched me in the face."

"It was my birthday cupcake. My mother put it in my lunchbox especially for me."

"You left it sitting out on the bench," Rafer said.

"I went to get a napkin."

"And then you looked like that in third grade when you lost the spelling bee to Norman Fuzcinski."

"He got all the easy words," Gabriela said. "It was rigged because his father was the principal."

"You had the twisted squinchy look a lot when we were married," Rafer said.

"It was my year of anger. I'm better now."

"You don't look better."

"This is different. I'm going to take him down and make him pay for what he did to Mickey and Thompson. I'm going to get the ring back and I'm going to make sure that psycho lunatic doesn't kill any more people."

And I'm not going to cry, she thought. She absolutely did not want to cry.

"Good goals, Gabs. Maybe a tad unrealistic since we're marooned on this island. Not to mention El Dragón's army of drugged-up, crazy-ass followers."

"He kidnapped Marcella, killed my neighbor, and blew up Mickey and Thompson."

"Don't forget Caballo's fingernail."

"We need to get off this island," Gabriela said.

"Do you have any ideas?"

"Fire. You could set fire to something; people would see the smoke and come to investigate."

"Good idea. Do you have any matches? Bic lighter?"

"No."

"Me either."

Gabriela looked out at the ocean. El Dragón's boat was a speck on the horizon. The debris from the *Juliet* was beginning to drift toward the island. Two orange objects caught her attention.

"Omigod," she said, taking off down the mountain. "I think those orange things are life vests."

Rafer was a step behind her. "It looks like there are bodies in the vests."

They reached the water's edge and Rafer and Gabriela plunged in and swam toward the wreck site. Flotation cushions, chunks of Styrofoam, coils of plastic rope, and unidentifiable flotsam were spread over a large area. The current was carrying it all toward the beach. The life jackets and their occupants were also caught in the current.

Rafer had a good lead on Gabriela. He grabbed the first vest and saw that it was holding Thompson, and that Thompson was alive. Rafer passed him over to Gabriela and went after Mickey in the second vest.

Gabriela began towing Thompson toward the shore. She was sidestroking, with one hand wrapped around a strap on the back of Thompson's vest. The vest was doing a decent job of keeping Thompson's face out of the water, but Gabriela was struggling with the small swells. A large chunk of Styrofoam floated close to her and she snagged it to use as a prop.

There were two-foot waves rolling onto the

beach. Rafer dragged Mickey out of the water, laid him in the sand, and ran back to help Gabriela get Thompson through the surf.

Mickey was on his stomach, eyes closed, mouth open. He coughed and some water gushed out. He rolled onto his back and opened his eyes. "Am I alive?"

"Looks that way," Rafer said, setting Thompson down next to Mickey.

"Are you okay?" Gabriela asked Thompson.

"Hell no, I'm not okay," Thompson said. "I just got blown up. It was like Mickey and me got shot out of a cannon. One minute I was flying through the air and then next thing I was in the water. And on top of that I've been shot in the foot. Lucky for me El Crappo is a lousy shot and he just nicked my little toe." He stretched out on his back, spread-eagle on the sand. "The sun feels good."

"So why aren't you dead?" Rafer asked.

"Mickey and me are a couple tough old guys," Thompson said. "We got skills. We can fake being all done in. Comes from being in a lot of bar fights and getting beat up by a bunch of drug thugs. And we know how to get out of those stupid worthless plastic handcuffs."

"You had explosives strapped to you," Gabriela said.

"Turned out to be fake. The wizard guy wasn't gonna blow himself up," Thompson said. "He had the real stuff in a nice package stashed in the fish locker at the back of the boat. Good thing we were locked in the cabin and not right on top of the explosives. We saw them leave and we knew their plans, so we got into the life vests and wrapped the v-berth mattress around us. We figured the explosion would blow the door apart and we could get out and swim for it. We weren't counting on Hiroshima."

Mickey was back to eyes closed. He had a nasty gash on his head and his skin was deathly pale.

"How about you?" Gabriela asked Mickey. "Are you doing okay?"

"I might need another stent. I already got seven but I feel like another artery is clogged," Mickey said. "I'm not feeling so good."

"We need to get off this island," Rafer said.

Thompson pulled a device out of his life vest. "Locator beacon. Water activated. The idiots locked us in the cabin with all the gear."

"Nice," Rafer said.

"Even better," Thompson said, "it looks like Mickey's got a boner, but it's a flare stuck in his pants."

Mickey pulled the flare out. "I only got one, so you want to save it for the right time."

"Same as a boner," Thompson said. "You get our age and it's all about your one shot."

"Something to remember," Rafer said.

A boat appeared on the horizon.

"I hope that's not the wizard coming back," Thompson said to Rafer. "He's a real whack job. He put curses on Mickey and me. And then he put a curse on you when you chucked Gabs overboard. That was the best. He was nuts! I have to tell you, I was impressed. That was a good throw. You could have a career in the majors."

"I played ball in high school," Rafer said. "I was pretty good."

"He knocked out his catcher once," Gabriela said. "Cracked his face mask and gave him a concussion."

"I think I got a concussion," Thompson said. "I got a killer headache."

"We should get off the beach in case that's not a friendly boat coming at us," Gabriela said.

"I don't know if I can walk," Mickey said. "I might have a broken leg."

Gabriela and Rafer got Mickey off the beach and into the vegetation. Thompson followed, walking slowly, limping and holding his head.

After fifteen minutes the boat got close enough to be recognized.

"That's an old Hatteras Sport Fisher with full

rigging," Thompson said. "It's Manny Ortega's boat. I can tell by the color. It's a solid boat and he got it on the cheap because nobody wanted a boat with a purple hull. Get the flare out. Go to the beach and flag him down."

Rafer took the flare and ran to the water's edge. He set the flare off and the boat answered with a blast on its horn. Thompson made his way out to Rafer and waved at the Hatteras as it slowly plowed through the debris from the wreck. The boat idled just beyond the breakers and dropped an inflatable into the water. A young man got into the inflatable and headed for shore.

"That's Manny's son, Raymond," Thompson said to Rafer. "He mates for his dad. He's a good kid."

Mickey was lying in the shade with his eyes closed. His breathing was shallow. Gabriela knelt beside him and put her finger to his neck. His pulse was erratic.

Mickey licked his lips. "Did you really find it?" he whispered.

"Yes," Gabriela said. "We found it in a cave halfway up the mountain."

"Is it wonderful? Is there a golden Madonna?"

"Yes," Gabriela said. "She's beautiful. When you're stronger we'll take you to see her."

"I'd like that."

"Hang on," she said to Mickey. "We're going to get you to a hospital." She stood and waved at Rafer. "I need help!" she shouted.

Raymond ferried Mickey and Gabriela out to the boat first. They put Mickey in a berth and Raymond went back for Rafer and Thompson.

"What happened?" Manny asked Gabriela. "I heard the call go out and I was in the area. From the debris it looks like an explosion."

"Mickey and Thompson were on the boat when it happened. Rafer and I were exploring on the island."

Manny shook his head. "Those two spent half their lives digging holes on that island."

"I'm worried about Mickey," Gabriela said. "His color is bad, and his pulse is erratic."

"I'll call ahead and try to get a medevac out of San Jose to meet us in Drake. We're about an hour and a half out."

Thompson came on board and Manny cruised away from the island and went full throttle. "What happened back there?" he asked Thompson.

"Pirates," Thompson said. "A bunch of damn pirates. They were after my treasure and when they didn't get it, they blew up the boat and took off."

"I almost believe you," Manny said.

"It's the God's honest truth," Thompson said.

Rafer and Gabriela exchanged glances. If it wasn't a hundred percent accurate, it was at least seventy percent. And it was a lot better than Thompson telling people he got blown up by a sorcerer.

Gabriela sat with Mickey on the way back, trying to keep him stable when the boat rocked. He asked about the Madonna a couple more times. He winced when he was lifted from the berth and transported to the airstrip.

"I'm going to fly with him," Thompson said. "I'll call and let you know how things are going."

Gabriela gave Thompson a hug. "Take care," she said.

Rafer gave him a hug, clapped him on the back, and stepped away.

Gabriela stared at Rafer. "Is that a tear on your cheek?"

"Sweat," Rafer said. "Stupid tropical jungle."

CHAPTER EIGHTEEN

The sun was just about to dip into the ocean. It was seventy degrees with a gentle breeze. There was a bottle of wine and a plate of fish tacos on the little round table overlooking the Pacific. Gabriela sipped her wine and relaxed back into her chair.

"I could get used to this," she said.

Rafer looked across the table at her. "This is my life every day . . . unless I'm chasing down pirate treasure with you."

"Does it get boring?" she asked.

"Yeah. It's good."

"You like boring?"

"Life at the dive shop isn't boring. When I get home, I want boring."

Gabriela set her wineglass down and took a taco. "Do you think El Dragón will immediately go back to Peru?"

"I think he'll want the ring analyzed, and I doubt he'll go back to New York for that. I'm sure he has antiquities connections in Peru."

"So, your answer is yes, he's probably on a plane to Lima."

"That would be my guess."

"Suppose the ring passes the test but the demon army doesn't materialize when El Dragón calls for them. What then?" Gabriela asked.

"I can only hope he gets a really bad spanking from Supay." Rafer drained his wineglass. "What about you? Are you still intent on getting the ring?"

"I'm intent on taking down El Dragón. Retrieving the ring would be a bonus."

"How are you going to manage this?"

"I'm going to get in touch with Pepe and see if he's interested in helping me. If we succeed, I get the ring and he gets the treasure from the cave in the slot canyon."

"You're counting on him bringing in all those armed guys who were on the drug plantation dock."

"Yes."

"You're gonna die."

Gabriela shrugged.

"It's a dumb idea," Rafer said.

Gabriela shrugged again.

"You're really going through with this?" Rafer asked.

"Yes."

"Okay, then," he said. "I'm in."

· · · ·

One day later, Rafer and Gabriela walked out of Jorge Chávez International Airport immigration and ran into Pepe.

"We were supposed to meet you in Cusco," Gabriela said.

"I thought this would be a better plan," Pepe said. "I have a plane here and it will save us some time. The truth is we were talking about raiding El Dragón's treasure cave when you called. We were hesitating because some of the men were worried about pissing off Supay."

"And now?" Rafer asked.

"Now they are okay with it," Pepe said. "I explained to them that Gabs is a more powerful sorcerer than El Dragón. I might even have told them that she is in service to Supay."

"In service?" Gabriela asked.

"Sexual favors," Pepe said. "It is well known that Supay has an eye for the ladies."

"Omigod," Gabriela said. "Your men think I'm sleeping with Supay?"

"Not necessarily sleeping with Supay. Maybe just an occasional BJ. It is a good thing," Pepe said. "The men will have much respect for your skill."

"As they should," Rafer said.

"Excuse me?" Gabriela said to Rafer. "What is that supposed to mean?"

"I'm being supportive," Rafer said, barely able to stifle the laughter. "And let's face it, Gabs, you do have some excellent skills."

"I suspected such was the case," Pepe said.

"We're done with this conversation," Gabriela said. "It's ended. Forever. Where is the plane?"

"It is a short walk," Pepe said. "This is not such a large airport. Everything is very convenient."

"Is this your uncle's plane?" Gabriela asked, following him to a small blue-and-white turboprop.

"No. It is my cousin's plane," Pepe said. "It is almost always living here in Lima."

Gabriela took her seat, and in an hour the turboprop landed on a private strip of grooved tarmac that could accommodate a large jet. There was jungle on all sides and a single dirt road at the end of the strip. A Jeep and driver waited at the road.

"This is Cocinero," Pepe said to Rafer and

Gabriela. "He's a good driver but he's a better cook."

Cocinero looked Gabriela up and down and smiled wide enough to show a gold tooth. "An honor," he said.

Gabriela acknowledged the honor and cut a death look at Pepe.

"We have very nice housing for you," Pepe said to Rafer and Gabriela. "It is a guest quarters attached to my uncle's house. My uncle is almost never here because it is too remote for his wife. She is a city girl."

It was a three-minute drive from the landing strip to the large adobe house on the edge of the compound. The guest quarters consisted of a two-bedroom bungalow with a small kitchenette.

"We will have dinner at seven o'clock," Pepe said. "Uncle's *teniente primero*, Miguel, will eat with us and we will discuss the raid. Miguel is also my uncle's first son and my cousin. He is very handsome. And a little ruthless."

"Looking forward to it," Rafer said.

Gabriela nodded. "Likewise."

Gabriela and Rafer entered the food line at seven o'clock. Cocinero was serving. He winked and smiled at Gabriela and slipped her a torta de chocolate.

Rafer looked down at Gabriela's tray. "I didn't get chocolate cake," he said.

"That's because you don't give BJs to Supay."

"Fair enough," he said.

A thirtysomething guy was sitting next to Pepe. His eyes were chocolate brown, his mouth was generous and smiling, his skin was tanned. His teeth were white and perfect. His black wavy hair was tucked behind his ears and curling against his neck. His crisp white linen shirt was open enough to display a gold chain with a cross and the beginnings of a tattoo.

"This is Miguel," Pepe said to Gabriela and Rafer. "He is going to tell you about our plan."

Gabriela took a seat across from Miguel. Rafer sat beside Gabriela. There were several bottles of wine on the table. Miguel chose one and poured glasses for everyone.

"What is your plan?" Gabriela asked him.

"It is a simple plan," Miguel said. "We kill everyone and take the treasure."

"I'll drink to that," Rafer said. "Cheers."

"Cheers," everyone said.

Rafer leaned in and whispered in Gabriela's ear. "Seems like a nice guy."

Gabriela grimaced and sipped her wine.

Rafer looked across the table at Miguel. "Is there a Mrs. Miguel?"

"Not at the moment," Miguel said.

"I'm interested in retrieving a ring that El Dragón took from me," Gabriela said to Miguel.

"The Seal of Solomon," Miguel said. "We will make all attempts to obtain this ring for you."

"Do you know if El Dragón is actually in residence?" Gabriela asked. "I understand that he has several houses."

"I have people watching," Miguel said. "El Dragón arrived this afternoon by helicopter. He does not have enough flat land for an airstrip, but he has a helipad at the far end of his compound. I'm told he spent the night in Lima and this morning he visited an antiquities expert."

"You aren't really going to kill everyone, are you?" Gabriela asked Miguel.

"Of course not," Miguel said. "We only kill bad people."

"How do you know if they're bad?" Gabriela asked.

"If they're shooting at us, they're bad. We might also have to kill people with knives and poison dart guns."

Rafer looked at Gabriela's chocolate cake. "Are you going to eat that?" he asked.

Gabriela passed it over to him. "When is this going to take place?" she asked Miguel.

"Tomorrow. Everyone in the compound stops

work at noon and goes to the dining hall to eat their midday meal. The dining hall and armory are close to the river. We will establish a presence at the armory first and then we will take over the dining hall. A special team will be in place well before noon to take down El Dragón when the order is given."

"How will you know El Dragón's location?" Gabriela asked.

"We have drones," Miguel said. "We have been mapping the compound for several days. We are able to follow El Dragón's movements."

"And you're doing this because you want the treasure in the cave," Rafer said.

"That will be a bonus," Miguel said. "We ignored El Dragón's presence when he was nothing more than a cult leader. He was in some ways useful to us, frightening away treasure hunters. He used a crude road through the jungle to access his compound and kept far from our plantation. His human sacrifices were more rumor than reality. Lately he has expanded into agriculture. He's taking over large swaths of the mountain and he's using the river to transport his product. His Supay worshippers are militant fanatics growing in number and his human sacrifices are no longer just rumor. If he continues, federal authorities will be forced to clean out this river valley. And this will impact our business."

"Don't forget Caballo's fingernail," Pepe said.

Miguel smiled. "The nail in the coffin." He pushed back from the table. "I have arrangements to make. Breakfast is at five thirty tomorrow. Pepe will bring you to our armory at six. You can choose your assignment."

"I want to be on the advance team that takes down El Dragón," Gabriela said.

Miguel nodded. "As you wish."

Gabriela and Rafer left the dining hall ten minutes later and followed the stone pathway that led to their guest quarters. Lights were on in the nearby two-story owner's house, and Gabriela assumed Miguel was staying there.

"What do you think?" Gabriela asked Rafer when they approached their bungalow.

"I think we're about to participate in a power struggle between two drug lords."

"Anything else?"

"The chocolate cake was amazing."

"And Miguel?"

"Give him half a chance and he'd eat you for lunch. Probably knows what he's doing when it comes to running a massacre."

"I agree."

"What about the ring?" Rafer asked.

"I think chances are good that El Dragón has the ring. He's not going to let the power of God out of his sight." Gabriela paused several feet from the front door. "Do you think this house is wired?"

"Yep. Sound and video. This is a large drug operation. They aren't going to chance bringing in an outsider with an agenda."

CHAPTER NINETEEN

*G*abriela started her day with a breakfast burrito and coffee.

"The food is good here," she said to Rafer.

"Better than the beds. Mine was two inches too short."

Pepe came to their table. "Are you ready to get outfitted?"

Gabriela and Rafer stood and looked around. Most of the men were still eating.

"Nobody else coming with us?" Rafer asked Pepe.

"They will come later. They have their own lockers and need little instruction."

Gabriela and Rafer took their coffee and walked along with Pepe.

"What team are you on?" Gabriela asked Pepe.

"I'm staying here and helping to coordinate. I will work with the drones and the radio dispatch. I'm not at my best with much shooting. I'm more a behind-the-scenes guy."

"What about Caballo?"

"Caballo came in last night with men from my uncle's other plantation. They have already been put in place upstream. They will secure El Dragón's armory."

Pepe opened the door to a large warehouse-type building made of corrugated metal. He walked Gabriela and Rafer past rows of lockers.

"These lockers are for the men who live and work on this plantation," Pepe said. "We have a storeroom at the far end of the building with a good selection of arms and tactical equipment. You can make your choices there."

Gabriela entered the storeroom and felt like she'd been given the keys to the candy shop. There were racks of automatic and semiautomatic weapons, handheld missile launchers, grenades, and knives. Nothing off-the-chart James Bond fancy. Just quality hardworking munitions.

Pepe opened a cabinet. "We have several types and a variety of sizes for body armor."

Gabriela selected one and put it on over her T-shirt.

"Do you think I need this?" Rafer asked.

"Wouldn't hurt," Pepe said.

Rafer Velcro-taped himself into a vest and moved on to the handguns.

Gabriela attached a knife and a two-pound Maglite to her belt, strapped a sidearm to her leg, shoved extra clips into her cargo pants pockets, and smiled when she hung a Heckler & Koch MP5 submachine gun over her shoulder.

"Are you kidding?" Rafer said, looking at Gabriela. "Who are you, Rambo? The Terminator?"

"I'm making the most of the opportunity," Gabriela said. "It's not every day that a girl gets to carry a Heckler & Koch MP5."

"It's an excellent choice," Pepe said. "And it looks very good on you."

Miguel walked into the storeroom. "Pepe is right," he said to Gabriela. "You've chosen the perfect accessories. I suspect you know how to use them."

"I can manage," Gabriela said.

Miguel was wearing a black ball cap. He took it off and placed it on Gabriela's head. "Now the outfit is complete," he said. "Supay would find this to be very attractive. I've heard rumors about you and the God of Death."

"They're all true," Gabriela said. "Every single rumor."

Miguel smiled. He was close to her. He adjusted the cap slightly and brushed a strand of hair back behind her ear. "You must have extraordinary talents. Is that true as well?" he whispered.

"There are some things a man should find out for himself," Gabriela whispered back.

Miguel's smile widened. "I believe Supay has met his match."

Rafer slipped a clip into his Glock 9 and glanced at Miguel. "When does this show get on the road?" he asked.

"I'm ready when you are," Miguel said. "I'll be leading our team. Pepe will give you an earpiece so we can communicate if we become separated."

The other three members of the team were waiting at the boat dock.

"Luis will take us a short distance up La Vibora," Miguel said. "He will drop us off and we will go the rest of the way on foot, skirting the compound. Once we are on land, we will maintain silence."

After three hours of hiking through the jungle, Gabriela was wishing she'd gone with lighter gear. At least she hadn't been designated to carry the rocket launcher, she thought. She assumed this was brought along in case El Dragón tried to escape in the chopper.

Miguel was on point. There was no trail that

Gabriela could see but Miguel seemed to know where he was going. He stopped and gestured for the team to sit. Gabriela could see light ahead. They were at the edge of the compound. It was almost eleven o'clock.

Miguel's three soldiers stretched out in the shade of the jungle. Rafer, Gabriela, and Miguel stayed alert. No one spoke. Occasionally, muffled voices carried from the compound. Gabriela knew El Dragón's house was set apart from the village. She wouldn't be surprised if he kept a contingent of armed guards patrolling the area around his house.

Gabriela heard the faint, high-pitched whine of a drone. She couldn't see it through the canopy.

Miguel was on his sat phone, speaking softly. He disconnected and brought everyone together.

"The helicopter isn't on the pad," he said. "It's believed that El Dragón is in the house alone. There are four armed soldiers in the area. Philip and Eduardo will take out the soldiers. Leonard will go to the back door. Rafer and Gabriela will go through the front door with me."

Miguel counted down the minutes and at precisely noon he made the motion to attack. Gabriela was running directly behind Miguel. She reached the front door to El Dragón's house and heard gunfire coming from the river area. Miguel rushed into the house and Gabriela followed on his heels. The gunfire was closer. Philip and Eduardo, Gabriela thought. They passed through the dining room. The table was set for one person. A bowl of soup was unattended. An elderly woman stepped out of the kitchen and gasped. She turned and ran back into the kitchen. Miguel's intel wasn't perfect. The drone knew only who came and went. It didn't know who stayed.

Miguel went after the woman. "Where is he?" Miguel asked.

"He left," she said.

Leonard was now in the house. "He didn't leave through the back door," he said.

"How?" Miguel asked the housekeeper.

"He comes and goes," she said. "He makes magic."

"He probably has a tunnel," Gabriela said. "This mountain is riddled with them."

There was an explosion deep in the village. Gabriela looked out a window and saw black smoke billowing skyward. A wave of nausea slid through her stomach. It was one thing to watch this on television. It was entirely different and awful when the destruction and injury were real. She didn't like it, but she was caught up in it and there was no turning back.

Rafer, Miguel, and Leonard were going room by room, opening doors and looking under rugs.

"Here!" Miguel shouted from a first-floor office. "Stairs to a tunnel."

Leonard stayed behind and Miguel, Rafer, and Gabriela went into the tunnel. There were no lights other than their Maglites. After several minutes they came to a fork. Miguel flashed his light into one of the tubes and there was a burst of gunfire from the far end. Miguel took a hit and went down. Gabriela threw herself on top of him and opened fire with the MP5. She stopped shooting and there was silence.

Rafer swept a beam of light down the tunnel and fixed on a body sprawled on the floor. He walked the tunnel with his gun drawn and stared down at the body.

"Not El Dragón," he said. "One of his tattooed henchmen."

"Is he alive?" Gabriela asked.

"Not even a little," Rafer said. "And there's another fork here."

Miguel was bleeding from a wound in his upper arm, and he had a bullet smashed dead center in his Kevlar vest.

"We have a bleeder here," Gabriela shouted to Rafer.

She shucked her body armor and stripped off

her T-shirt, wrapping it around Miguel's arm, twisting it into a makeshift tourniquet to stop the bleeding. Rafer knelt beside them, removed his vest and T-shirt, and gave the T-shirt to Gabriela.

"I'll trade you my shirt for your bra," Rafer said. "It'll make a better tourniquet."

Gabriela handed Rafer her bra and slipped into his shirt. "I hope you know what you're doing," she said. "That's a $465 La Perla Balconette."

"And it's worth every cent. Supay is a lucky guy," Rafer said.

"The Supay thing is getting old," Gabriela said.

Rafer smiled. "Understood."

Gabriela took Miguel's sat phone and called Pepe. "Man down," she said. "We need medical at El Dragón's residence. How's the war going?"

"Doing cleanup," Pepe said. "Do you have El Dragón?"

"Negative," Gabriela said. "He escaped into the tunnel system."

"What kind of medical do you need?"

"Miguel got shot in the arm. We have a tourniquet on it, but he's lost blood and he's probably going to need surgery."

"I'll send the chopper," Pepe said.

"We also need people to go into the tunnels to search for El Dragón."

"I will put Caballo in charge."

Twenty minutes later, Gabriela stood back and watched the plantation chopper lift off and glide over the treetops. Miguel and Rafer were on board with the pilot.

Leonard was next to Gabriela. "It is fortunate that your friend Rafer has some first-aid training," Leonard said. "He seems very competent."

Gabriela nodded. "I'm sure Miguel will be okay. Rafer will monitor the bleeding until they get to the hospital." She turned her attention to the village. "What happens to El Dragón's followers now?"

"The women will be sent away. There are not many of them. And there are no children. The men will stay. Their loyalties will change if El Dragón does not return."

Gabriela wanted to ask about the casualties, but she didn't want to hear the answer. From the amount of gunfire she heard, she knew there had to be injuries and possibly deaths. She returned to the house and stood by the stairs that led to the tunnel entrance. Leonard went with her.

An hour later, Caballo appeared and climbed the stairs.

"No sign of El Dragón," Caballo said. "The men are still searching. The tunnels are complicated. They lead everywhere. We are using fluorescent spray paint to mark our way so we don't get lost."

"My fear is that he'll escape through the canyon system that connects his compound to the ruins where we found the treasure," Gabriela said.

"That is a good fear," Caballo said. "My men would be reluctant to follow El Dragón beyond the slot canyons. They would not want to intrude through the sorcerer's forest and to the mountaintop where the snakes rule."

"You didn't have a problem with the snakes."

"I try not to step on them and make them mad. And I wear boots and canvas hiking britches."

"You're not superstitious."

"I'm Catholic. I have a fear of God, not snakes."

Pepe called Gabriela on the sat phone. "Are you outside?"

"No. I'm in El Dragón's house."

"Go outside and look to the Dragon's Head mountain."

Gabriela and Caballo went outside and looked beyond the compound to the slot canyons and the mountain.

"Do you see the helicopter?" Pepe asked.

"No," Gabriela said. "Wait, yes. I see it now. It's hovering just beyond the slot canyons."

"One of the men on another plantation saw it fly over. Have you found El Dragón?"

"No."

"Is it possible the copter is picking him up?" Pepe asked.

"We've been in that area. There's no place to land. It's either rain forest or rocky slope."

"We didn't explore every inch. He could have cleared an escape pad."

"The copter just dropped below the canopy," Gabriela said.

Gabriela and Caballo watched the sky and minutes later the copter reappeared and flew off.

"The chopper's gone," Gabriela said. "El Dragón must have made it through the tunnels, to the canyons, and up to the top of the mountain. Can you trace the helicopter?"

"We'll try," Pepe said. "And I'll get a drone in the air over the slot canyons to see if we can find a landing pad."

"Tell your men to come back here," Gabriela said to Caballo. "Let's see how far they got and if they found anything."

There were six men plus Caballo, Leonard, and Gabriela at El Dragón's dining room table. Caballo had a crude map of the compound and the mountain, with the slot canyons drawn on a yellow pad. He had another map of the tunnels as his men remembered them.

"No one in our group got to the slot canyons,"

Caballo said. "Marko and Cesare came close, but we called them back. They thought from time to time they saw footprints made by a single man."

"Did any of the other tunnels look like they'd been recently used?" Gabriela asked.

Caballo translated.

The men shook their heads.

"Only the tunnel leading to the slot canyons," Caballo said. "Do you want me to have the men continue to search?"

"No," Gabriela said. "I doubt El Dragón is still in the tunnel system. Thank the men for putting out a good effort. I appreciate it."

Caballo translated and the men smiled and nodded.

"There is still some activity by the armory and the kitchen," Caballo said to Gabriela. "If you are ready to return to the plantation you should avoid those areas. The road to the highway is on the other side of the temple. It is a longer route than using the river but it is necessary. Leonard can drive you. It should be safe but keep your weapon close just in case."

Gabriela left the house and climbed into a modified Jeep Gladiator. She thought the only thing missing was a gun turret. Probably not necessary since one of the two men in the backseat was carrying a rocket launcher.

Leonard drove away from the compound and the road immediately deteriorated into brain-rattling ruts and waist-high overgrowth. A half hour into the trip the Jeep careened down a gully and hit a hundred-and-twenty-pound peccary. The men in the back jumped out, gutted and quartered the pig, and threw it into the back of the truck.

"Dinner," Leonard said to Gabriela. "Very tasty."

After two hours of bone-jarring driving through the jungle on a barely there road, Gabriela was wishing for an ambush. She was starting to think the pig was the lucky one. His innards had been removed. He was feeling no pain.

"How much further?" she asked Leonard.

"Minutes," he said. "We are almost at the high-way. You can see it just ahead."

"How long will we be on the highway?"

"Just a short distance until we reach the plantation road."

"And then?"

"A half hour," Leonard said.

Leonard burst out of the brush onto the paved highway and Gabriela heard the unmistakable *wup, wup, wup, wup* of a helicopter. She leaned forward to search the sky and caught sight of the chopper.

"It's probably bringing Rafer and possibly Miguel back to the plantation," Leonard said.

Gabriela looked down at herself and saw that her hand had gone to her heart. Okay, so Rafer was going to be there when she arrived at the compound. Any civilized human being would be relieved that a colleague was safely returned. No need to read any more into it than that, right? Wrong. There was a lot more to read into it. She was actually liking the guy. She was depending on him. She thought he was hot!

"*Oh God*," she moaned.

Leonard looked at her. "Are you okay?"

"Backache," she said. "Damn rutted road."

Rafer was waiting on the porch of the guest quarters when the Jeep pulled up to the house. He smiled wide when Gabriela swung out.

"Gabs!" he said, grabbing her and hugging her to him. "You're okay! You're not dead or maimed or anything. I was afraid you'd go back into the tunnel with a new team and have to throw yourself on a live grenade. Holy crap, I couldn't believe you pumped all those rounds into that crazy-ass Supay soldier. I looked down at him and he had holes everywhere. You made Swiss cheese out of him."

"I was shooting blind into the dark. It was sheer luck that I took him down."

"It wasn't sheer luck. It was bravery and quick thinking. Thanks. If it wasn't for you, he might have killed all of us."

Rafer released her from the hug but kept an arm around her, moving her into the house. "I heard El Dragón got away," he said.

"I'm pretty sure he was picked up by a helicopter. How's Miguel?"

"He's good. He was a couple pints down when we arrived at the hospital, but he was looking better when I left. They're keeping him overnight."

"I've been in some ugly situations since I went into the recovery business," Gabriela said. "This is right up at the top of the ugly list."

"Yeah, I would have joined the army if I wanted to be in a war." He pulled her bra out of his pocket and dangled it from his finger. "I brought this back. It's been washed, disinfected, and delicately dried. The nurses were all jealous of your lingerie. And Miguel said the sight of you half-naked kept him going when he was in a lot of pain. He sends his thanks."

Gabriela took the bra. "If you don't mind, I'm going to keep your shirt. I see someone gave you a new one, and I'm running low on clothes."

"Wear it in health."

Pepe walked into the open doorway. "Knock, knock," he said. "I have food for you. And wine."

"You're my hero," Gabriela said. "I'm starving."

Pepe set the cardboard box on the table. "Cocinero put this together. I have no idea what he gave you. I suspect it's something of everything."

Gabriela got plates and knives and forks and Rafer set the containers of food on the table.

"Chicken, rice, beans, some kind of fish, tortilla, sautéed vegetables, several kinds of sauces that are unlabeled, mystery meat in very dark gravy, and chocolate cake. Enough cake for everyone," Rafer said.

"Word got back that you saved Miguel's life," Pepe said. "We are all grateful."

"We were ambushed," Gabriela said. "It was pitch-black in the tunnel. We came to a fork and a soldier was covering for El Dragón."

"His soldiers are fanatics, and many are fortified with drugs. We do not allow our workers to use drugs."

"Coca leaves?" Gabriela asked.

"Of course, that is allowed," Pepe said. "It is a major food group."

Rafer poured wine for everyone.

Gabriela filled her plate. "I'm not sure where to go from here. El Dragón has a city house in Lima. He might also have one in Cusco."

"The helicopter took him to Lima," Pepe said. "We were able to learn that much. It is thought he might leave the country. My uncle is very power-ful, and he could make things difficult for El Dragón if he stayed here. Actually, he could make it fatal. Are you still determined to have the Seal of Solomon?"

"More than ever," Gabriela said.

CHAPTER TWENTY

*G*abriela ran into Pepe at the breakfast line. "Any word on El Dragón?" she asked.

"Yes," Pepe said. "We believe he is going to his estate in California. He left late last night. Uncle has offered the use of his plane if you wish to follow El Dragón. Uncle is grateful that you and Rafer saved his son's life. And he would like to see El Dragón brought to some kind of justice."

"That's very generous of him," Gabriela said.

"Uncle's plane will be flying in shortly and can be ready to take off at nine o'clock. Will that work for you?" Pepe asked.

"Absolutely," Gabriela said.

Pepe left and Rafer sauntered over to Gabriela. "Mind if I cut the line?" he asked.

"I thought you were sleeping in."

"I got hungry."

"You look like you just rolled out of bed. Did you comb your hair?"

"No. I'm going for the sexy tousled look."

Well, you've achieved it, Gabriela thought. "Pepe just told me that El Dragón flew out of Lima last night. They think he's headed for his estate in California."

"That makes sense," Rafer said. "Get out of Dodge."

"Pepe's uncle is making his plane available to us. He's grateful that we saved his son's life."

Rafer added two coffees to their tray. "He's giving us his plane so we can hunt down El Dragón for him."

"I'm surprised you could figure that out before coffee," Gabriela said.

"It wasn't hard."

"The plane will be ready to leave at nine o'clock."

"Are we going?"

"Yes, we're going, but I'm not sure if we're going on Uncle's private plane."

"You would rather fly cattle car?"

"I don't want to be tied to a drug lord."

"Okay with me," Rafer said. "You can fly commercial, and I'll go on the drug lord's plane. I bet he'll have churros and hot chocolate on board.

And might I remind you that you flew *here* on his private plane."

"I hate when you're right," Gabriela said.

Pepe and Caballo picked Rafer and Gabriela up at nine o'clock and drove the short distance to the airstrip. Two uniformed pilots were waiting beside a midsize business jet.

"Nice plane," Rafer said to Pepe.

"It is a Challenger 350," Pepe said. "It seats eight passengers and two pilots, and it has a nice cargo area. We will make a very short fuel stop in Mexico, but we will not have to deplane. Caballo and I will be traveling with you. My uncle thought you might need help with El Dragón."

"Have you heard any more about him?" Gabriela asked. "Has he been seen at his California residence?"

"His plane landed at LAX. We do not know beyond that."

Gabriela climbed the stairs and paused at the small refreshment area.

"Help yourself," the pilot said to Gabriela. "We have a coffeemaker and a microwave. There are churros and chocolate for a late breakfast. Also, fruit and cheese plates and boxed lunches in the undercounter refrigerator. Feel free to explore."

Rafer was standing behind Gabriela. "Churros and chocolate," he said. "You gotta love the uncle."

Gabriela took a forward seat and Rafer sat across the aisle. Pepe and Caballo took seats at the back of the plane.

Gabriela buckled in and looked out the window as the plane raced down the runway and did a steep vertical climb. She was having doubts about her quest, doubts about her own abilities. She worried that it was arrogant of her to assume she could take down El Dragón without Uncle's army backing her up. Even with Uncle's army she hadn't been able to capture El Dragón, and she'd almost been killed in her attempt. And for what? To save a town. Really? There was no guarantee that the Seal of Solomon was authentic. And there was no guarantee that anyone would pay millions of dollars to have it. El Dragón wanted it, but he was insane. And even if she did get millions of dollars for the Seal, would that actually save the town? Who would want to stay under the threat of another hurricane? She let out a sigh. She knew the answer to the last question. Her grandmother would want to stay. Her mother and father would want to stay. Rafer's family would want to stay. So, capturing the ring was still important and hopefully it was worth some money. Making sure that El Dragón was locked away for the rest of his life was even *more* important. And that was the dilemma. There were people who were better equipped to take down El Dragón. The police, the FBI, DEA. Should she bring them in?

The plane leveled off and Rafer unbuckled, went to the refreshment station, and returned with churros and chocolate. Gabriela pulled her table out. Rafer set everything on the table and took the seat opposite her.

"This is so civilized," Rafer said. "These drug lords know how to live. Too bad they produce stuff that kills people. It makes it difficult to like them."

"Do you think we're on a suicide mission?" Gabriela asked. "I mean, is there any chance in hell we'll be able to capture El Dragón?"

Rafer dipped his churro into the chocolate sauce. "There's always a chance. Probably not a good one."

"Do you think we should give up and go home?"

"Is that what you want?"

"No," Gabriela said, "but I don't want anyone else to get shot, either."

"I got a text from Thompson this morning. Mickey is getting released from the hospital today. Thompson said Mickey is just as good as ever. I don't know what that means. Mickey *never* looked all that good to me."

"What about Thompson? Is he okay?"

"He said half his little toe got shot off, but they bandaged it up and gave him special sandals at the hospital and he's getting around."

"I'd like to turn this over to the police, DEA, FBI, whatever," Gabriela said. "They're better equipped to bring El Dragón to justice. Problem is, I might lose the ring. At the very least it would get bogged down in bureaucratic red tape."

"So, you aren't going to any of those guys for help."

"No."

"Do you have an idea about how you're going to pull this off?"

"No."

"Do you want to make out in the restroom?"

"No." She locked eyes with him. "Do you?"

"Maybe."

"Only maybe?"

"It's a toss-up between that or getting another churro."

"I need more coffee," Gabriela said, sliding out of her seat. "I'll get you another churro while I'm at it."

• • • •

The plane began to descend and the *cinturón de seguridad* light came on. Gabriela turned in her seat and looked back at Pepe.

"We are stopping in Mexico to refuel," he said. "It will only take some minutes, and we will stay on the plane."

They were flying over an area of dense vegetation and terrain that was ribboned with valleys. There was an occasional small village with the hint of a road that seemed to lead nowhere. The plane banked and turned, and Gabriela was able to see a wide, flat area between two mountains. A long landing strip stretched in front of the plane and a plantation very similar to Uncle's at La Vibora sprawled alongside the landing strip. Fields dotted with short green trees clung to the side of the mountain.

Gabriela looked back at Pepe again.

"Coffee," Pepe said.

The plane rolled to a stop and a tanker truck approached. A white van followed the tanker truck. The van went to the cargo door and parked. Two armed men got out of the van and loaded a dozen jute bags onto the plane.

Gabriela shot a look at Rafer.

"Don't ask," Rafer said.

Gabriela relaxed into her seat, closed her eyes, and told herself it was coffee. And it was probably normal to carry automatic weapons when you worked on a coffee plantation. True, it was a well-known fact that drugs were often hidden inside bags of coffee because the coffee scent threw off the sniffer dogs, but this was of no concern to her, Gabriela thought. She had her eyes closed, and she knew nothing. If she was arrested in California, she would tell them she was just on board for the churros. And when she was eventually released from prison, she would find Rafer and surgically remove his penis.

A half hour later they were in the air. Gabriela went to the back of the plane to talk to Pepe.

"What happens when we land?" she asked. "Are we flying into LAX?"

"Not LAX," Pepe said. "It is always very crowded, and immigration is annoying. Uncle finds it is better to use smaller airports. I believe we are scheduled to use a nice quiet airstrip near Bakersfield."

"Oh boy."

"No, really," Pepe said. "It is perfectly okay. There is a pleasant man who comes to the plane and performs all the necessary duties. There will be a car waiting for us and we can drive to our hotel."

"Where is our hotel?"

"I don't know exactly. There will be information with the car. The arrangements were made very quickly. I imagine our hotel will be near El Dragón's fortress."

"Do you know anything about his fortress?"

"Only what I have seen on real estate sites. I googled it last night. The photographs were ten years old but it looked very nice."

"You don't have any operatives in California?" Gabriela asked.

"My uncle has California business associates who might not be entirely trustworthy."

Gabriela returned to her seat and found that Rafer had set out their box lunches.

"How did that go?" he asked. "Do you have everything planned out?"

"Yep," Gabriela said. "No problem. This is going to be easy peasy."

· · · ·

The California airstrip was in the middle of nothing. The runway was paved but everything else was hardscrabble dirt. Some rocks and some bare sticks that used to be plants cluttered the landscape. A couple of corrugated-metal buildings were hunkered down at one end of the strip. A gray Camry, a tan panel van, and a black Escalade with tinted windows were parked by the buildings.

"It will be best to unload the coffee first," Pepe said. "I will send Caballo out to make sure it all goes smoothly."

Gabriela pulled the shade down on her window and turned to Rafer. "You had to have churros."

"With chocolate," Rafer said. "Don't forget the chocolate."

Ten minutes later Caballo came back with a short, stocky man dressed in a suit that was a size too big.

"This is Bucky," Caballo said. "He will stamp your passports if you wish."

Bucky carefully stamped each passport and, without saying a word, left in the gray Camry.

"I like the service here," Rafer said. "I'll have to remember this airport. Does it have a name?" he asked Pepe.

"It does not have a name and you do not want to remember it," Pepe said.

Rafer grinned. "Okeydokey."

Caballo drove the Escalade up to the plane and began unloading luggage into the SUV.

"More churros?" Rafer asked Pepe, looking at the stack of soft-side rifle bags and tactical pistol cases.

"Exactly," Pepe said. "You can never have too many churros. Uncle did not want us to be left without quality churros."

"What's in the crates?"

"*Boom!*" Pepe said.

Rafer leaned close to Gabriela and whispered

in her ear. "You were concerned for no reason. Uncle thought of everything. He flew us into a nonexistent airport so there wasn't a problem off-loading his drugs and illegal weapons. Nothing to worry about."

"Clever," Gabriela said. "I'm sitting in the backseat of the Escalade so I can say I've been kidnapped when the police stop us."

"It is unlikely they will stop us," Pepe said. "Bucky is the mayor, and his brother is the chief of police. I will do the driving since I am very good at it. This is not my sweet Angelina, but it will be satisfactory for our purposes."

The road out was single-lane dirt for several miles before joining up to a paved highway. Gabriela was scanning the area on her iPad. They were in the Santa Ynez Mountains, northeast of Los Olivos. There were sporadic signs to wineries and horse farms but none of these were visible from the road they were traveling.

"I'd like to see El Dragón's estate before going to the hotel," Gabriela said.

"Excellent plan," Pepe said. "I have the address programmed into my GPS. It is not far ahead of us."

After forty minutes Pepe pulled to the side of the highway. "I'm told the address is down this dirt road and that it is private and not accessible."

"This is far enough," Gabriela said. "Most likely there are security cameras at some point. I have a satellite view pulled up on my iPad. It looks like the dirt road ends at a manned gate. The property is fenced, and a dirt road runs along the inside of the fence.

"I'm guessing the fenced area might be around fifty acres. A lot of it is barren scrub that would make it difficult to reach the house without being seen."

"Only if someone is watching," Rafer said.

Gabriela nodded. "True. There are several buildings in the middle of the property. A fairly large house with a swimming pool, what appears to be a detached garage for multiple vehicles, and a smaller house that might be a guesthouse."

"What is next?" Pepe asked.

"We go to the hotel," Gabriela said. "I need to think about this."

The hotel was a budget-priced chain. It wasn't luxurious but it was clean, and it was close to El Dragón's lair. It was also close to a strip mall with a Target. Gabriela checked into her room, dropped her pack on the bed, and went in search of Pepe.

"I need the car keys," she told him. "I want to go shopping."

"Be careful driving," Pepe said. "You would not

want to explain the many things in the back of the SUV to Mr. Picky Policeman."

Gabriela hit the women's clothes section of Target first, moved on to men's, picked up some essentials in toiletries, and ended in produce. She rolled into checkout with a full basket. She was behind a man dressed in black fatigues. He was rail thin, his long black hair was braided, and he had Supay symbols tattooed on his face.

The man paid with a credit card and left. Gabriela stepped up to the checker.

"That man had such unusual tattoos on his face," Gabriela said.

The checker nodded. "There's some kind of religious cult stuck away in the hills. They shop here all the time, and they all have the same tattoos."

Gabriela checked out and loaded her packages into the SUV. She slid behind the wheel just as the tattooed man drove by in a black crew cab pickup.

It's almost always better to be lucky than to be good, Gabriela thought, pulling out of her parking place, keeping the pickup in sight.

The tattooed man stopped at a supermarket and twenty minutes later came out with bags of groceries. He left the strip mall, got onto the highway, and drove toward El Dragón's compound. Gabriela followed him at a distance until he turned onto the private dirt road.

End of the line, she told herself. Time to go back to the hotel.

Rafer was in Gabriela's room when she returned.

"How did you get in here?" she asked.

"I told them we were married."

"And they believed that?"

Rafer shrugged. "I'm cute. Women believe me."

"I don't believe you."

"That's because you know me. I'm superficially believable." He looked at the bags she dumped on the bed. "Looks like you went shopping."

"I didn't pack for a globe-trotting adventure. I expected to be back in New York by now."

"Does Target sell La Perla undies?"

"No. Target sells Jockey undies and Jockey happens to be another of my favorites." She grabbed a couple of bags and handed them to Rafer. "I got some clothes for you, too."

He looked in the bags. "This is great. Everything is the right size. One of the advantages of traveling with an ex-wife."

"I also got our never-fail emergency staples—bread and peanut butter and a bag of cookies."

"If you got a six-pack we'd be all set for dinner."

"I got a six-pack."

Rafer grinned. "I'm falling in love all over again."

Gabriela found the box of plastic utensils,

opened the jar of peanut butter, and made herself a sandwich.

"You were gone a long time," Rafer said, opening the beer and passing one to Gabriela. "I was starting to worry."

"There was a Supay guy in front of me in the checkout line at Target. Dressed in black, long braided hair, full-on tattoos. The woman at the register said the tattoo guys shop there all the time. She said they come from a religious cult stuck back in the hills."

"So, El Dragón isn't just living the good life in his expensive house. He's got his militia with him."

"Looks that way," Gabriela said. "I followed the tattooed guy to a supermarket and waited for him to come out. Then I followed him to the private road. He was driving a black crew cab pickup. It looked new."

"And you were driving a tank that was loaded with enough firepower to take down a small country."

"It was oddly exhilarating," Gabriela said.

Rafer gave a snort of laughter. "You said the same thing after you were rushed to the hospital with a burst appendix."

"Scoots Bartlet was driving. He had the siren going and I could see the lights flashing through the back window of the ambulance."

"Scoots had the siren and the lights going when he went home for lunch," Rafer said. "He loved the siren and the lights."

"He had the siren and the lights going when he drove Mr. Ratkowski to the cemetery after the Scoon Mortuary hearse broke down and they had to transfer the casket to the EMT."

Rafer made a peanut butter sandwich and opened another beer. "I went online while you were gone, and I found something interesting. It's difficult to see on the satellite photo but it looks like there's a connecting road between El Dragón's property and the neighboring vineyard. The neighboring vineyard is also entirely fenced, with an inner road running along the fence line."

Gabriela opened her iPad and pulled up the satellite photo of the two properties. "I see the connecting road. It's toward the back. Were you able to get a name for the vineyard?"

"No. It's an LLC. No owner name available."

"I can get it," Gabriela said. "You have to know where to look." She searched around the internet and sat back. "It's owned by our good friend Leon Nadali. It's a hundred and fifty acres and the wine it produces appears to be for private consumption. From the photo I'd say about half of the property is devoted to grape production. The rest of the property reminds me of El Dragón's La Vibora compound. Two large warehouse-type buildings, a collection of small huts, and a smaller warehouse. There's another structure that I'm guessing is a garage for farm vehicles and equipment."

She phoned Pepe. "Do you have an equipment inventory?"

"I do not."

"After it's dark and there's not a lot of people wandering around, I want you to bring everything to your room. I need to see what we've got."

"Some of the crates are very heavy. We could use Rafer's help."

"You got it," Gabriela said. "Call him when you're ready."

Gabriela disconnected and smiled at Rafer. "Pepe needs muscle."

"That would be me," Rafer said.

CHAPTER TWENTY-ONE

*G*abriela looked at the weapons lined up on Pepe's bed.

"A nice variety," she said. "Everyone, pick out a handgun and a razzle-dazzle. I have dibs on an MP5." She moved on to the open crates. Flash grenades, smoke bombs, hand grenades, pepper spray that could take down a grizzly, various explosive devices, climbing gear, flashlights, walkie-talkies, body armor, a selection of knives. All good stuff, she thought, but not what she was looking for. She moved to the crate marked SURVEILLANCE.

"Jackpot," Gabriela said, pulling out a padded case that contained a drone. "Is anyone here proficient at flying a drone?"

Crickets.

"I've seen them used but I've never flown one," Rafer said. "It looked like it required some skill."

"I've flown a couple with mixed results," Gabriela said. "Some require more skill than others. I'll take this with me and try to figure it out. I want to get it in the air tomorrow at eight o'clock."

Rafer walked Gabriela back to her room. He paused at her door while she opened it, and he instinctively leaned in for a kiss. He caught himself midway, redirected his angle, kissed her on the forehead, and tugged her ponytail.

"Good luck with the drone," he said. "See you in the morning."

What the heck was that? Gabriela thought, closing and locking her door. He kissed me on the forehead. What does that mean? You kiss kids and dogs like that.

She set the drone case on the small desk, opened the lid, and gave a low whistle. "Nice," she said.

It was a DJI Mavic 2 Pro-Drone Quadcopter UAV with Hasselblad Camera 3-Axis Gimbal HDR 4K video and more. It was packed with a smart controller with a screen. She was familiar with this particular drone and it was perfect for her purposes. She put the drone together and did a short test run in her room. "All in working order," she said to herself. She packed it up and called her mom.

"Just checking in," she said to her mother. "Is everything okay?"

"The gray cat had kittens," her mother said. "They're adorable."

"I thought the gray cat was a boy."

"Apparently not."

"Anything else new?"

"Your father has been working at painting the house. Your grandmother wanted her bedroom to be peach and once your father got started, he just kept going room by room. Where are you? Are you in New York?"

"I'm in California. Is Grandma with you? Can I talk to her?"

Gabriela's grandmother came on the line. "How's the treasure hunt going?" she asked. "Are you getting any closer to the Seal of Solomon?"

"I'm working on it," Gabriela said.

"Annie stopped in last night to see the new kittens, and we had a nice chat. She said that you clearly had the grit of your ancestors, and that you were on the right road."

"Anything else?"

"We mostly talked about kittens. Annie is a cat person."

"If you see her again, tell her I could use some help."

"Of course. And when you get back to Scoon you can have your pick of the kittens. Annie said she thinks you should take the tiger-striped with the white bib."

Gabriela hung up and slouched back in her chair. Annie thought she had the grit of her ancestors. Gabriela hoped that was a good thing. Her intentions were righteous but lately she found herself operating too far left of the law. She was okay with an occasional breaking and entering for a legitimate cause. She was okay with retrieving a stolen bauble and sneaking it back to its owner. She was okay with fibbing. She was uncomfortable with her current level of vigilantism.

Gabriela dialed Rafer. "Are we doing the right thing?" she asked him.

"Can you be more specific?"

"Is the ring worth risking lives?"

"It seems to me this isn't about the ring anymore. This is about stopping a madman. The ring is a bonus."

"What about the uncle? Is he a madman?"

"He's a businessman. We don't agree with his business. His business is bad, but as far as we know he doesn't sacrifice humans on the altar of Supay."

"No, but his business kills people all the same."

"True," Rafer said, "but right now we need to focus on taking out the killer in front of us."

"You're right," Gabriela said. "I just needed a reminder."

. . . .

It was 9:00 a.m. and sixty degrees when Gabriela and Rafer left Pepe in the Escalade and set out walking under a cloudless sky. Gabriela had a Glock 9 discreetly tucked under her waistband. She had the drone and the MP5 in her backpack. Rafer was also carrying concealed. Pepe was parked on the side of a secondary road that ran through a sloped forested area behind the vineyard. He almost immediately lost sight of Gabriela and Rafer as they pushed into a stand of oak trees and tall scrub.

"The satellite photo shows a small clearing about a quarter mile off the road," Gabriela said. "It looks like a good place to launch the drone. We'll be hidden but we'll be close to the vineyard."

"I'd just gotten used to trekking through jungle," Rafer said. "This requires an adjustment. The ground cover is woodier. I'm not sure a machete would cut through it. This stuff needs a chain saw."

"Easier going than dense chaparral," Gabriela said. "Watch for rattlers."

"Remember last night when you asked if this was worth risking lives?"

"Yes."

"Can I revise my response?"

"No."

"It might have been the beer talking," Rafer said.

"Too late."

Gabriela was following the GPS route mapped out on her watch. She was walking carefully and as quietly as possible, but the undergrowth was making it difficult. She periodically stopped and listened. The sounds of men talking carried uphill to her. They were speaking in Spanish. She could only make out an occasional word. Their conversation sounded casual. Field-hand banter.

She reached the clearing and paused. The open space felt safe. She didn't hear anyone walking in the woods. A couple of mature oak trees grew on the border of the area.

"Do you think you can climb one of the oaks?" Gabriela asked Rafer. "Maybe you can get a visual on the vineyard."

"I can't reach the lowest limb on the larger tree, but I should be able to get up the smaller one," Rafer said. He hung his binoculars cross-body style, ran at the tree, and grabbed a limb. He did a pull-up, swung a leg over, and went up the tree.

He settled himself in a crook and looked down at Gabriela. "Limited view," he said, "but I'll be able to see the drone and help direct it."

Gabriela opened the drone case and put the drone together. She set it on a cleared spot of level ground and took the smart controller in hand. She powered on and raised the drone high enough to get a broad panorama. The controller screen showed six men repairing vine supports on the north end of the vineyard. Gabriela moved the drone away from them and flew it toward the buildings. She decreased the drone's altitude to get a closer look at the village of huts, moving the drone over the huts and toward the large warehouse. A pickup truck drove onto the property and parked in front of the warehouse. Two men got out and ran into the building. Gabriela hovered the drone in place. Seconds later the door to the warehouse burst open and a dozen armed men ran out. She heard three gunshots and the screen went blank.

Rafer instantly scrambled down from the tree. "Pack it up," he said. "They took the drone out and I think they spotted me."

Gabriela shoved everything into her backpack and ran through the woods with Rafer.

"I hear dogs," Gabriela said.

"No shit," Rafer said. "Run faster."

They reached the road and jumped into the Escalade.

"Drive!" Gabriela yelled at Pepe. "Get us out of here."

They were a half mile from the highway when Gabriela saw a black Range Rover speeding toward them.

"That Range Rover is riding the white line," she said to Pepe.

"I can see it," Pepe said. "It is filled with the crazy tattoo people."

At the last moment Pepe jerked the Escalade to the right and the Range Rover took off Pepe's side mirror.

"What assholes," Pepe said. "This is a new Escalade. They have no respect."

The Range Rover spun around and raced after the Escalade. Two men leaned out the side windows and opened fire. A barrage of bullets shattered the rear window on the Escalade and pinged off the back quarter panel.

"Sunroof," Rafer shouted to Pepe.

Pepe opened the sunroof. Rafer popped up, pulled the pins on two grenades, and tossed them into the road. Seconds later the Range Rover exploded, sending car parts in all directions.

Gabriela looked wide-eyed at Rafer. "Holy crap. You blew up the Range Rover!"

A tire fell out of the sky and bounced on the road behind them. A beat later a chunk of something bloody smashed against the Escalade windshield.

Pepe flipped the windshield wipers on, and they flicked the bloody chunk away. "We are a very good team with my excellent driving and your use of explosives," Pepe said to Rafer. "Would you like to return to the hotel now?"

"Good idea," Rafer said. "Maybe you could stop at a drive-thru on the way. I didn't have time for breakfast this morning."

"I know just the one," Pepe said. "It is a coffee-and-donuts drive-thru with greasy sausage-and-cheese breakfast sandwiches. One-stop shopping. And after we get our food, Caballo and I will drop you off and then we will park this very recognizable car in the parking lot of a hotel down the road."

• • • •

Gabriela and Rafer carried bags of food and containers of coffee back to Gabriela's hotel room.

"Blowing cars up gives me an appetite," Rafer said.

"I was wondering what you had in your daypack. I guess it was filled with explosives."

Rafer opened his coffee and took a sip. "It was

a last-minute decision. I figured you never know when you might need a grenade."

Gabriela gave Rafer a breakfast sandwich and took one for herself. "I got some decent information before the drone died. The building we thought might be a temple has Supay markings on it, so temple is probably correct. There are eleven small huts that look like basic housing. They all show signs of being occupied. The one large building is definitely a garage. The doors were open, and I could see trucks and a baby backhoe. There are large storage tanks by the garage. I'm guessing gasoline or propane. The two big warehouse buildings remain a mystery. One might be a communal mess hall. There were exhaust fans on one side that could suggest a kitchen. The properties are connected by two gates. One at the rear and one at the front. Both properties have their own driveways in from the highway. Both are gated and both have a small guardhouse inside the gate."

"Do you have any idea how you're going to get to El Dragón?"

"No, but it's going to be something sneaky. There are only four of us," Gabriela said. "If we go in like gangbusters, we'll get mowed down. If we bring in the police, we stand a chance of losing the ring. We need to slip in somehow. Pull a con. Impersonate Pacific Gas and Electric."

"They shot down our drone and sent the dogs out after us," Rafer said. "We've lost the element of surprise. I think the ship sailed on a con."

"Then we'll go in at night and do the ninja thing."

Gabriela called Marcella. "I need a digital copy of the floor plans for Leon Nadali's Santa Ynez house."

"No problem," Marcella said. "Over and out."

"Did Uncle supply us with nunchucks? What about the black clothes?" Rafer asked.

"You're being a wiseass," Gabriela said. "Anything dark will be okay."

"You're serious," Rafer said.

"Hell yes, I'm serious." She opened another bag, took a donut out, and handed the bag over to Rafer. "Have a donut. Enjoy yourself. When you're done with the donuts tell Pepe and Caballo that we're meeting here at six o'clock. I should have the floor plan by then and we can work out the raid details. I don't want to waste time. I want to go in tonight."

"How is Marcella going to get the floor plans?"

"From the architect or a realtor or the county review board. Blueprints pass through many hands before a house is completed. You can obtain those plans by hacking into a system, paying someone off, or by following legitimate protocol. Marcella is excellent at pursuing all those channels."

"You've done this before," Rafer said.

"I'm a recovery agent. If the object was easy to find and recover, it wouldn't be necessary to hire me. I've obtained floor plans of palaces, museums, hospitals, office buildings, and factories. Frequently they aren't completely accurate, but they at least provide a basic traffic map. And they show exit points. It's important to be able to find an exit if things don't go down as planned."

The reality is that things almost never go as planned, Gabriela thought, but they aren't usually as horrifically complicated as recovering the Seal of Solomon.

"Anything else?" Rafer asked.

"I need some art supplies. I need a couple markers and a big drawing pad."

CHAPTER TWENTY-TWO

*E*l Dragón was alone in his vineyard temple. The ceiling and walls were decorated with prayers to Supay. Pictographs of human sacrifice and fanged snakes were intermingled with the prayers. Gaslight torches lit the room, casting eerie flickering shadows. El Dragón was kneeling at an altar that was embossed with gold leaf and dotted with precious stones. He was staring up at a six-foot-tall, solid gold statue of Supay.

"She's here," he said to Supay. "She arrived yesterday, and she was on vineyard property earlier today. She can't resist the allure of the ring. She desires it, my lord."

El Dragón paused, listening for the voice of Supay, but Supay was silent. Lately Supay had been angry. El Dragón understood Supay's displeasure. He was enraged because the Seal of Solomon was authentic, but it had no power. It had been damaged by the woman's touch. El Dragón's faith and sorcery weren't enough to repair the ring and amass the demon army. Supay understood all this and had decreed that the woman must die. Only her intense suffering and death would erase her touch from the ring.

"She will soon be yours," El Dragón said to Supay. "And once she's sacrificed on your altar, the full power of the ring will be restored." El Dragón took the knife that was lying on the altar and cut a small cross into the flesh of his arm, just above the wrist. He let the blood drip onto the altar. "Soon her blood will mingle with mine on this altar," he said to Supay. "You will be pleased."

El Dragón bowed as a sign of respect for his lord and left the altar. He was at peace for now. The angry voice of Supay wasn't in his ear. He gave a small, rare smile to his personal guards who were standing at the door.

"Take me home," he said, getting into the shiny black Mercedes that was idling in front of the temple.

He thought he might swim in his heated pool. It was a California luxury. Later he might call for a woman. Perhaps two or three. And he would prepare his house for Gabriela Rose. He was certain she would come for the ring tonight when it was dark. She would cross his yard like a shadow and slip into his house. And then she would be his to give to Supay.

· · · ·

At six o'clock Gabriela held up a diagram of El Dragón's two properties. "I want to go in at one a.m. Most of the men should be asleep then. I want this raid to be quiet and with as few casualties as possible. Rafer and I will go into the estate house and capture El Dragón," Gabriela said to Pepe and Caballo. "You will be responsible for securing our exit."

Pepe raised his hand. "How are we getting past the fence and the guards?"

"I've been reviewing the drone video and the blueprints," Gabriela said. "The weak link is the fence system on the estate property. It's six feet high but it's not topped with razor wire, and I see nothing to indicate that it's electric. Security seems to be counting on the surveillance road running inside the fence line and the expanse of barren scrub surrounding the house. The vineyard is better protected. There are electric fence warnings at intervals and the entrance gate is serious. The entrance gate to the estate is more for show than for security."

"So, we will go over the fence?" Pepe asked.

"Yes," Gabriela said. "There's an ATV that constantly drives the perimeter road of the two properties. I saw it on the drone video. I don't know its schedule, so we'll just have to listen for it. There's a clump of shrubbery about an eighth of a mile from the gate." Gabriela drew an X with the red marker. "This is where we'll go over the fence. We're helped by the fact that there's only a sliver of moon tonight. Hopefully we'll be the only ones wearing infrared goggles. Once we're over the fence we'll run to the house. We'll be coming at it from the side where the garages are located. Rafer and I will enter through the side door. Caballo and Pepe, you'll stay outside and do whatever you have to as a diversion. I'm assuming I'll set off an alarm when I pick the lock and open the door. Nothing I can do about that. Rafer and I will go directly to the second-floor master. When we secure El Dragón and the ring, we'll go out the same way we came in."

"Do you think this will work?" Pepe asked Gabriela.

"Maybe," Gabriela said.

"Dios mio," Caballo said.

Rafer was grinning. "This is going to be a complete cluster—"

"If anyone wants to drop out, I'll understand," Gabriela said.

"Hell, not me," Rafer said. "I love a good screwup. I'm in."

"Me, too," Pepe said. "I can screw up good."

"I'm in," Caballo said. "I will divert the crap out of everything."

· · · ·

A little after midnight Gabriela picked through the weapons spread around Pepe's room. She didn't want to be encumbered with heavy artillery. She chose lightweight body armor, a Glock 9 that she strapped to her leg, a two-pound Maglite, and an MP5. She had some extra ammo and a couple of flash grenades in her daypack. Rafer carried a heavier pack and Caballo took a submachine gun, the rocket launcher, rockets, and a bunch of grenades. Caballo was ready for Armageddon. Pepe chose another of the MP5s. Everyone had infrared goggles hung around their neck.

"Showtime," Rafer said.

They all trooped out to the parking lot and stopped when they got to the Escalade.

"I thought you might have swapped this in," Gabriela said to Pepe.

"I didn't think to do that," Pepe said. "It is a quality vehicle. It seemed sufficient to hide it until this appropriate time."

"It's full of bullet holes and it doesn't have a side mirror or a back window," Gabriela said.

"Does this bother you?" Pepe asked.

"Nope," Gabriela said. "Everybody, get in the car."

It was almost 1:00 a.m. when Pepe slowly drove down El Dragón's driveway. He had his lights off and his goggles on.

"This is far enough," Gabriela said. "We'll walk from here. Pull off the road and park."

"It will be difficult to hide this big Escalade," Pepe said.

"I doubt anyone is going to be on the driveway at this hour," Gabriela said. "Pull it into one of the clumps of stunted trees and it will fade into the darkness."

Gabriela led the way through the softer sand and scrub brush. No one spoke. She was following a route on her watch. She reached the fence at a place where they would go over the fence into the taller shrubbery. Rafer tapped her on the shoulder and pointed left. The ATV was approaching, making its rounds. Everyone backed up and went flat to the ground. The ATV passed and everyone stood.

One less thing to worry about, Gabriela thought. The ATV wouldn't be back for an hour. She went over the fence first, easily climbing it and dropping to the ground on the other side. Rafer and Pepe followed. Caballo got up and couldn't get over.

"I am stuck," he whispered. "I'm built like a donkey, not a monkey. My legs don't do these things."

Rafer climbed up to meet him. He took the rocket launcher and passed it to Gabriela. He grabbed Caballo by his backpack straps, pulled him over, and they both crashed to the ground and lay there stunned for a moment.

"I landed on my rocket," Caballo said. "Ow!"

Rafer pulled Caballo to his feet. "It's all good. The rocket looks okay."

"Moving on," Gabriela said, keeping her voice soft. "We're going straight to the house. Side door."

"It is far away," Pepe said. "There will be tarantulas. They are more active at night. They are as big as dinner plates here. And they can jump into your face!"

"I'm going to pretend I didn't hear that," Gabriela said. "We are going to quietly and carefully cross this field without stepping on tarantulas."

They silently jogged across several acres of

dark yard and paused at the side door. No tarantulas, no guards, no vicious dogs, Gabriela thought. This was all good. She removed the set of picks from her pocket and in seconds she had the door open. No alarm sounded but she could see the light blinking on the alarm pad on the wall. An alarm was sounding *somewhere*. She closed the door and left Caballo and Pepe standing watch outside.

With Rafer following close behind, she moved through the kitchen to the butler's pantry and the back staircase, taking the stairs two at a time. She was working from memory, recalling the digital floor plan Marcella sent her. She turned left into the hallway that led to the master.

Something's wrong, she thought, moving down the hallway. The house is too quiet. An alarm went off somewhere. People were alerted, but no one is up and about in the house. There are no lights on anywhere. The lights should have gone on by now.

Rafer was behind her. She glanced back at him and saw that he had his sidearm in hand. She drew her gun and put her hand on the doorknob to the master. She opened the door, stepped inside, and looked around the room. It appeared to be empty. The bed hadn't been slept in.

Her first reaction was disappointment. El Dragón wasn't in residence. She approached the bed and saw that there was a note on the quilt.

I've been waiting for you. I knew you would come. It is your destiny.

Gabriela felt her skin crawl at the nape of her neck. She'd underestimated El Dragón and walked into a trap.

"This guy needs to dial it down," Rafer said, close enough that she could feel him pressed against her back. "He had me until the destiny line."

That got Gabriela smiling. Classic Rafer, thumbing his nose at a bad situation.

"Cheesy Hollywood melodrama," Gabriela said.

"Yeah, Supay is probably down in hell, cringing. It's embarrassing."

Gabriela did a fast scan of the room. "I suppose we should try to find him."

"Or we could leave and let him find us," Rafer said.

Gabriela nodded. "That would have some advantages."

"I don't see any clues," Rafer said. "He could at least have left some clues."

"Inconsiderate," Gabriela said.

A light went on in the hall.

"Here we go," Rafer said, removing his goggles. "Follow the light."

The light led them down the hall to the main staircase. The light switched off in the hall and path lighting blinked on, illuminating the wide curving stairs that ended in the large formal ground-floor foyer. A living room that was just slightly smaller than a basketball court extended beyond the foyer. A single lamp was lit at the far end of the dark living room. Rafer and Gabriela walked toward the lamp and stopped at an area rug. There was movement on the rug. Snakes. At least a dozen.

"Just like being in the jungle," Rafer said.

Gabriela flicked the beam from her Maglite across the floor. "There are more snakes by the table with the lamp."

They walked around the snakes and looked past the table into the adjoining dining room. Candles were lit on the dining room table and there were more snakes on the floor.

"This guy needs serious help," Rafer said. "I get that some people have a snake as a pet, but this is ridiculous."

"Are you freaked out?" Gabriela asked.

"Yes! Are you?"

"Yes."

A light was on in the butler's pantry. Gabriela moved toward the galley pantry and Rafer grabbed her arm and pulled her back.

"There's a snake coiled on the counter," Rafer said. "This game has ended. It's time to leave."

There was a green flash and El Dragón appeared at the far end of the pantry.

He was dressed all in black. His pants had a side loop that held a large knife with a flamed blade and a handle embossed with gold images of Supay. His black satin cape was trimmed in gold embroidery and small gemstones. His hair was severely pulled back, showing off his prominent facial tattoos. He was backed up by four similarly tattooed soldiers.

"The game hasn't ended," El Dragón said. "It has only begun."

"Getting ready for Halloween?" Rafer asked, raising his gun, pointing it at El Dragón. "I like your cape."

"This cape is to honor my lord, Supay," El Dragón said. "It has been consecrated by the blood of many sacrifices and tonight it will again honor my lord with a sacrifice on his holy altar."

Rafer looked around. "I don't see an altar. I think you're full of baloney."

"Kill him," El Dragón said. "And take the woman to the vineyard."

A soldier stepped forward and shot Rafer, twice. Rafer looked stunned for a beat and crumpled to the floor. Gabriela brought her gun up but was stun-gunned from behind before she could get off a shot.

CHAPTER TWENTY-THREE

Pepe and Caballo were a short distance from the house, keeping watch over the side door. The estate property was dark. No lights anywhere on the grounds. A light would appear in the house and then be extinguished. They'd assumed this was Rafer and Gabriela moving room by room, searching for El Dragón. First upstairs as planned. Then the lights moved downstairs.

"This is not a good sign," Pepe said to Caballo. "If they found him in the bedroom, they would contact us. They would not be walking through the downstairs."

Two gunshots rang out and Pepe and Caballo drew their weapons and ran for the house. Pepe opened the door and listened. He cut a quick glance to Caballo. The house was silent. There was a faint light ahead. The kitchen was dark but there was light in the butler's pantry. They crept forward and saw a man on the floor. Rafer. A snake was moving over his legs.

Caballo pulled his machete out of the loop on his belt, chopped the snake's head off, and kicked the snake away from Rafer. Pepe turned Rafer over and Rafer squinted up at him.

"Crap," Rafer said.

"Have you been shot?" Pepe asked.

"Yeah," Rafer said. "Twice. Both got me in the chest at close range. I'm wearing body armor, but it knocked the wind out of me. I feel like I got hit with a sledgehammer." He looked around. "Where's Gabriela?"

"She's not here," Pepe said. "Nobody is here but us."

"And many snakes," Caballo said. "Why are there many snakes in this house?"

"They're here because this house belongs to a crazy man," Rafer said, getting to hands and knees, taking in a couple of deep breaths and getting to his feet. "We need to find Gabriela."

"We didn't see anyone come or go from this house," Pepe said. "We were not able to watch the front door, but we were able to see all across the yard in the back."

"And we didn't hear any footsteps or vehicles," Caballo said.

"They were already in the house, waiting for us," Rafer said. "We were at the butler's pantry and El Dragón appeared at the other end with four of his soldiers. One of them shot me and I don't know what happened after that. The bullets didn't penetrate the vest, but I think my heart stopped for a couple beats."

"El Dragón wasn't in his bedroom?" Pepe asked.

"No. He knew or assumed we might go there first and he led us down to the butler's pantry."

Caballo had walked through the pantry, carefully avoiding snakes, and was standing at the far end. "Here," he said. "There is a door disguised as a bookcase. It is not entirely closed. It appears that there are stairs."

Pepe went down the stairs and called back to Rafer and Caballo. "It's a tunnel."

"Are you kidding me?" Rafer said. "Another freaking tunnel? It isn't enough that he has half a mountain dug out in Peru."

"Should we follow it?" Pepe asked.

"No," Rafer said. "Been there. Done that. Too easy to get trapped in a tunnel. Besides, I'm pretty sure I know where they're going. Just before I was shot, Dragón told his soldiers to take Gabriela to the vineyard. We can cut across the yard. I feel more comfortable doing that than taking the tunnel."

They left the house and ran to the gate that linked the two properties.

"Not locked," Rafer said, pushing the gate open.

A wide expanse of open field stretched out in front of them and ended at the two warehouses. They crossed the field and pressed themselves against the side of a building. Somewhere in the distance they could hear the ATV making its rounds.

Rafer eased around the building, carefully opened a door, and looked inside.

"Armory," he said. "She's not in here." He moved to the neighboring warehouse. "She's not in here, either. This looks like a common kitchen and storeroom. I'm looking for the temple."

The cluster of huts was off to one side. A rectangular, high-roofed building was directly opposite the huts. An acre of open field was between the two. Light suddenly flickered in the small windows located just below the roof.

"That has to be it," Rafer said, running to the building, taking in the Supay symbols when he got closer.

He tried the front door. Locked. He found a

back door. Locked. He motioned for Caballo to stand against the building under one of the windows. He removed his infrared goggles, climbed up Caballo, and looked through the window.

Gabriela was lying on an altar that had clearly been designed for human sacrifice. Her hands were bound, and she was perfectly still. El Dragón was in front of her with his back to Rafer. He had his arms raised and he was chanting to a gold statue of Supay. The four soldiers were at attention at a distance from El Dragón.

Rafer silently dropped to the ground. "I need a distraction," he whispered. "Get me chaos."

"That is my job," Caballo said. "I have been looking forward to this." He ran into the open field and fired off a rocket at the gas storage tank by the garage. There was an instant explosion that blew the garage apart and ignited other storage tanks. Black smoke billowed into the air and flames shot out and raced through what was left of the garage and surroundings.

Half-naked men tumbled out of the small huts and the front door to the temple burst open. Two soldiers stood in the temple doorway with their guns drawn. Pepe raked the doorway with his MP5 and took out the soldiers. Rafer ran into the temple with Pepe on his heels. There was a flash of green smoke at the altar and by the time Rafer reached it and the smoke cleared, El Dragón and the other two soldiers were gone. Gabriela was left on the altar. Her eyes were open but unfocused. Her fingers were twitching. Rafer pulled her off the altar, and draped her over his shoulder like a sack of flour.

Caballo kicked the two soldiers out of the way and closed and locked the front door. "There is a crazy mob coming here," he shouted to Rafer. "We should leave now."

"Back door," Rafer said. "Behind the altar."

Pepe and Caballo reached the altar and stopped, staring up, open-mouthed, at the gold Supay.

"Dios mio," Caballo said.

"Seriously," Pepe said.

The front door to the temple crashed open and several men rushed in. Pepe opened fire with the MP5 and Caballo threw out a couple of grenades. The grenades went off on impact. There was a lot of smoke and screaming and Pepe, Caballo, and Rafer ran from the building, Gabriela still unconscious, draped across Rafer's shoulder. They reached the kitchen warehouse and stopped to catch their breath. Men were combing the area and rooftop security floodlights had both properties lit like daylight.

"We cannot get across the field to the car," Caballo said.

Gabriela was beginning to function. "Whaz waaa?" she said.

"Hang on," Rafer said. "I'm looking for a back door."

"Here," Pepe said. "Side door but it's locked."

Rafer kicked it and it popped open.

Everyone ducked inside and Rafer set Gabriela on her feet.

"Are you okay?" he asked her.

"Yes," she said. "No. They kept stun-gunning me. Where are we?"

"We're in the vineyard kitchen," Rafer said.

"Not exactly a kitchen," Pepe said, shining his flashlight at the equipment and supplies. "More like a big-time drug lab. There are bags of cocaine stacked on the far table. No surprise there. You'd expect El Dragón to fly in with his homegrown. It's the boxes from China that are stacked against the wall and the bags on the table next to the cocaine that tell you what's happening here."

"The bags all look the same," Rafer said. "White powder."

"El Dragón is cutting his cocaine with fentanyl," Pepe said. "It is very profitable to do this. It is also superior in potency. Of course, if you use cocaine and fentanyl, it has the side effect that it is likely to kill you."

"He's got some meth going over here," Caballo said.

"Corporate diversification," Pepe said. "Smart."

Footsteps could be heard passing close to the building. Everyone clicked their lights off, ducked under the tables, and listened. The footsteps faded and everyone stood.

"Can you walk?" Rafer asked Gabriela.

"Yes," she said. "I'm a little shaky but I can manage."

"We should get out of here," Pepe said. "Some of the lab chemicals are flammable and they are all toxic. I can hear more explosions happening outside this building."

They crept out the side door and took a beat to get their bearings. Sirens were wailing in the distance and flashing red lights could be seen at the vineyard gate. El Dragón's soldiers were disappearing into the woods behind the vineyard. A transformer exploded and the lights blinked out on both properties.

"I want the ring," Gabriela said. "El Dragón had it on a chain around his neck. And I want El Dragón."

"Maybe you should let it go," Rafer said.

"No way am I going to give up now," Gabriela

said. "I'm going to bring that son of a bitch to justice."

"I'm with you," Caballo said. "He pulled off my fingernail. And it was my favorite."

He held his hand up, displaying his pointer finger without a nail.

"I'm sure he escaped into the tunnel," Gabriela said. "Here's the plan. Rafer and I will go to the house and search for him. Caballo and Pepe, you will go back to the temple and make sure he doesn't return through the tunnel."

"Good plan," Pepe said. "What should we tell the police and all those people who are arriving in the emergency vehicles with the flashy red-and-blue lights?"

"Try to avoid the police," Gabriela said.

"We are good at this," Pepe said.

Rafer and Gabriela moved away from the warehouse and Gabriela fell over.

"Crap!" she said. "My legs aren't working right."

Rafer picked her up and made sure she was standing straight. "You just have some neurons scrambled. You need a little more time."

"We don't have time. Run to the house and I'll follow."

"Are you sure?" Rafer asked. "I'm not comfortable leaving you like this."

"I'm fine! Go!"

"You have your gun, right?"

"Yes."

He reached into his cargo pants pockets and pulled out some grenades. "Here. Take these just in case."

"Omigod, you're carrying grenades in your pants?"

"I've got condoms in there, too. I like to be prepared."

"Are you serious?"

He pulled a couple out and put them in her hand. "Take these, too. They're good ones."

"I don't need condoms," Gabriela said.

"I was thinking maybe later tonight . . ."

"Maybe," Gabriela said. "Get the ring and then we'll talk."

Rafer took off at a run and Gabriela concentrated on walking. Fire trucks and EMT trucks were rolling through the vineyard gate and taking positions on the property. Police cars were parking on the side of the driveway and in the cleared acre between the huts and the temple. Chunks of debris from the garage had settled among the grape arbors and the grapes were on fire. Some of the huts were in flames.

Gabriela thought it looked like the end of the world. She tried running. She fell down and got up and tried running again. She made it to the house and went in through the side door. Rafer stopped her halfway through the kitchen.

"Don't go any further," he said to Gabriela. "It's not safe."

"What's the problem?"

"There's no electricity and there are snakes everywhere. Even with flashlights and goggles I don't think it's safe."

Rafer flashed his Maglite on a figure on the floor. It was one of El Dragón's soldiers and snakes were swarming over him.

Gabriela was breathless for a couple of beats. She swallowed down the nausea, pulled herself together, and focused on the figure.

"What happened?" she asked.

"I don't know. I found him like this. I don't know a lot about snakes, but I know the ones on his body aren't harmless."

Gabriela had her flashlight trained on the snakes. "At least two of them are black mambos and deadly. I've had some previous encounters."

Rafer looked at her. "Sometimes you really scare me."

"It was job related," Gabriela said.

"No shit," Rafer said.

"Do you want your condoms back?"

"Hell, no."

"What about El Dragón?" Gabriela asked.

"Not here. Maybe he's still in the tunnel. I didn't go into it. There were snakes there, too."

"You don't like snakes?"

"Not my favorites," Rafer said. "I could deal with them better in the jungle. They're supposed to be there. This is creepy."

Gabriela called Pepe. "What's going on at your end?" she asked.

"Police are in the tunnel and will be heading your way. We are in a vehicle, and we will pick you up at the side door."

"They're picking us up at the side door," Gabriela said to Rafer.

"How are they doing that?"

"Didn't say. I don't want to leave until we're sure El Dragón isn't in the tunnel. As soon as we know that the police are at the stairs we'll leave."

"Works for me," Rafer said.

Minutes later Gabriela heard talking in the tunnel and saw light from flashlights and torches. There was the sound of footsteps on the wood stairs. Red lights flashed in the kitchen window and there was the *wop wop* of a siren. Gabriela and Rafer went to the side door and looked out. Pepe was driving an EMT truck.

"Get in," he said. "*Now, please!*"

Gabriela and Rafer climbed into the back.

Caballo was already there, sitting on a jump seat. A body was on the stretcher, covered with a sheet. Gabriela and Rafer sat on the bench seat alongside the stretcher.

"Who is this?" Gabriela asked, looking at the shrouded body.

"Supay," Caballo said.

"Excuse me?"

Caballo raised the sheet enough to show Gabriela the face. "It's Supay. We took him."

Rafer gave a bark of laughter. "I love you guys."

"How did you get him into the truck?" Gabriela asked. "He must weigh a ton."

"He was not so heavy," Caballo said. "He is clearly not solid gold. El Dragón made a cheapskate version, but even so there is some good gold on his outside."

"What are you going to do with him?" Gabriela asked.

"Melt him down," Caballo said. "Pepe has people who can do these things."

Pepe pulled up to the gate and stopped. The gatehouse was abandoned. Pepe got out, pushed the button in the gatehouse, and the gate opened. Pepe got back into the EMT truck and drove down the driveway to the Escalade that was hidden off-road.

"I think we should leave this borrowed ambulance here," Pepe said. "We can put Mr. Supay in the back of the Escalade."

Everyone helped off-load Supay and shove him into the cargo space of the Escalade.

"He doesn't fit here," Pepe said. "I can't close the tailgate. His feet are sticking out."

"He'd fit if we didn't have all these boxes of ammo and explosives," Gabriela said.

"No problem," Rafer said. "The rear window is smashed. Stick his feet out the window."

They angled Supay so that his golden feet were sticking out the rear window. Everyone got into the Escalade and Pepe drove to the highway.

"I have called ahead and made arrangements," Pepe said. "We will take Supay to Happy Acres. It is officially a cemetery and crematorium, but they have a smelting operation on the side."

"Are you sure you want to leave Supay there?" Gabriela asked.

"He will be well taken care of," Pepe said. "My uncle owns Happy Acres, and my cousin Ralph manages it. Ralph is very reliable. He is a good smelter."

Forty minutes later they left the highway and drove through the gates to Happy Acres. Caballo was asleep, riding shotgun next to Pepe. Rafer was asleep, in the backseat, next to Gabriela. Gabriela was wide awake.

Okay, so it's three in the morning, she thought. Not a lot of people were on the road. Nevertheless, she was riding in a bullet-riddled Escalade that had part of a stolen golden idol sticking out of the rear window. Thank goodness they were finally cruising through the dark, rolling hills of the cemetery. A fitting place for the God of Death. Probably, he wouldn't be happy to see his likeness melted down and reformed into little gold bars, but these things happen. Life isn't perfect. For instance, she didn't have the ring. After all the time wasted, damage done, and money spent, she still didn't have the ring. Or El Dragón.

Pepe drove around a circular driveway and parked in the loading area for the crematorium. Lights were on. They were expected. A short, stocky fortysomething man with serious bed-head was waiting beside a rolling gurney designed to hold a casket.

"That's Ralph," Pepe said. "He'll take it from here."

Ralph looked in at Supay and grimaced. "This is a monster. I'm going to have to break him up before I melt him down. Do you know the composite?"

"No," Pepe said. "You'll have to do some testing."

"And you found him lying on the side of the road, right?"

"Right," Pepe said. "Must have fallen off a truck."

"He looks angry."

"His night didn't go in a good way for him," Pepe said. "And I have noticed that frequently men who have grown horns are angry."

"What else do you have back there?" Ralph asked.

"A little of everything," Pepe said. "Do you need anything?"

"I could use some flash-bangs and maybe a box of hollow-points for a nine."

"You got it," Pepe said, pulling out two boxes and setting them on the cement apron to the crematorium door.

Caballo and Rafer came around to help wrangle Supay out of the Escalade. They got him on the gurney, Ralph and Pepe did a man hug, and Ralph rolled Supay into the building.

"Another job well done," Pepe said.

"Uncle will be happy," Caballo said.

It was almost daybreak when they returned to the hotel.

"I'm going to bed and I'm not getting up until Christmas," Gabriela said to Rafer.

"You'll miss Thanksgiving, which is flat out the best holiday. You don't have to give anyone a present and there's gravy and pie. You've always been a sucker for gravy."

"I need sleep," Gabriela said. "G'night."

She closed and locked her door, dumped her guns and grenades on the floor, stripped down to her underwear and a tank top, and crawled into bed.

It'll be better when I wake up, she told herself.

"Sorry," she said to Annie. "I tried."

CHAPTER TWENTY-FOUR

*G*abriela met Rafer in a restaurant close to the hotel. He was seated in a booth and he was looking at the lunch menu. He looked up when she sat across from him.

"Gabs," Rafer said. "You don't look good. Did you sleep okay?"

"No," Gabriela said. "I kept waking up, thinking about the ring and gravy."

"I hear you," Rafer said. "It's disturbing that El Dragón is in the wind."

Gabriela did a fast read of the menu and set it aside. "I had Marcella make some phone calls. Preliminary reports indicate that El Dragón's soldier died from multiple snakebites. Another soldier was found just outside the front door of the estate house. Also died from multiple snakebites."

"And El Dragón?"

"He hasn't been found," Gabriela said.

"Have you talked to Pepe or Caballo?" Rafer asked. "I haven't seen them."

"They're on a flight back to Peru. Commercial."

"Probably wanted to leave before someone finds the Escalade."

"I'm sure the Escalade is spare parts and compressed metal by now," Gabriela said. She slouched back in her seat and closed her eyes. "Have you heard anything about demon armies marching on Santa Barbara?"

"No, but I haven't tuned in to the news today," Rafer said. "Personally, I think the ring is a dud."

"The snakes bother me. Why did they suddenly turn on those men?"

"Maybe they were hungry. Maybe the shipment of frozen mice didn't arrive on time. Maybe El Dragón stepped on one of the black mambas and it got pissed off."

Gabriela's phone buzzed with Marcella's number.

"Holy hell," Marcella said when Gabriela picked up. "Are you watching the news?"

"No," Gabriela said. "We're still in California and we're just about to order lunch."

"The news coverage on Leon Nadali's estate and vineyard just broke and it's bigger than the Super Bowl and the royal wedding combined. I'm talking about helicopter pictures of the smoking vineyard and close-ups of a creepy tattooed guy with snakes crawling over his dead body. Lots of video of the fentanyl and meth lab. And there's some really good footage of his creepy temple to the God of the Dead. Apparently, a gold statue of the god was stolen, and someone blasted the crap out of the temple's front door, scattering a bunch of devil worshippers' bloody body parts around. I don't suppose you know anything about that?"

"Who, me? Nope."

"Anyway, your man Nadali was worth a billion from drug sales, and everyone seems to be convinced he was certifiably batshit crazy."

"They've got that right," Gabriela said. "And I'd rather you didn't refer to him as *my man*."

"Gotcha," Marcella said. "Any luck with the ring?"

"None. The ring has disappeared with Nadali."

"It's for sure one of your more frustrating jobs. On that note, I also heard some news about Simon Gitten. Apparently, he was injured awhile back. Someone broke into his home and threatened to kill him, but he fought the guy off. Gitten had some knife wounds but he was able to get his gun out of his desk and he shot the intruder."

"What happened to the intruder?"

"He ran off, gushing blood all down the hall and stairs. He died on the sidewalk outside Gitten's building."

"Did the intruder have tattoos on his face?"

"You know it."

"I'm glad Simon is okay."

"He might be out of the ring authentication business," Marcella said. "Do you want me to make any travel arrangements? Like, for you to return to New York?"

"Not yet. Nadali and the ring are here, somewhere."

"This might fall into the obsession category," Marcella said.

"I'll consider that after I have my turkey club sandwich and iced tea."

"Okeydokey. I'm here if you need me."

"One last thing," Gabriela said. "Check around to see if you can find Nadali. Try local hospitals and news sources."

"I'm on it, boss."

"What's up?" Rafer asked when Gabriela hung up.

"Leon Nadali made the news. Big splash. Film, photos, financials."

"He was a bad guy," Rafer said.

"Evil," Gabriela said.

"Yeah, but he was good at the green smoke thing. Damn, I wish I could do that."

"I'll get you a copy of *Magic for Dummies*. I'm sure green smoke is in there."

Twenty minutes later, Gabriela was considering dessert and Marcella called.

"I found something," Marcella said. "A man with no identification checked himself into a twenty-four-hour clinic in Santa Thomas last night. He'd been bitten by a snake. That's a couple miles from Nadali's property. His face was covered with odd tattoos. Police are looking for anyone who might know him."

"Where is he now?"

"I'm not sure. I'll text you the clinic's address."

Gabriela finished the last of her iced tea and pushed the dessert menu aside. "I have a lead," she said to Rafer. "Let's go."

Rafer dropped a wad of money on the table and followed Gabriela.

"What's the lead?"

"Tattooed guy checked into a clinic last night. Snakebite."

"Where is he?"

"Marcella is texting me the clinic address. We need wheels."

Rafer pulled rental cars up on his phone. "Nothing close," he said.

"Get creative."

He went into the kitchen and came back with keys. "One of the line cooks said I could use his bike for two hours for two hundred bucks."

"What kind of bike?" Gabriela asked.

"It's the hog parked in front of the restaurant in the Employee of the Week spot. A Harley Fat Boy."

"Okay, but I get to drive."

"Like hell you get to drive. I made the deal. I drive."

The small town of Santa Thomas was ten minutes from the hotel. Rafer motored down the main street and parked in front of the clinic.

Gabriela went inside and approached the woman at the check-in desk.

"I'm here about the snakebite victim," Gabriela said. "I think I might know him. Is he okay? Is he here?"

"He came in around three a.m. and he left an hour later. It was a nasty bite on his hand, but it turned out not to contain venom. We gave him a shot of antibiotics in case of infection. He was a real odd duck. We get a lot of strange ones here, but he was at the top of the list. The police came asking about him, too. I guess he was involved in the fire at the vineyard."

Gabriela walked back to the Harley with Rafer. "This is a real downer," she said. "After everything we've been through only to have El Dragón disappear with the ring."

"I hear you," Rafer said. "I feel bad for Scoon, but the ending pretty much fit the whole rest of the trip. Every day I thought things couldn't possibly get more screwed up, and then they did. And now we just had the final screwup. The grand finale of all screwups. It's kind of satisfying . . . in a screwed-up kind of way."

"Consistent," Gabriela said.

"It's all about meeting expectations. This met my expectations."

"You have low expectations," Gabriela said.

"Not always," Rafer said, straddling the Harley. "I've got this for another hour. Let's go for a ride."

CHAPTER TWENTY-FIVE

*I*t was four o'clock when Gabriela drove through Scoon. It was cold and rainy, and the gloom did nothing for her mood.

"I'm not looking forward to this," Gabriela said to Rafer. "Thanks for sticking with me."

"I needed to touch base anyway," he said. "I've been away too long. My life is on the island, but I still have friends and relatives here." He watched the town roll by. "It's shocking what's happened in just a couple years. Scoon is a ghost town."

"We could have turned that around with money from the ring."

"We could have turned it around with money from the treasure you found in Peru and the Treasure of Lima, but you promised it to other people."

347

"Stupid me," Gabriela said. "Stupid Annie."

That got a bark of laughter from Rafer. "Way to go, Gabs. Throw Annie under the bus."

"Truth is, I don't believe this is over," Gabriela said. "Leon Nadali will turn up sooner or later. Pepe is keeping his eyes open in Peru. The FBI and DEA are looking for him. The facial tattoos will make it difficult for Nadali to entirely disappear."

Gabriela pulled into her parents' driveway and parked the rental car. "I'm surprised you let me drive," she said to Rafer.

"It's a four-cylinder, five-year-old economy Chevy. Nothing I could get excited about."

Five cats came running to say hello and Gabriela's mother and grandmother were at the door.

"Omigosh, it's Rafer," Gabriela's mother said. "This is such a surprise. I didn't think I'd ever see you again."

"I had to make sure Gabs didn't get lost driving out of the airport in the rain," Rafer said.

"Do your parents know you're here?" Grandma asked.

"I called them when we landed," Rafer said. "I told them I would be over later."

"You're welcome to stay for dinner," Gabriela's

mother said. "We're having chicken pot pie. You always liked my chicken pot pie."

"I'd love to stay for dinner," Rafer said. "Thank you. It's good to see everyone again."

"How are things going?" Gabriela asked her mother. "The town looked a little empty."

"It's a struggle," her mother said, "but we're all hanging on. I was hoping this homecoming would bring good news."

"Things took a bad turn yesterday," Gabriela said. "We're at a dead end."

"Oh dear," her mother said.

"Are you sure?" Grandma asked.

Gabriela's father came into the kitchen. "Welcome back, kitten," he said to Gabriela. "You, too," he said to Rafer. "What's going on? Nobody looks happy."

"We don't have the Seal of Solomon," Gabriela said.

"I always thought it was a bunch of baloney anyway," her father said. "Do I smell chicken pot pie in the oven?"

"It will be ready at six o'clock, just like always," Gabriela's mother said.

Her father nodded and went back to the living room to watch television.

"He sold his boat last week," Gabriela's mother

said. "We haven't got much else left, but he found a job in Greenville. You have to be flexible in these times. It might even all work out for the best. People say Greenville is very nice."

"Well, I'm not leaving," Grandma said. "I'm going back to my house with the tree in the living room."

"I can help you get your living room repaired," Gabriela said.

Rafer took Gabriela aside. "I want to talk to you on the porch."

Gabriela followed him out.

"I haven't got enough money to save the town, but I can help my parents keep their house," Rafer said. "And I can help your parents, too." He pulled a handful of precious stones out of his pocket. "I helped myself to some baubles along the way."

Gabriela smiled wide. "I did, too." She pulled a handful of gems out of her pocket and showed them to Rafer.

"There's about a hundred thousand in gemstones there plus four condoms," Rafer said.

"You never know when you might need one. And you said they were top of the line."

"Gabs!"

He pulled her to him, and he kissed her.

"Don't expect this to happen every day," she said. "This is a special deal."

"Whatever." He kissed her again and his hand slid under her shirt.

"It's not like I want to rekindle anything long-term."

"Okay, I get that. What is it that you *do* want?"

"I want to get you naked."

"I'm up for that, but we're on your parents' porch in the rain. If I'd known this was going to happen, I would have rented a bigger car. I'm not sure I can do my best work in a four-cylinder Chevy."

Gabriela knew the extent of Rafer's best work, and she thought on this one occasion she might be willing to settle for slightly less since this was the farewell tour. He'd make her happy, have dinner with her family, and tomorrow she'd return to New York and never see him again. Maybe.

Lights appeared on the road and turned into the driveway.

"More company for dinner?" Rafer asked.

Gabriela adjusted her shirt. "I don't recognize the car."

The car parked next to Gabriela's rental and a man got out. He was wearing a suit and carrying an attaché case. He ran through the rain to the porch and approached Gabriela and Rafer.

"Is this the Rose house?" he asked. "I'm looking for Gabriela Rose and Rafer Jones."

"I'm Gabriela Rose," Gabriela said. "And this is Rafer."

"Sorry to be disturbing you at the dinner hour," he said, "but your office manager, Marcella, said it would be all right. We need to conclude some business that was begun in South America. Is there someplace private where we can talk?"

"It's a small house," Gabriela said. "Private spaces don't exist."

"Then the porch will do," he said. "I must first ask you for a photo ID."

"What's this about?" Rafer asked.

"This is a private business transaction," he said. "If I can see your identification, I can give you a note from my employer that will explain everything."

Rafer showed him a driver's license. Gabriela retrieved hers from the house and returned to the porch.

"This is the note of explanation," the man said, handing each of them an envelope. "Both notes are precisely the same."

My cousin Ralph said Supay was mostly of high-quality gold and that he melted down very nicely. I took the liberty of quickly transforming the holy remains of the God of Death into Bitcoin. I am hoping this meets

*with your approval. Your one-quarter share
is in the accompanying envelope and is only
minus the necessary expenses of smelting
and handling.*

Your friend,

Pepe

The man handed Rafer and Gabriela a second envelope. "These envelopes contain your digital wallets plus your private and public key to your wallet. I'm sure you will want to immediately transfer the Bitcoin to your own address that is accessible only with your own private key. I'm pleased to tell you that the Bitcoin amount for each of you, less expenses, is $8,245,000. And now I'll be on my way if you'll simply sign this form verifying payment."

Rafer and Gabriela signed the form and the man left.

"Holy crap," Rafer said.

"It's Bitcoin," Gabriela said. "The criminal currency of choice. No one can trace it."

"Thoughtful of Pepe."

"Absolutely. And honorable. He didn't have to share the gold money with us."

"So, my choice of guide turned out to be good," Rafer said. "Right?"

"Wrong! You hooked us up with a drug lord."

"Okay, I'll give you that, but Pepe might not be very involved in the business."

"You think he's only connected by birth."

"Exactly!"

"Are we rationalizing this?"

Rafer draped his arm across her shoulders. "We're giving him the benefit of the doubt."

"Do you have a Bitcoin account?" Gabriela asked.

"Yes," Rafer said. "Do you?"

"Yes."

"The God of the Dead saved Scoon," Rafer said.

CHAPTER TWENTY-SIX

*G*abriela was alone at the kitchen table. The kitchen was lit by a nightlight and by the glow from Gabriela's laptop. The rest of the house was dark and quiet. Rafer was with his parents. Her parents and grandmother were in bed. Everyone was resting easier knowing that there was money to rebuild the town. Everyone but Gabriela. It was midnight and Gabriela was still awake, catching up on email and sorting through her thoughts.

Now that the money was available it would have to be managed. Rebuilding a town was a complicated undertaking. She didn't want to assume that responsibility. She would have to find someone to take on the job. And she would have to make sure the money got transferred correctly. At least she no longer had to worry about capturing the ring to take care of the town. In fact, she found herself surprisingly free from the entire El Dragón obsession. She attributed it to obsession exhaustion. Good riddance, she thought.

She heard the whisper of fabric behind her, and she turned to see El Dragón, standing in the kitchen. He was dressed in street clothes that looked borrowed, the ring was on a chain around his neck, and he was wearing a blood-red cape. The hand holding the gun was bandaged. The other hand held a small duffle bag.

Gabriela took a moment to steady herself and call up some bravado.

"What are you doing here?" she asked.

"I've come for you, of course," he said. "It's the only way to repair the ring and regain the good grace of Supay."

"How did you know I was here? Three days ago, we were in California and you were bitten by a snake."

El Dragón looked down at his bandaged hand. "It was a justified warning from my master Supay. I failed him. He is a demanding lord and quick to punish. I must not fail him again."

"Has it occurred to you that you might be insane?" Gabriela asked.

"That is a typical comment from a nonbeliever,"

El Dragón said. "I have seen Supay. He speaks to me. He holds my heart in his hand. I sent one of my trusted followers to New York, but you weren't there. This was the obvious second choice. In times of crises the weak go home."

"Do you go home?"

"My home is in hell," El Dragón said. "I haven't had that sweet pleasure yet."

"Okay," Gabriela said. "What's next?"

"Supay has chosen a place for the sacrifice. It will be necessary to go outside. You will do this quietly so you don't wake your family. If you wake your family, I'll have to kill them."

"It's raining."

"Rain isn't significant. The sacrifice will take place tonight. Move, now."

Gabriela got up and moved toward the door. "Where are we going?"

"We're going to the lighthouse."

The lighthouse was less than a half mile away on a rocky promontory. It was no longer in use. Gabriela knew every inch of it. She'd played there as a kid and made out there with Rafer as a teen.

El Dragón was behind her as she stepped off the porch into the darkness and the light rain. The silhouette of the lighthouse could barely be seen against the night sky. She walked toward the lighthouse, heard El Dragón close in on her, and felt the sting of the stun gun on her neck. When her synapses unscrambled, she realized she was wearing a spiked collar that attached to wrist shackles. El Dragón held a leash that was attached to the collar.

"We can proceed," he said, when Gabriela got to her feet. "You can avoid pain and bloodshed by walking carefully in front of me."

And I can avoid being sacrificed by waiting for the right moment, Gabriela told herself. This man is a psychotic disaster. He's come here alone because his faithful followers have probably deserted him. If I stay calm, I can lose him in the lighthouse. The spiked collar is a problem, but I just have to take it one step at a time.

She was drenched by the time she reached the lighthouse. The wind had picked up and she could hear the waves crashing against the rocks. El Dragón was also drenched, and she thought the long, wet cape and the duffle he was carrying had to be a burden when he was climbing the stairs of the lighthouse. She made an effort not to focus on the contents of the duffle. No doubt it contained the tools necessary for a bloody sacrifice to Supay.

The lighthouse was 135 feet tall. It was made of red brick with a beacon at the top. There was a room below the beacon that controlled the light.

She suspected that was where the sacrifice was supposed to take place. Before reaching the room, the winding staircase led to a door that opened to a narrow balcony that encircled the lighthouse. Gabriela thought this was where she would make her move. She needed to get control of the tether and escape through the door. It would be hard for him to shoot her or stun her on the balcony. Beyond that, she hadn't a clue how she would survive.

She entered the lighthouse and began climbing the spiral staircase, counting the steps as she went. It was pitch-black in the lighthouse and she wouldn't be able to see the door, but she knew it would be on step 100. It had been years since she'd been out on the balcony. She was hoping nothing had changed. She was hoping a lock hadn't been installed on the door and that the door would still open with a push.

El Dragón was several steps behind her, and he was slowing down. He had a gun in one hand and the duffle in the other. This left no hand free to hold a flashlight. He couldn't see her ahead of him. He wouldn't know about the door.

The tether pulled the spikes against her neck.

"The spikes are cutting me," Gabriela said. "You have to give me more rope. I can't climb the steps like this."

"Climb slower," El Dragón said.

"I'm doing the best I can," she said. "I can't see where I'm going. Please, just a little more rope."

She felt the rope go slack and realized that he was no longer holding it. She said a silent prayer to whoever was listening. She was on step 95. She maneuvered her body so she was able to grab the rope and gather it up. She counted the steps off in her head. She leaned her shoulder against the wall at step 100 and the door opened. Her heart was beating hard from surging adrenaline. She slipped through the door to the balcony and was instantly buffeted by the wind and rain. She avoided the three-foot-high, rusted railing, pressed her body against the brick building, and quickly moved around the curve.

She heard El Dragón shout at her and shoot through the door. She saw him step out onto the balcony and she moved out of sight. She heard him drop the heavy duffle bag on the metal floor, and he emerged from around the curve. His cape was whipping around him in the gusting wind. Gabriela ducked down and charged him, coming in low, below the gun. Her shoulder glanced off him, he crashed through the rusted railing and did a free fall off the lighthouse. Gabriela slipped on the rain-slicked metal grate and partially slid off the balcony after El Dragón. She felt hands grab her and pull her back to the safety of the building. She forced herself to breathe, to slow her heart rate. After a moment she was able to look over the side. There was a dark form on the rocks below her. No one else was on the balcony. She called out but no one answered. She could see a flashlight bobbing in the rain, someone making their way across the field, from her parents' house to the lighthouse.

Gabriela carefully inched her way around the curve, found the door, and began the slow journey down the narrow stairs. She was being careful. The last thing she wanted was to trip and fall and break her neck after what she'd just been through.

Bright light flashed through the open door at ground level. The light moved forward, swept up the spiral staircase, and caught Gabriela. It was Gabriela's grandmother, Fanny.

"Are you all right?" Fanny shouted to Gabriela.

"Yes," Gabriela called back. "Shine the light lower so I can see where I'm stepping."

Gabriela reached the bottom and Fanny gasped when she saw the collar. "Don't move any more than necessary," she said to Gabriela. "You're bleeding. We have to get this thing off you."

"I need air," Gabriela said, leaving the lighthouse, walking out into the rain and wind, tipping her face up to feel the salt spray.

Headlights raced toward them, the rental car skidded to a stop on the slick grass, and Rafer jumped out and ran to Gabriela.

He stopped just short of her and reached out to carefully touch her. "You're alive, right?"

"Yes," she said.

"I'm not having a nightmare, am I? This is real?"

"Yes. This is real."

"Gabs, you're bleeding. Are you okay?"

"Sort of," Gabriela said. "I'd like to get out of this dog collar. El Dragón probably has the key on him."

Rafer looked around. "Where is he?"

"He's on the rocks. He fell off the balcony."

Rafer ran to the rocky point. Gabriela and Fanny followed at a slower pace. Rafer reached El Dragón and a wave crashed onto the point and knocked Rafer over onto his back. He scrambled to his feet and another wave came in and sucked El Dragón into the sea.

Rafer was about to go in after him and Gabriela shouted to him.

"Let him go," Gabriela said. "Let him go. I don't want to lose you. Just let him go."

Rafer got knocked around by another wave and retreated back to Gabriela and Fanny.

"He was wearing the ring on a chain around his neck," Rafer said. "I could see it."

"We don't need it," Gabriela said. "No one needs it. He left a duffle bag on the balcony. Maybe there's something in it that will release the collar. I can't walk anymore. Every time I move it cuts into me."

Rafer ran up the spiral staircase and returned with the duffle bag. He dumped everything on the ground and pawed through the knives and Supay icons while Fanny held the flashlight.

"Here are the keys!" Rafer said.

He unlocked the collar and the wrist shackles and hugged Gabriela.

"A hug is great," Gabriela said, "but what I really need is a stiff drink."

"Me, too," Fanny said. "That was the scariest thing that's ever happened to me. And I'm in my nightgown! And I'm wet!"

Rafer looked down at his bare feet. "I didn't waste time on shoes or a shirt." He shoved everything into the duffle bag. "What should we do with this?"

"It belongs with El Dragón," Gabriela said.

Rafer zipped the bag and heaved it into the ocean.

. . . .

Gabriela, her grandmother Fanny, and Rafer assembled at the kitchen table with a bottle of whiskey, a jar of peanut butter, and a box of Ritz crackers. They were wrapped in blankets while their wet clothes tumbled in the dryer.

"How did you know I was at the lighthouse?" Gabriela asked, speaking softly so she didn't wake her mother and father.

"I had a dream that you were screaming at me to wake up," Rafer said to Gabriela. "You kept screaming, 'Wake up, wake up. Go to the lighthouse.' It was so real and so urgent. I ran out half-dressed and rushed over here. I have to tell you I'd have felt like an idiot if there was no one at the lighthouse."

"It was Annie telling you to wake up," Fanny said. "She woke me up, too. She said Gabriela needed help."

"I knew every step of that lighthouse by heart," Gabriela said. "And I knew my only chance was to get onto the balcony. El Dragón followed me out and we were getting pushed around by the wind and getting pelted by rain and I charged him. I barely touched him with my shoulder, but I guess he lost his balance and crashed through the railing."

"That's a metal railing up there," Grandma said. "It must have been all rusted to break that easy. Even then I'd think he needed a good push. What happened next?"

"I slipped on the wet grate, and partially slid off the balcony," Gabriela said. "I would have ended up on the rocks with El Dragón, but something stopped me. It almost felt like a pair of hands pulling me back onto the balcony." Gabriela paused. "It must have been that my shirt got caught on something." Another long pause. "Or maybe . . ."

Everyone was dead still, exchanging glances.

Gabriela blew out a sigh. "Thank you, Annie," she whispered.

"Really?" Rafer said.

"I thought I should say it," Gabriela said. "Just in case."

Fanny nodded in agreement.

"This is too weird," Rafer said. "We aren't going to tell anyone else about this, are we?"

"Not me," Gabriela said.

"Nobody ever believes me anyway," Grandma said.

Gabriela raised her whiskey glass. "To Annie."

Fanny and Rafer raised their glasses. "To Annie!"

Stephanie Plum returns in

Dirty Thirty

by Janet Evanovich,

coming from Atria Books

in November 2023.

I'm Stephanie Plum. Jersey girl. Rutgers graduate. Successful underachiever working for Vincent Plum Bail Bonds as a recovery agent, hunting down losers who've skipped out on their bond.

A half hour ago, I heard police chatter about Duncan Dugan exhibiting erratic behavior in an office building downtown. Dugan is a big-ticket bond who failed to show for his court appearance. He's been accused of robbing a jewelry store on King Street at gunpoint, almost hitting a crossing guard in his effort to leave the area, and leading seven police cars on a high-speed chase before running out of gas. Since I'd been assigned the task of finding Dugan and dragging his sorry butt back into the legal system, I rushed to the scene with my coworker Lula. We found Dugan standing on a fourth-floor ledge. He was flattened against the front of the building, and he was looking down at the crowd that was gathering below him.

"He's gonna jump," Lula said to me. "I got him pegged for a jumper."

There was a large police presence in the area. There were fire trucks and ambulances, and a satellite news truck was parked not far away. It was lunchtime, and the outdoor eating area attached to the building's café had been cleared of diners.

"I'm thinking this might be partly your fault on account of he knows you're after him," Lula said to me. "He probably don't want to go to jail. You should yell up to him and tell him jail isn't so bad. Tell him he'll get free room and board and he'll have a chance to make new friends."

"I'm not yelling that up to him," I said. "That's crazy talk."

"Yeah, but is it true?" Lula asked.

"Technically, yes."

"Hunh," Lula said. "There you have it."

It was a nice October day in Trenton, New Jersey. The sky was as blue as sky gets in Trenton, and the sun was shining. I was wearing jeans and sneakers and a hooded sweatshirt over my V-neck, fitted T-shirt. Lula was wearing spike-heeled, thigh-high boots, and as usual she'd managed to squeeze her plus-size body into a spandex dress designed for a much smaller person. Her hair was frizzed out into a big puffball, and her fake lashes were furry-black-caterpillar quality. Lula is a person of color, and I'm a person of less color. My eyes are blue. My hair is brown, naturally curly, and shoulder length. I lack the patience to iron my hair into straightness or blow-dry it into luxurious waves, so it's almost always in a ponytail. I make up for this by wearing lip gloss and smiling.

A woman pushed her way through the crowd and stepped out onto the street. "Duncan, you moron!" she yelled up to Dugan. "What the hell are you doing?"

"I'm gonna jump," Dugan said. "I screwed up. It's over. I'm jumping to my death."

"Well, you better take a header then because you're only on the fourth floor. If you don't fall right, you could just end up with a bunch of broken bones or maybe paralyzed."

"I don't like heights. Four is as high as I can go."

"You need to crawl through that window next to you and get down here," the woman yelled at him.

"I'll go to jail."

"Big deal. My Uncle Charlie went to jail, and he said it wasn't so bad. He got free room and board and he got to make a bunch of new friends."

"Charlie said that?"

"More or less. Anyway, it won't be for so long, and in the meantime we can talk."

"What would we talk about?"

"Stuff."

He looked over at the window. "I don't want to get broken bones."

"You see?" Lula said to me. "You could have been the hero if you'd been the first one to tell him about making friends in jail. Although, the business about broken bones was a good addition."

Dugan turned to get to the window, his foot slipped, and he fell off the ledge. There was a collective gasp from everyone watching as Dugan crashed through the yellow-and-white awning that stretched over the sidewalk café and landed like a sack of wet cement on the pavement.

I'm not normally a fainter, but I came close to fainting when I heard him hit. I bent at the waist, sucked in air, and fought the nausea. When I straightened up, Dugan was surrounded by paramedics and police.

"Do you think he's okay?" Lula asked.

"Not even a little," I said.

"They're bringing a stretcher over," Lula said. "That might be a good sign."

One of Dugan's arms came up, and he did a little finger wave. "I'm okay," he said. "Sort of."

The crowd dispersed after the wave and

message from Dugan, but Lula and I stayed. The woman who had shouted up to Dugan approached the outer rim of the first responders, stood there for a couple minutes, and left.

The paramedics finally lifted Dugan onto the stretcher and rolled him over to the ambulance. I knew one of the men. Jerry Fisher.

"Where are you taking him?" I yelled to Jerry.

He turned and waved at me. "The Medical Center."

I gave him a thumbs-up, and Lula and I walked down the street to my car.

. . . .

I dropped Lula off at the bail bonds office on Hamilton Avenue and drove a couple more blocks to the hospital. The ambulance was parked in the ER drive-through. I bypassed the drive-through and went to the parking garage.

The bail bonds office and the medical center are on the fringe of the Burg. I grew up in the Burg, and my parents still live there. It's a residential chunk of South Trenton clinging to Hamilton Avenue, Chambers Street, and Liberty Street. Houses and yards are small. Televisions are large. Secrets are nonexistent. A few people cheat on their taxes, but it's okay because they're grandfathered into the mob.

I checked in at the desk in the ER, showed them my papers for Dugan, certifying that I had the right to capture him, and took a seat in the waiting room. After an hour, I was told Dugan was in surgery. Three hours later, he was out of surgery and in the ICU, hooked up to a bunch of machines. He wasn't in any shape to flee, so I went back to the office.

. . . .

"I was just closing up for the day," Connie said. "Lula told me about Dugan. How's he doing?"

"He's in the ICU. I didn't get a chance to talk to a doctor. His condition was listed as stable. He got lucky. His fall was broken by the café awning."

Connie Rosolli is a couple years older than me. She's the office manager, the guard dog for Vinnie's private office, and, like Vinnie, she's certified to write a bond. She has a lot of black hair, thinks there's no such thing as too much mascara, and likes bright red lipstick and polka dots. She wears heels to work but keeps a pair of running shoes in her bottom drawer next to her Glock 9. She can shoot the eyes out of a grasshopper a quarter mile away.

She took two folders out of her top drawer and handed them to me. "Two new FTAs came in today. Nothing exciting. Both are low bonds.

A smash-and-grab who left with a couple bags of chips and a six-pack, and a low-level drug dealer. Hooter Brown."

I slipped the files into the messenger bag I used as purse and mobile office. "These two FTAs aren't going to pay my rent."

Being a bond enforcement agent has its highs and lows. One of the lows is that I don't get a salary. I get a percentage of the original bond when I make a capture. If I don't make enough captures, I'm forced to mooch food off my parents and moonlight for rent money.

Connie took a business card off her desk. "This might help. A man came in about an hour ago, looking for you. He said he had a job that required your special skills."

I took the card from her. "I don't have any special skills."

"He asked me if you were good at finding people, and I said you were our best skip tracer."

"I'm your *only* skip tracer." I looked at the name on the card. "Martin Rabner. He owns Rabner's Jewelry, right? That's the store Duncan Dugan robbed."

"Yeah, small world," Connie said. "Rabner told me he'd be in the store until eight o'clock if you were interested. He also left his cell number on the back of the card."

I dropped the card into my messenger bag.

"Are you going to talk to him?" Connie asked.

"Maybe," I said. "Probably."

I left the bonds office, got into my Jeep Cherokee, and drove downtown to Rabner's Jewelry. I parked across the street and watched the store for a couple minutes. The special-skills thing had me worried. I hoped it didn't involve anything kinky. I needed money, but not that bad.

I crossed the street and entered the store. It was five o'clock, and there were no customers in Rabner's. A nicely dressed man who looked to be in his late sixties to early seventies was seated at a writing desk. He stood when I walked in.

"Stephanie Plum," he said. "Sorry I missed you at the office. Thank you for coming to the store."

"Do I know you?"

"We've never officially met. I recognize you from the Leoni viewing. I was there when you put Bella Morelli in cuffs and hauled her out of the funeral home. That took guts. I don't think I could have done it."

Bella Morelli is a Sicilian immigrant stuck in a Marlon Brando *Godfather* time warp. Her hair is gray. Her dresses are always black. Her posture is vulture-on-the-attack. She's crazy like a fox, and she's my boyfriend's grandmother. She was being her usual disruptive self at the Leoni viewing, and the funeral director begged me to take her away.

"Bella wasn't really all that upset about leaving in cuffs. She loves a dramatic exit," I said to Rabner.

"She scares the heck out of me. She put a curse on Stu Carp, and he got shingles."

I nodded. "She scares the heck out of a lot of people. Connie said you mentioned a job."

"Yes. I thought of you because you're obviously good at finding people and surviving dangerous situations."

"Like arresting Bella."

"Exactly! Like arresting Bella."

"About the job?" I asked.

"I want you to find a former employee. I've reported him as missing to the police, but nothing has come of it."

"How long has he been missing?"

"Three weeks. He disappeared on the same day that the robbery occurred."

"Before or after the robbery?"

"After," Rabner said. "Actually, I fired him. He was supposed to provide security. I hired him so I wouldn't get robbed, and I got robbed."

"But now you want to find him?"

"Yes," Rabner said. "He stole a tray of diamonds valued at close to a million dollars."

"Seriously?"

"The man who robbed the store got low-hanging fruit. He cleaned out the cases. I don't want to trivialize that. It was terrifying. It was a smash-and-grab without the smashing. He had me dump everything into a garbage bag while he held me at gunpoint. Fortunately, all the pieces he took were insured and he left the cases intact."

I glanced around the store. "It looks like you got everything back."

"Unfortunately, no. The bag of stolen jewelry wasn't in the car when the police arrested the driver. Everything you see here is new. My displays are a little skimpy, but at least I'm still in business."

"How could it not be in the car? I thought the police were on him when he pulled away from the curb."

Rabner shrugged. "I don't know. It wasn't in the car. And it gets worse. The real loss was with the unset gemstones that were stolen separately. A large part of my business is in engagement rings. Couples come in and select a setting and a stone. So, like most jewelers, I keep an inventory of gemstones. Mostly diamonds of varying sizes and quality."

"And you think your security guy stole the unset stones."

"Yes. I do."

"Have you told the police?"

"Yes, but I have no proof. After the robbery when I locked up for the night it was just me and a couple cops. Andy left a couple hours earlier."

"Andy the security guard."

"Yes. He always worked from noon to eight. Six days a week. He left at eight o'clock on the day of the robbery, and he never returned."

"Because you fired him."

"Yes."

"And you haven't heard from him."

"Not a word," Rabner said.

"Why do you think he stole the diamonds?"

"My routine is that every night I take the jewelry out of the display cases, and I put the jewelry in the safe. When I open in the morning, I take the pieces out of the safe. The morning after the robbery I opened the safe to get the few items that were left to display, and the diamond tray was missing."

"The diamond tray always stays in the safe?"

"Yes."

"Did Andy know how to open the safe?"

"I never gave him the combination, but he was there when I closed every night. If he was motivated, I suspect he could have watched me punch in the numbers. The thing is there's no other way the diamonds could have disappeared. There were no signs that the safe had been tampered with. Someone opened it."

"There are people who have skills when it comes to opening safes."

"They would also need to have skills picking locks. The man who robbed me shot out the security cameras inside the store. Not that it did him any good. I tripped an alarm at my desk and the police arrived just as he was getting into his car. I have a camera at the rear entrance but not at the front door. I didn't think I needed one there. Whoever took the stones came in through the front door without damaging the lock. He disarmed the alarm, opened the safe, and took the diamonds."

"Andy had a key?"

"Yes, and he knew the code to disarm the alarm."

"Have you been in contact with his family?"

"His parents don't seem to be very concerned. They said he's always been a free spirit. He doesn't have siblings, and he isn't married."

"And you want me to find Andy?"

"Yes."

"Why?"

"I want the diamonds if any are left. Truth is, they were underinsured. And I'm angry. I trusted Andy. I want him arrested and sent to jail."

"Does Andy have a last name?"

"Andy Manley."

Holy crap. Sucker punch to the brain. I knew Andy Manley. I went to school with him. His nickname was Nutsy. He felt me up at a party when I was fourteen years old, and he told everyone I stuffed my bra with toilet paper. It was a lie, of course. I stuffed my bra with Kleenex. Fortunately, halfway through high school I managed to grow breasts that were acceptable and only required a push-up bra on special occasions.

"I might be able to find Andy for you," I said to Rabner, "but I can't guarantee that he'll be sent to jail."

Rabner nodded. "Understood."

. . . .

It was six thirty when I pulled into my apartment building's parking lot. The building itself is an unimaginative three-story chunk of brick and mortar. I live on the second floor, in a one-bedroom, one-bath unit that's mostly furnished in hand-me-downs from dead relatives. I share the apartment with a hamster named Rex, and honestly, it's all very comfortable. Rex is the perfect housemate and best friend. He's nonjudgmental, he never complains, and he's ecstatically happy when he gets an occasional Ritz cracker or a corner of my Pop-Tart. He lives in a large glass aquarium, he sleeps in a Campbell's soup can, and he runs all night long on a hamster wheel, going nowhere. I feel like his life mimics mine.

I saw that lights were on in my apartment and Joe Morelli's SUV was parked in my lot. Morelli is a Trenton cop working plainclothes. I have a long history with him and possibly a future. For as long as I've known him, no one has ever called him Joe. His mother, grandmother, and my mother call him Joseph. Everyone else has always known him as Morelli. At present, for lack of a better word, he's my boyfriend. He has a key to my apartment, and I keep a couple T-shirts and a toothbrush at his house. I parked next to Morelli, bypassed the unreliable elevator in the lobby, and took the stairs.

Morelli's dog, Bob, lunged at me the instant I opened the door to my apartment. Bob is big and orange and overly friendly. He put his two massive paws on my chest, knocked me flat on my back, and gave me Bob kisses. Morelli shooed Bob away and pulled me to my feet.

"Sorry about that," Morelli said. "Are you okay?"

"Yeah, he caught me by surprise."

Bob was still in front of me, tail wagging, eyes bright.

"Who's a good boy?" I said to Bob. "Who's a good boy?" I gave him a hug and scratched him behind his ears. He snuffled me for food, didn't find any, and went back to his place on my couch.

"This is a surprise," I said to Morelli. "I don't usually see you on a Monday."

Joe Morelli is six feet of lean muscle. His hair is dark brown and wavy. His eyes are soft brown and expressive when he's feeling romantic, and they're laser focused and unreadable when he's being a cop. He was wearing his usual outfit of running shoes, jeans, and a casual cotton knit sweater.

We were standing in the small foyer that led to my kitchen. I flicked a glance into the kitchen and saw a thirty-five-pound bag of dog food resting against a cabinet. This might suggest that either Bob or Morelli or both were moving in with me.

"Oh boy," I said.

Morelli grinned. "I'm guessing the 'Oh boy' is about the dog food in your kitchen. I need to go out of town for a few days. I was hoping I could leave Bob with you. Last time I left him at home with a dog sitter he knocked her down when she opened the front door and he ran away. It took half the force to find him."

"Sure. How many days are a few?"

"I don't know. Police business. I've been tagged as a witness in the Wisneski trial."

"I read about that. It was a drug bust gone bad in Miami."

"Yeah. I'm not supposed to talk about it. I heard you were babysitting Duncan Dugan this afternoon."

"He's FTA. Lula and I were there when he jumped. I followed the ambulance to the Medical Center and waited for him to get out of the OR. I'll check up on him tomorrow."

"Dugan was operating above his pay grade when he robbed Rabner," Morelli said. "He's a quality control inspector for one of the lines at the button factory. No priors."

"If I had to stand around all day making sure buttons were round, I might decide to rob a jewelry store. Were you one of the guys investigating?"

"No," Morelli said. "I only investigate when there's a lot of blood. I learned about it from my mom because Rabner accused Nutsy of stealing a tray of diamonds. She heard about it at bingo."

"Rabner came to the office today. He hired me to find Nutsy."

Morelli's eyes narrowed ever so slightly. "You're kidding, right?"

"No. He hired me to find Nutsy. He said he reported it to the police, but they haven't had any luck locating him."

"Walk away from it," Morelli said. "Let the police do their thing."

"I need the money."

"Do you get paid by the hour or do you only get paid if you find him?"

"I get paid when I find him."

"Then you're wasting your time. Chances of you finding him are slim to none," Morelli said. "The police can't find him, and Ranger can't find him."

Ranger is the other man in my life. Riccardo Carlos Manoso, a.k.a. Ranger. Former Special Forces. Tall, dark, and dangerous. More muscle than Morelli but not so much that he doesn't look good in or out of clothes. I've seen him both ways, and he's not a man you can easily forget. He was my mentor when I first became a bond enforcer. He was a bounty hunter then. Now he's the owner of a high-end security business.

"Why is Ranger looking for Nutsy?" I asked Morelli.

"Don't know. It's street chatter. Nutsy was a private hire, but Rangeman installed and monitored the security equipment. Maybe Ranger's just protecting the Rangeman brand. Maybe there's something more."

"Rabner didn't share that information with me," I said.

"This robbery smells bad. You don't want to get involved," Morelli said.

"It's all good. I can partner with Ranger."

"My worst nightmare," Morelli said. "I'll be stuck in Miami, and you'll be doing God knows what with Ranger. He's built a premier security company, but he's a threat as a human being. He's fearless. He plays by his own rules. And I don't like the way he looks at you."

"Like I'm lunch?"

"Yeah," Morelli said. "Plus, he has skills and resources to back him up when things get bad. You have Lula."

All this was true.

Morelli leaned in and gave me a quick kiss. "I have to run. I'm catching a plane out of Newark and I'm late. Bob's leash is on the counter. Probably you want to lock the bag of food up somewhere, so he doesn't binge-eat it and throw up on your couch.

The story continues in *Dirty Thirty*
by Janet Evanovich,
coming in November 2023.